A Battle for Hope

A Novel

by
Nancy Manther

Formatted, Converted, and Distributed by eBookIt.com
http://www.eBookIt.com

ISBN-13: 978-1-4566-3907-5 (hardcover)
ISBN-13: 978-1-4566-3905-1 (paperback)
ISBN-13: 978-1-4566-3906-8 (ebook)
ISBN-13: (audioebook)

To Chuck, for always believing in me...

Table of Contents

Leah

Stacks of cardboard boxes stand at attention in the living room, guarding the jumbled collection of furniture huddled there. In order to save money, Mom told the movers to leave the boxes and most of the furniture in the living room, that we'll do the rest. Fortunately, she's having them put my bedroom furniture where it belongs because I don't know if we could carry it up the narrow stairway to the second floor by ourselves. It's going to be hard enough moving the furniture that's staying on the main level.

All of a sudden, I hear my little sister whisper, "Leah! Betcha can't find me!"

Clara loves to play Hide and Seek—it's her very favorite game. The room is full of great nooks and crannies at the moment, and I can see why she can't resist the urge. She's been a good sport all day, so I figure she deserves to have a little fun.

"Okay, Clare-bear, ready or not, here I come!"

As usual, Clara can't keep her giggles in, but I pretend to be clueless. Instead of finding her right away, I make a big production of looking in the most unlikely places—inside an end table drawer, under a sofa cushion, inside a lampshade—making her giggle even more. When Mom pops in from the front porch, I hold my finger to my lips, our Hide and Seek signal.

"What are you doing, Leah?" She asks, giving me a wink.

"I'm looking for Clara. I'm kind of thinking she might be on the moving van or something. Have you seen her,

Mom?" I use my most serious voice which is hard to do when I want to laugh out loud.

"Oh dear!" Mom plays along. "I wonder where they'll bring her? I'm sure going to miss our Clare-bear!"

"Same here! I've looked and looked, but I can't find her *anywhere!*"

Clara jumps up from behind the sofa, the giggles spilling out of her like confetti. "Here I am!"

"Oh, thank goodness!" Mom says and rushes over to give her a hug. "I was really worried for a second there!"

"Were you *really*?" Clara asks, clearly thrilled to have fooled us.

"Of course!" Mom ruffles her hair.

"We really need your help, Clara," I add, pointing to all the boxes. "Look at all the stuff we have to unpack!"

We know which rooms the boxes go in since Mom labeled them, and the movers stacked them accordingly. The last time we moved, all the boxes were randomly piled in the garage which made finding things and unpacking a nightmare. This time, Mom declared that she's working smarter, not harder. Of course the last time we moved, we couldn't afford to hire movers, so this feels like a luxury no matter what they do with the boxes.

It's the second time we've moved in three years, but this time I'm excited and happy about it. The last time was after Dad died. Clara, Mom and I had to move into an apartment above my Aunt Kathy's garage. One day, I'd overheard a conversation between Grandma Mo (I call her Momo) and Kathy. Being only eight years old at the time, it didn't make much sense.

"I can't believe that man didn't have any life insurance," my aunt said. "Talk about irresponsible!"

"Well, I don't think *that man* had a responsible bone in his body, so it's no surprise to me," said my grandma. "It's a wonderful thing you're doing, Kathy, letting them live here for free."

"Diane would do the same for me, although I sure hope she never has to."

"I'm just glad Jim helped her get into that court reporting program," said Momo. "Once she finishes that, she'll be able to get a good job."

"Yeah, it should all work out really well," Kathy said. "I just hope she doesn't throw this opportunity away like she did when she married Bill. If she'd finished college, she wouldn't be in this pickle."

"Now, now," said Momo in a stern voice, "then we might not have our Leah, and that would be truly awful."

From the tone of their voices, it sounded like life insurance was a pretty important thing to have—and we didn't. Apparently, if you had it you didn't need to live with relatives for free. It also made my tummy hurt to hear what Kathy said about my mom. Sometimes listening to adults isn't the best idea.

As it turned out, Mom didn't throw away the opportunity because she graduated and got a good job as a court reporter. She even managed to save enough money to buy our new house. That's pretty impressive if you ask me! She hasn't saved enough to pay for the whole thing—I guess only really rich people have enough money to do that —but has enough for a down payment, whatever that is, and enough to pay the bills every month.

All I know, is that it's going to be wonderful to have my own room again! For the past few years Clara and I shared the only bedroom, while Mom slept on the foldout couch in the living room/kitchen area. Having a room to myself and some privacy is something I've dreamt about for a long time. Clara is nice enough as sisters go but is also a pain in the neck sometimes. I'm glad I get to have the room upstairs—it even has its own small bathroom! There's only a toilet and a sink, so for showers or baths I'll have to use the bathroom downstairs, but that's fine with me. Clara's room is downstairs near Mom's, partly because she's younger and partly because of the frequent nightmares she's had ever since Dad died. She usually ends up crawling into bed with Mom at least three nights a week. I feel sad for her but also wish the bad dreams would stop for all our sakes. Maybe the new house will help.

Our new house is called a *story and a half* because the second floor is a little smaller than the main level. I think it's a strange name because it isn't *half* as big, it's just different. The ceiling is slanted on both sides and one of the windows is in what Momo calls a dormer. The dormer even has a window seat! It's the most amazing thing ever! I've always wanted a window seat and now I have one all to myself! Momo is going to make cushions for it out of whatever fabric I want. She's going to make curtains too! I can't wait for everything to be finished. I picture myself sitting there, reading a book or even just daydreaming.

"Hey Leah-loo!" Mom's voice drifts up the stairs. "Here comes the last box for you!" Then I hear her chuckle to herself, "I'm a poet and don't even know it!"

I look in the direction of the stairs to see Mom lugging one more box labeled **Leah's room, second floor.** She sets it down on the floor at the top of the steps and looks around, her hands on her hips.

"You've got your work cut out for you up here, don't you, sweetie? Are you sure you don't want some help?"

"I'm sure, Mom. I've got a plan!" I can't conceal my smile.

"Of course you do! You're my little planner; always have been." She walks over to where I sit on the bed and plants a kiss on my cheek. "That helps me more than you know."

I just grin and soak in her praise. It's not that she's stingy with praise, but I thrive on pleasing people, and Mom is right at the top of the list. Even before Dad died, I decided that it was my responsibility to help Mom in any way I could and that meant not making more work for her. I've made it my job to do the dishes, clean the apartment and help with Clara. This past year, I've started doing the laundry too. There were a few mistakes at first. The worst one was when a red sock got in with a load of whites and turned everything pink. I thought I'd get in big trouble for that when Aunt Kathy found me crying in the laundry room. Instead, she gave me a hug and told me about the wonders of bleach. I felt like she'd saved my life!

"Well, don't stay up too late. Tomorrow will be just as busy as today. Nighty-nite, Leah-loo. I love you!" She gives me a big squeeze and heads back downstairs.

"Nighty-nite, Mom. Love you back."

I hear the door at the bottom of the stairwell close and suddenly feel very much alone. Alone is something I haven't been for years, and I'm not exactly sure what to do with myself. I know I could start unpacking, but there's all day tomorrow for that. Tonight, I decide it would be more fun to explore my new room. There are so many cool features, like the window seat bench and the built-in bookshelves. There's also an amazing walk-in closet. This way, when I begin to unpack tomorrow, I'll know exactly where to put everything.

The first place I want to check out is the window seat bench. The top has hinges on it so the seat can open. I've been thinking about what I'll store in it since the first moment I'd laid eyes on it. I have to be careful not to just throw things in there without a plan. That could turn into a disaster very quickly! No, I'll have to be very methodical about it; very organized. I've always joked that *Organized* is my middle name. (Which it's not, by the way; it's Ann!)

After I wash my face, brush my teeth, and change into my pajamas, I tiptoe over to the window seat. The dormer is on the front of the house, and the street lights cast enough of a glow so I don't need to turn on the ceiling light. Kneeling down, I quietly open the seat and peer inside. It's empty except for a few cobwebs and some dust bunnies. It looks like the previous owners haven't used this for a long time, if ever. I'm relieved when no spiders crawl across the space but know they're probably hiding somewhere. I hate spiders with a passion and try to think of them all as Charlotte from Charlotte's Web. That helps a little, but I still panic and scream every time I see one.

I can make out the outline of some sort of little door in the back that I didn't notice at first. It's too dark to see it clearly, so I scramble over to my nightstand and get a small flashlight out of the drawer. It's not very bright because it needs new batteries, but it's better than nothing. Shining it down into the window seat, I see a narrow, black ribbon sticking out of one side of the compartment. Before I give it too much thought, I reach in and tug on the ribbon. With a muffled pop the small door opens, revealing a seemingly empty compartment inside.

I sit back on my heels, unsure of how to proceed. What if a family of mice is living in there? I don't mind mice too much if they stay away from me, but if I've just disturbed their little lives, what would that mean? Suddenly, my perfect room takes on an ominous feeling. I don't hate mice as much as spiders but prefer not to share my new room with *anyone,* human or otherwise.

Gathering all my courage, I know what I have to do if I'm going to get any sleep tonight—I have to investigate the mysterious little compartment. New batteries for the flashlight are the first order of business, so I creep downstairs to find some.

Thanks to Mom also being organized, I find the box labeled **Junk drawer** right away, and it's already been opened. I start rummaging around for the batteries, trying not to make too much of a mess or too much noise.

"Whatcha doin'?"

I jump at the sound of Clara's tiny voice.

"Aren't you supposed to be in bed?"

Clara comes closer, her thumb in her mouth. "Yeah, but I can't sleep. I miss you." She burrows into my side.

I want to remind her not to suck her thumb but decide against it. So what if she's six years old and still does that? This is a big change for all of us. I actually think Clara's smart to find a way to comfort herself.

"I miss you too, Clare-bear, but remember what Mom said about sleeping in our own rooms?" I give her small shoulders a reassuring cuddle.

"Yeah, if we sleep in our own rooms for two nights in a row, we get to have a slumber party in the living room with movies and popcorn." Clara repeats what Mom promised us in a monotone voice and an expressionless face. She's so tired, she can hardly keep her eyes open.

"That's right, so let's not blow it. We can do this, right?" I give her a gentle fist bump and a hug. "Now get back in bed before Mom catches you out here!"

"Okay, okay," mumbles Clara, and she leaves the room, dejected.

My heart aches for my little sister. Clara was only three years old when Dad died in the car accident. Once we moved to the garage apartment, all she ever knew was sleeping not only in the same room with me but in the same bed. Clara must have felt more alone than I did and was too young to understand it all, not that I did. Understand it all, that is.

After I find the flashlight batteries, I sneak back upstairs, silently closing the door at the bottom of the steps behind me. There isn't another door to my room, since the upstairs is the entire bedroom. As I replace the old batteries in the flashlight, I wonder if Mom will ever let me put a lock on the door. I'll wait a while to make that request—maybe next year.

I make my way over to the window seat again and aim the now brighter beam of light at the small rectangular opening. With my heart nearly beating out of my chest, I lean over and reach my hand into the bench.

"Here goes nothing," I whisper. "Please don't have spiders, please don't have mice!" I've never been so scared in my life. Actually, that's not true; I've been way more scared than this before.

I don't feel the scurrying of little mouse feet or the tickle of spider legs, thank goodness, but instead my fingers land on something that feels smooth and flat. I pull it out of the opening and see that it's a small book covered in a thick layer of dust. As I lift it out, some of it flies in my face, making me sneeze.

Sniffling, I set the book down inside the bench so I won't get the dust all over everything. Mom gave me a few trash bags to use until we buy a wastebasket for my room, so I bring one over to the bench. Putting the bag inside the bench, I take the book and shake off as much dust as I can into the bag, preventing a few more sneezes. Peering at the book with my flashlight in hand, I can see fancy gold letters on its red cover that say: *My Diary*.

I've always wanted a diary where I could write my private thoughts and feelings. In school last year, we read *The Diary of Anne Frank*. I became obsessed with the story of Anne and her family, who'd lived in hiding from the Nazis during World War II. I was also obsessed with the idea of having my own diary. I'd asked for one for my birthday but didn't get it. Mom had explained that we didn't need more things cluttering up the apartment. It seemed like a lame excuse to me, but I kept my disappointment to myself. If she had just said it was because we couldn't afford it, I would've understood. We couldn't afford lots of things.

I wipe the remaining dust from the diary with my fingers and then rub my hand on the carpet, making a mental note to vacuum tomorrow. Diaries usually come with keys, but this one doesn't seem to have one. It has a lock, but if there's a key I have no idea where it is. Pushing up on the small gold button on the latch with my thumb, I'm pleasantly surprised when the lock pops open. Maybe the owner of the diary felt the hiding place was a good enough lock in itself.

A small voice in my head warns me not to start reading since diaries are private, but I have to look in it to see who it belonged to, don't I? I can't imagine throwing it in the trash without at least looking inside for a name. Sitting with my back against the bench, I pause to think about my options. It's an invasion of privacy to read another person's diary but doesn't that rule mostly apply if you *know* the other person? What harm could come from reading a complete stranger's diary? I can't think of any at all. It might even solve some mystery I don't know about yet.

Outside my window, I hear the eerie hoot of an owl. Goosebumps sprout on my arms, but it's not the owl that makes me feel afraid. I look at the book in my hands, say a silent apology, and begin to read.

Hope

December 25,1965 (Christmas Day)

Dear Diary,

I'm so excited to finally have you! I asked for you for Christmas and there you were in my stocking this morning! We just read *The Diary of Anne Frank* in school. That's what made me want to have a diary of my own. You are my favorite Christmas present this year! Maybe ever!

First things first—I need to name you. I think I'll call you Daisy. I like how the first letter is the same as the first letter in Diary. *Dear Daisy*....I like it! Next, I need to find a good place to hide you and your key. Pete, my brother, is 16 and couldn't care less about what I do, but you can never be too careful, right? I would hate to have you fall into the wrong hands! Just the idea of a diary being someone's private thoughts is enough to make people want to snoop. I know that's what I'd want to do! I'll have to think about that some more.

Let me introduce myself, Daisy. My name is Hope Ann McMillan and I am 11 (almost 12!) years old. I'm in the 6th grade at Holy Saints School. Pete goes to the public high school. My parents wanted him to go to the Catholic boys' high school, but he threw a giant fit and refused. He always gets his way, so my parents gave in. From what they say, I'm still going to go to the Catholic girls' school for high school, but that's two and a half grades away, so I'm not going to worry about it now. Most of my friends are planning to go there too, so it won't be that bad. I think it would be great not to have any nasty boys around at school. They can be so annoying!

Well, that's all for now, Daisy. I promised my mom I wouldn't stay up too late.

Love,
Hope

Leah

The girl in the diary is my age! She and her brother are five years apart, just like Clara and me, only in the opposite direction. She's in the same grade as me, and we both have the same middle name! How cool is that? Hope—that's her name—also just read *The Diary of Anne Frank* in school. She named her diary Daisy, the same thing I'd name a pet if I'm ever allowed to have one. There are just so many coincidences! I feel as though I've just found a new friend. This is fantastic!

Before going to bed, I tuck Daisy away in the secret compartment to keep her safe, looking forward to reading more tomorrow. I can't help but wonder if we'll have even more things in common.

Once I'm lying in my old bed in my new room, I find myself missing Clara. I didn't realize how used I'd gotten to having her near by, softly snoring and grinding her teeth all night long. It's been sort of inconvenient sharing a bed with Clara because I've also been sharing the same bedtime, just to make things easier When I was eight it was fine, but once I turned eleven, I was embarrassed to have the same bedtime as a six-year-old. If the kids at school found out, they'd never stop teasing me. Life is hard enough without doing things to make it harder. That's a life lesson I learned from my dad.

Sleep isn't coming as easily as it should after a busy day of moving and unpacking. I flip back and forth to get comfortable, but it's not being in a new room that's the problem. Try as I might, I can't get the memories of Dad out of my head. Watching him struggle with drinking too much alcohol was hard, mostly because I didn't really understand what was happening. It wasn't too bad when I was really little, but after a while it got worse; *everything* got worse. In fact, it's all I can think of when I remember life before the accident. It makes me sad for Clara; she doesn't have hardly any memories of the good times.

We moved a lot, mostly because Dad kept losing jobs. That made it challenging for me to make friends. I always felt like I didn't belong, like I wasn't good enough. It was awkward to find my footing on the social ladder of every new school; by the time I found it, we'd move again. At least this house is within the same school boundaries as Aunt Kathy's, and that's a huge relief. It was one of our *must haves* in a house. Mom had seen how I'd blossomed (her word, not mine) by staying at the same school for three years and didn't want to spoil that. I'm going to be starting middle school, so everyone will be in the same boat as far as the actual school building goes. At least I'll have some friends on the first day this time, my besties, April and Nora.

I wake to the sounds of birds chirping outside my window and the hum of voices downstairs. I can't figure out who the voices belong to until I remember that Kathy and Momo are coming over to help us get settled. Rolling over onto my back, I soak in my new room. It sparkles in the morning sunlight, and I can't imagine how a room could be any more perfect. As my eyes settle on the window seat, my thoughts drift back to the diary named Daisy. My heart sinks a little as I realize I'll probably have to wait until the end of a very busy day to be able to visit Hope and Daisy again. Sometimes life is so unfair.

The thought of getting the boxes unpacked and the house settled makes me spring into action. I hop out of bed and stretch, ready to conquer the day. After making my bed—something I do first thing every morning—I get dressed, wash my face and brush my teeth. It feels like I just did those things but do them again anyway. An article I read online stressed how important regular face-washing is in order to prevent acne breakouts. I don't have any zits yet and don't want any, *ever*. Last year, one of my classmates had a particularly epic outbreak of acne and kids had been so mean. I felt so bad for him! That's when I decided I better learn how to keep the same thing from happening to me. It can't hurt to try.

"Good morning, family!" I call as I enter the kitchen.

"Good morning, Loo-loo!" My grandma opens her arms wide and gives me a big hug and a sloppy kiss on my cheek, her usual way of greeting me.

"Hi, Momo!" Momo's hugs are the best because she's so soft and cuddly.

From the time I was a baby, I've been called Leah-loo by my mom, but my grandma calls me Loo-loo. I loved it when I was a baby and still do. When I shortened Grandma Mo, which is what my cousins called her, to Momo, it stuck. It's our special thing.

"How did you sleep last night? Did your new room keep you awake?" Momo sits down in the breakfast nook, returning to her bagel slathered in strawberry cream cheese and her mug of piping hot coffee. (The breakfast nook is another thing that I love about this house!)

"Good—it was weird at first, but then it was okay." I glance over at Clara, who has a sleepy thumb in her mouth. "How did you sleep, Clare-bear?"

She lets out a dramatic yawn. "Not so good."

I peek over at Mom and smile. "But she stayed in her new room all night! Isn't that great, Leah?"

"That's awesome! Only one more sleep and we get our slumber party. We're almost there!" I give my little sister a high five, hoping she doesn't tattle on herself.

"Whatever." Clara is clearly not enthused, but she tends to be grouchy without enough sleep. It could be a long day.

Once breakfast is over, we set to work unpacking. I really want to help the grown-ups in the kitchen. I love listening to the conversations my mom, Kathy and Momo have together. There's always some little tidbit of gossip or information to tuck away in my mind for later. If I had a diary, I could write those gems down shortly after I hear them. As it is, I just try my best to remember them. Quite often, their conversations turn to diets and how much weight they need to lose or what parts of their bodies they hate the most. Momo usually tries to change the subject because she doesn't believe in that stuff, but Aunt Kathy just ignores her. Mom is somewhere in the middle, not saying too much, but she still complains plenty. It's always struck me as odd that no one ever says they want to *gain* weight. That makes me assume that gaining weight is one of the worst things you could ever do. The other thing that's strange is that they all look perfectly fine. After hearing one of those conversations recently, I've become more aware of how the waistband of my pants feels and keep tugging it away from my stomach. It's not too tight, but I've decided that I don't ever want it to be. What would my mom and aunt think of me if my pants ever got too small? Maybe they wouldn't love me as much anymore or they'd be ashamed of me. It's a terrifying thought.

"Actually, Leah, I'd like you to help Clara get her room situated," says Mom. "She needs a little direction, if you know what I mean." She gives me a quick wink.

"Okay—c'mon, Clare-bear, let's go!"

It doesn't take long for the two of us to unpack the boxes stacked in Clara's room and to arrange the bed, dresser, desk and bookshelf. We've always shared the bookshelf we had in the garage apartment, but now Clara has it all to herself.

"I wish I had as many books as you do," Clara says as she pulls books from a box. "It looks empty with just mine."

I glance up from the dresser where I'm arranging Clara's t-shirts, shorts and jeans. It's strange to see the clothes I'd worn when our dad was still alive, filling my sister's dresser. Some of those memories make me sad, so I shut that part of my brain off for the time being.

"It took my whole life to collect my books. You'll have more before you know it." What I don't say is that I'd accumulated my books before the really hard times hit. "Maybe Mom will let us go to the book sale at the library next week to get you some more. They always have lots of good ones, really cheap."

Clara brightens at this idea and continues working in a much better mood. Before long, her room is completely put together. Momo has shown me how to flatten the cardboard boxes so they won't take up so much room in the garage. The plan is to store them out there in case we ever need them again. Clara even tries to help me carry them, although she drops more of them than she holds onto. I hope we won't need these boxes for a very long time but know better than to get my hopes too high.

Even though Clara wants to hang out with me as I get settled in my new room, I'm relieved when Momo invites Clara to ride along to the hardware store with her and Aunt Kathy. I'm excited to spend some time by myself, not only to unpack and organize my room but to read some more of the diary.

The built-in bookshelves run all along the short walls on opposite sides of the room and can also work as a headboard. I've never had a headboard before, so it's nice to have something there besides a bare wall. It will be perfect for late night reading or writing. I can just set whatever I'm working on right behind my head. It's so perfect!

The last box to unpack is full of photo albums from when I was a baby. For some reason, Mom thinks I should be the keeper of these books stuffed with a potpourri of memories. I know my parents weren't always happy, but they weren't always unhappy either. It surprises me that my mom doesn't want them in her room. Sure, there are pictures of my dad that might upset her, but there are also pictures of me. Doesn't she want those close by? I place the photo albums on the shelf across the room from my bed; that's where my desk sits, along with a comfy chair and ottoman from the garage apartment that Aunt Kathy has given me. Every time Kathy came over to the garage apartment, I was curled up in that chair either reading a book or doing my homework. She says she wanted to get rid of it anyway, but I still think it's kind. 'You and that chair belong together, Leah,' Kathy said the day she gave it to me. 'Nobody loves it like you do.'

I stack the albums on the shelf behind the chair so I won't be able to see them so easily. 'Out of sight, out of mind,' I've heard Momo say a gazillion times. I'm not exactly sure what it means or if it's a good saying, but it seems to fit the situation. As hard as I try to ignore the photo albums, the 'out of sight, out of mind' thing isn't working—I'm drawn to them like a magnet.

There are three albums—one red, one blue and one gold. The red one is from when I was a baby, the blue one is from when I was a toddler and the gold one is from right before Clara was born, the year I started kindergarten. After that, there were never as many pictures.

Settling into the chair, I clutch the red photo album close to my chest. Do I really want to go down this road on a day that's been so happy so far? I know that looking at pictures from when I was little will make me sad; there's no doubt about it. My heart pounds and my palms grow clammy as I sit there deciding what to do. I'm just about to open the album when Mom's voice floats up the stairs.

"Hey, Leah-loo! How's it going?" Footsteps follow the voice until Mom's in the middle of the room. "This is looking great, sweetie! You've been busy! I love how you've arranged the furniture."

She says all of that before her gaze lands on me, sitting in the chair with the red photo album on my lap. She makes her way over to me and sits on the arm of the chair, putting her arm loosely around my shoulders.

"Whatcha got there?"

I don't know why she says that because she knows *exactly* what I've got here. Not wanting to hurt her feelings, I keep my snarky thoughts to myself.

"My baby pictures. I haven't looked at them in a while." I brush a tiny speck of lint off the cover with my thumb, avoiding my mom's eyes.

"Can I look with you? Maybe I can fit my big butt in this chair with you if you skooch over a little bit." She gives me a gentle nudge as she says it.

Mom is always saying things like that about different parts of her body, and I can never figure out why. I think she looks, well, like Mom, which to me, is perfect. Whenever she says anything bad about herself, I always wonder if I should feel bad about my body too. From what I've heard Mom and Kathy say, hating your body is something that just happens by a certain age. I sort of assume it's something *all* women do whether they want to or not. (Momo doesn't talk about herself like that, but maybe by the time you're a grandma, you don't care about it as much anymore.) Thinking about it makes my stomach hurt.

"I thought you didn't like looking at these, Mom." My voice comes out in a tiny squeak. I say it so quietly that for a second I wonder if she heard me.

"I love looking at your baby pictures, sweetie!" She drops into the chair next to me with ease. "You were so cute, and I was so in love with you!" She kisses me on the cheek. "Of course you're still cute, and I'm still in love with you."

"I know, Mom. I love you too." I feel my cheeks getting warm.

As we flip through the plastic-covered pages, I'm transported back to a time when I didn't have a care in the world, when all I did was eat, sleep, and have my diaper changed. Do babies even *think* about anything if they have nothing to worry about?

"Oh my God, I was so *thin* back then!" Mom's exclamation brings me back to the moment. "If only I looked that good now!"

I examine the picture my mom is looking at, squinting to make sure I don't miss a thing. I look from the picture to Mom and back again.

"You *do* look that good now!"

"You're so sweet! Do you really think so? I sure don't feel like it. I mean, I *have* had another baby, and I *am* ten years older…." Her voice trails off into a heavy silence.

I feel helpless. I don't know what I'm supposed to do or say to make Mom feel better. Listening to her complain about her body makes me question my own judgment and eyesight. To me, she's amazing and always has been. I see nothing wrong with her at all—except the way she complains about herself. *That* gets old.

Finally, I say, "*I'm* the one that's gotten bigger, not you, silly!"

I hope my weak attempt at humor will shake her out of the funk she's quickly fallen into. This has been a good day, a happy time, and I don't want it to be ruined.

Smiling, she ruffles my hair. "That's just baby fat, sweetie. You're growing into a beautiful young woman, and I'm so proud of you." She gives my leg a squeeze, and I cringe inside. "Maybe we should put the pictures away for now and go fabric shopping for your cushions and curtains. Grandma Mo told me how much she needs and said we should pick it out ourselves. Sound like a plan?"

"Yes!" I can't wait to have the cushions and curtains. I'm also relieved for the diversion.

I take the photo album and place it back on the shelf behind the chair. For some reason, thinking about how much bigger I've gotten since then doesn't make me feel proud. All I feel is a strange, icky knot in my stomach, like I've done something wrong by growing at all.

Hope

January 1,1966

Dear Daisy,

Happy New Year! It's so exciting to be in a new year, isn't it? Mom always says it's nice to have a clean slate, a fresh start. I didn't think the old year was so bad, but looking forward to new things is always exciting, I guess.

We had a little New Year's Eve party last night with the neighbors who live on either side of us. The adults claimed that no one would have to worry about drinking and driving. Mr. Hartley joked that as far as he knew there were no laws about drunk *walking*. I think he already drunk-walked to our house, and he just got worse as the night went on. I could tell that Mrs. Hartley was super embarrassed. Susie, their daughter, is a year older than I am. She has a HUGE crush on Pete, and he doesn't even know she's alive. It's kinda hard to watch because she's not very sneaky about it. At midnight, when everyone was kissing each other, Susie ran over to Pete with her chin tilted up, hoping he'd kiss her, but he just ignored her. She started crying and ran home. Pete's friend, Mark, was there, and teased Pete about Susie liking him until Pete was ready to punch him (but he didn't). I'm usually just annoyed by my brother, but Mark was being such a jerk about it, that I felt sorry for Pete. He doesn't have to like Susie if he doesn't want to. She *is* four years younger than he is. They don't even go to the same school!

After midnight, the party sort of fizzled out—at least all the kids went home, along with the moms. The dads stayed longer and drank more. I thought it was super annoying because the more they drank, the louder they got. It was hard to fall asleep with all that commotion. This morning, Mom was mad at Dad, mostly because he wanted to sleep all day. She said he has a hangover, a bad headache from drinking too much. It's not like it happens all the time, if *ever*, so I thought Mom was being kinda mean. He felt *really* crummy. Mom thought she was funny when she made all kinds of noise, like vacuuming around him, just to make him feel worse. I was worried for a while but then they kissed and made up, so now things seem okay. They get super annoyed with each other a lot, and that's kinda worrisome. It's probably just a phase they're going through. At least I hope so!

Love,
Hope

Leah

It's way past midnight when I close the diary. I don't realize I'm crying until a tear drops onto my arm. I've just discovered something Hope and I do *not* have in common: two living parents. It sounds as though her parents were way more normal than mine ever were. After all, they actually entertained their friends by having a New Year's Eve party. They actually *had* friends. The other normal thing was that they made up after they had a disagreement. Hope's dad hadn't kept drinking and her mom hadn't stayed mad. Everything turned out okay. I feel jealous of how normal her family was and that she *had* a family. I chase those thoughts away, however, because I also have a family, and they love me very much. Besides, it's pointless to wish for something I'll never have.

I'd always thought my family was like everyone else's, until I went to school. That's when I found out that everyone's dads didn't stay out all night or go missing for days at a time. I'd been invited to my first birthday party for a friend when I was in kindergarten. I remember being amazed to see how nice my friend's house was and how well-behaved her father was. He was very funny and helpful and kind the whole time, not only after he'd had a few big gulps from his drink. As it turned out, my classmate's dad had been drinking lemonade just like the rest of us—plain old lemonade. My dad would've drunk lemonade, but he would've poured something from a small silver flask into it first. After that, everything would change, usually for the worse.

I've never had a birthday party of my own because we couldn't afford one. I also think Mom was ashamed of our rundown house. She and Dad bought it right after they were married and at first, Dad had taken pride in it, mowing the lawn and repairing things that had broken. He'd even painted it once. As the years went by, even before Clara had been born, he had less interest in the house and more interest in meeting his buddies at the bar. It always makes me sad to think about it. I've never been able to talk to anyone about it because there's no one I feel safe confiding in. If I had a diary of my own, I'd be able to tell it everything, just like Hope told Daisy everything—at least that's how it seems. I've only read the first few entries, so I don't really know how much she shares, but I hope I'll get to know her better—even the ugly parts, if there are any. That's what friends do.

I get out of bed to return Daisy to her hiding place. It's tempting to just put the diary on the shelf near my bed, but it can't hurt to be careful. What if Mom finds Daisy and gets upset with me for reading it? Worse yet, what if she throws it away? On some level, I feel like I'll fall apart if I can't look forward to reading Daisy at the end of the day. I'm amazed that I've grown so attached in such a short amount of time. Before placing it in the window seat bench, I give it a little kiss on the cover and gently tuck it away for the night.

A loud clap of thunder wakes me from a deep sleep, making the windows rattle and shake. My heart pounds along with the rain, and I'm disoriented for a couple of seconds until I look at the window seat and get my bearings. I'd been dreaming about our old house, the one we lived in when we were happy. It had been a nice dream, and I'm not ready for it to be over just yet. The weather, however, has other ideas. Bright flashes of lightening and deafening claps of thunder keep rolling through, making sleep impossible. Peeking at my alarm clock, I see that it's six o'clock; not that early, but not that late either

In a flash as quick as the lightening, I decide to make breakfast for Mom and Clara. After I make my bed, I wash my face, brush my teeth, get dressed and tiptoe downstairs. If they're still asleep, I don't want to wake them and spoil the surprise.

Once downstairs, I see a soft glow coming through the kitchen door. Poking my head in the doorway, I see Mom in her robe, sitting in the breakfast nook. There's a coffee mug in front of her, and she's staring at a letter that's laying on the table. The expression on her face makes me want to sneak back upstairs and pretend I'm still asleep. My heart fills with fear to see that look on her face; it's the same look she has when there's more bills than money. In other words, it's an expression I've seen many, many times.

"Leah-loo! You're up early! Did the storm wake you?"

"Yeah, it was really loud." I stand in the doorway, not sure if I should intrude.

"Were you scared being up there all alone?"

"Not really, it just woke me up."

"Well, don't just stand there, sweetie, come on in." She gives me a weak smile.

"I was going to surprise you and Clara with breakfast," I say as I slide into the nook across from her.

"Aww—you're sweet, but I'm just having coffee for breakfast today. Maybe another day, huh?" She glances down at the letter again.

"What's that?" I nod toward the document on the table. Since Dad died, I've been used to having Mom tell me her troubles, financial and otherwise. I don't understand most of it, but it seems to help her feel better to tell me about things.

"It's a letter from the school district." The smile she gives me is way too big and much too bright. "School starts in less than a month, you know."

"I know! I'm getting excited. It'll be a new school but at least April and Nora will be there with me."

Mom takes a long sip of her coffee, sets the mug down and looks at me with sad eyes. "Well, that's the thing. This letter says the district had to redo the school boundaries. You'll be going to Shady Creek instead of Rolling Hills."

For a minute I just sit there, wondering what the big deal is. "So?"

"Well, from the way they drew the boundaries, it looks like April and Nora will still be going to Rolling Hills." She slides the map that came with the letter across the table so I can see it. "See—here's our street and way over there are your friends' houses. I'm so sorry, Leah."

I stare at the paper, wishing I'd paid more attention when we'd studied maps in social studies last year. There's a line drawn with yellow highlighter over the outline of the new boundaries. I don't think our new house is that far from Rolling Hills, but apparently the school district does. Our new house is just inside the highlighted line. We miss Rolling Hills by a smidgeon.

"But I thought when we picked this house, I'd be going to Rolling Hills with my friends." I try really hard not to sound whiny, but it's not easy, especially when I feel like crying. I *am* only eleven, for Pete's sake!

Mom reaches across the table and puts her hand over mine. "It was, sweetie. I didn't know they were going to change the boundaries. I'd heard rumors, but I also heard that nothing would change until you were in high school."

Panic snakes through me as I try to stay calm. Mom has enough going on without me getting all emotional right now. April and Nora are not only my best friends, they're my *only* friends. We call ourselves The Three Amigos and The Three Musketeers; 'all for one and one for all.' Now they'll be friends without me, and I'll be alone. I want to scream and throw a fit, but that won't change anything. The sky grows as dark as my mood, and I can't help but wonder if it's a bad omen. Just then, another deafening clap of thunder shakes the house and my happiness right along with it.

Hope

March 9 1966

Dear Daisy,

Today was the WORST day EVER!!! I wish I could DIE! First of all, it's Girl Scout Week. That started out being a good thing because we get to wear our Girl Scout uniforms on Wednesday(that's TODAY!), if we have one or regular clothes if we don't. It's such a treat to not have to wear my ugly school uniform! It's even cooler because the girls who aren't in Scouts still have to wear their school uniforms. HA! The boys don't even have uniforms, which is so unfair, but it's fun to feel special for being a Girl Scout.

Anyhow, because as my mom says, 'we're not made of money,' I have a hand-me-down Scout uniform. That's fine and dandy, except that it's the old style, like from the fifties, so I stick out like a sore thumb. It's a darker shade of green and has long sleeves instead of short ones. The newer ones are so much neater looking, but beggars can't be choosers. (My mom says that too.) I guess it's better than no uniform at all. The girls in my troop are nice about it, but I've been kinda worried about the other kids at school teasing me. I know it shouldn't bug me, but it does. No one likes to be made fun of. Of course some kids made fun of me, especially the cool kids. They made jokes about getting my uniform at the Goodwill or asked me if I thought I was the troop leader and stuff like that. I felt like crying almost all day. Why did I decide to wear the stupid thing? I could've just worn regular clothes, like my favorite outfit that I feel great in, and it would've been so much better—but then it wouldn't have been. You'll never believe what else happened!

In the middle of the afternoon, during geography class, my tummy felt really strange—sort of achy. It didn't feel like I had to go to the bathroom, so I waited until my class's bathroom break to go. When I did, I couldn't believe what I saw! There was *blood* on my underpants! There wasn't any on my petti-pants (that's like a culotte slip), so I didn't think it went through to my uniform, but still! I thought I was dying from cancer or something! I didn't know what to do. I put some toilet paper in my undies in case it happened some more. I also looked at the back of my uniform and nothing showed. The rest of the day went by SO slowly. All I wanted to do was go home and hide. I also worried all afternoon about how I was going to tell my mom and dad that I'm dying. How do you tell someone something like that? The achy feeling never went away either. In fact, it got worse. In music class, I asked our music teacher, Mrs. Olsen, if I could use the bathroom (she's really nice about that type of thing, not mean like the nuns). There was a little more blood, so I changed the toilet paper for new stuff and hoped I'd be good until I got home.

As soon as I got home, my mom asked me to run down to the drug store on the corner to buy some new shoelaces for Pete. I asked why he couldn't buy his own shoelaces, but she just gave me a heavy sigh and rolled her eyes. That's code for: 'You know how busy your brother is.' That's baloney because he's not *that* busy. So I went to the store and wouldn't you know it? Kevin, the cute high school boy who lives across the street from us, was working. He's SO cute! Anyhow, I told him I needed some shoelaces and followed him over to the display where the laces are kept. I told him which color and length and when he pulled out the little plastic drawer they were in, he pulled it out too far and the shoelaces spilled all over the floor. I wanted to DIE! I figured it happened because I was bleeding to death, even though he had no idea. I felt so ashamed.

On the way home, I decided I had to tell my mom right away. I couldn't wait until Dad got home to tell them together. As soon as I got inside the back door, I blurted it out.

"Mom,I think I'm dying."

She looked from the pillowcase she was ironing, surprised. "Why do you think that, honey?"

"Because I'm bleeding…down there." I pointed to 'down there.'

She put her hands to her face and said, "Oh my goodness! I didn't think it would happen so soon!"

What?! She *knew* I was going to die? Then she sat me down and told me about getting my period. She had a little kit with a booklet that explained all about it. It also had a weird elastic belt with a clip in the front and one in the back and something called a sanitary napkin that fastens onto the hooks. You're supposed to wear that stuff to soak up the blood every month. EVERY MONTH?!?!? She said something else about my body getting ready to have a baby someday, and that really freaked me out! Why so soon? I'm only 11 years old! The other thing she said, and she was VERY serious about this part, was that I'm not to tell ANYONE about it, not even my friends. She said it's very, very private and nobody's business. That made me feel ashamed and dirty, like it's not a good type of secret to have.

Tomorrow when I go to school, I have to wear one of those thick, yucky napkin thingys. Mom said I should probably wear TWO of them, just so I have a spare. *Two* of them? How will I even be able to walk? She said my teacher probably isn't used to dealing with girls 'like me.' I know she meant girls having their period so young, but it made me feel like it was my fault, that *I* was a problem. Tomorrow's going to the WORST! You're lucky you're not a girl, Daisy!

Love,
Hope

Leah

Clara and I are both starting new schools tomorrow. The biggest difference isn't the grades we're in, it's that Clara is super excited and I, well, am not. Clara can't wait to make new friends and has no doubt she'll have many. I feel just the opposite.

Mom and I went to the Open House last week where I met Ms. Wilcox, my homeroom teacher, and got my schedule and locker, but it was terrifying. The only kids I saw that I recognized were a few kids from the popular group. They'd already formed their stupid clique, making it seem even worse. Since everyone wasn't there all at once, I had no idea if I'd know anyone else.

To make matters worse, I've just finished reading a rather disturbing entry in Daisy about Hope getting her first period. Poor Hope, to have gotten it without being prepared! It's sort of a coincidence that it happened during Girl Scout Week, with Scouts promising to be prepared and all that, but I doubt she appreciated the irony. I wonder if she ever did, like years later, when she'd tell the story to her own daughter.

Fortunately, Mom has already told me all about periods, so I'll be ready. She told me how back in the day, like when Momo was a girl, it was much more hush-hush. Now, it's just accepted as a normal part of growing up, but it still seems sort of embarrassing. Normal or not, I hope I don't get it until high school. It mostly sounds inconvenient, but hopefully it won't hurt too much. April's sister, Anna, always gets really bad cramps and needs to lie on the couch with a heating pad on her tummy for a whole day every month. That would be terrible! At school last year, after they showed the fifth grade girls a movie about puberty, it had become a frequent topic of conversation with April, Nora and me. We'd giggled about how boys' voices would change and how their 'boy parts' would grow. Nora laughed so hard the Pepsi she was drinking came out through her nose! I feel bad that Hope couldn't talk to her friends about it. That would be the worst kind of awful.

When I wake up, the first thing I notice is a sticky feeling in my undies. I've *never* felt that way before. With a sinking feeling, I know what's happening: my period. My *first* period. No, not today! Not on the first day of middle school! Could life be anymore unfair?! If April and Nora were there it wouldn't be so bad, but so far I'm not sure if I know a soul—at least a *kind* soul.

I sneak downstairs to the main bathroom. There's a small linen closet in there where Mom keeps towels and extra toilet paper. I figure she stores the stuff for periods in there but don't know for sure. I suppose I should have asked her, but I wasn't ready to know yet. Especially since it's the first day of school, I have no idea how she'll react. I hope she doesn't get all sentimental about it. (She tends to do that about "firsts.") For now, however, I'm on my own.

I peer past the neatly folded towels and stately stacks of toilet paper, looking for...I don't know what. I've never paid attention to the packaging for those things because Mom is always so secretive when she buys them. She always hides them in the bottom of the grocery cart, like they're something to be ashamed of. Suddenly, I feel ashamed of myself for needing them.

There's a rustling sound outside the door and then someone gently jiggles the crystal doorknob.

"Leah? Are you in there?" Mom's whisper slips in under the closed door.

"Uh-huh."

"You okay?"

That's a loaded question if I've ever heard one. I don't know what to say, but I also don't know what to do, so I simply open the door and the tears begin to fall. It's weird because I didn't know I was going to start crying.

"My period started." I whisper, trying not to wake Clara. I certainly don't need an audience for this.

"Oh, sweetie, it'll be okay." Mom wraps her arms around me. "Let's get you all set up." She reaches into the cupboard, extracting a turquoise plastic package of pads. "It's so much easier now than it used to be. When your grandma was a girl, they used to have weird elastic belts to hook the pads onto. Now they just stick in your undies by themselves. Easy-peasy!"

She says it like I should be grateful or something. She also must have forgotten that she already told me all that when we had The Talk, but I'm not about to remind her. She hands me the package and kisses the tip of my nose.

"Do you have any cramps?"

"Um, no, I don't think so."

"Oh, you'd know! Well, that's good. Do you think you can go to school?" Her eyes are filled with so much compassion, I feel as though this is a much bigger deal than they said it was in the movie.

"I'm *not* missing the first day," I say, a little hotly. How could she think I'd want to stay home (even though I do)?

"Good, that's good. You're right—it's not a reason to stay home from *anything*. You can keep those in your bathroom. I guess these will be a regular item on the grocery list now." She nods towards the package in my hands. "Bring some in your backpack so you can change it at school if you need to—but you know that. I forget—can you carry your backpack around in middle school or does it stay in your locker?"

My mind is blank; I don't remember. "I don't know. I'll figure it out."

"Maybe I should call the school and ask how they handle this." Mom thinks out loud.

"It's okay, Mom, I'll figure it out. I can probably just go to the nurse's office or something." The last thing I need is for everyone in the office to know about this, especially on the first day. To them, I'll always be Period Girl or something. "They'll be busy enough in the office as it is."

She puts her hand on the side of my face and gazes at me. "I know you'll figure it out, sweetie. You're so responsible and sensible." She kisses my nose again.

I shrug, her praise making me feel self-conscious. What do I say to that? I don't know if I would've been this responsible naturally, but I've always thought it was because of how things were after my dad died. No kid really wants to be this conscientious. Now that things are more settled, it's just how I am. I know that part of me wants to stay in control to help my mom in case something bad happens again.

"Okay, I'm going to get ready for school," I say, moving towards the stairs to my room. "Thanks, Mom."

There's no other way to describe my first day of middle school besides awful, horrible, and *more* horrible. At least that's how it starts out. I really am trying to have a positive attitude, but it's close to impossible given the circumstances. I feel like I don't know anybody, and I miss April and Nora so much. There's one girl in my homeroom who's new to the school district, so she doesn't know a soul. I know a few souls who have to come to this school like me, but she's totally new. Her name is Prudence, but she goes by Prudy. She seems really nice, so I'm going to try to be friends with her. Prudy also has a few classes with me: English, math and science, so maybe we'll get to know each other even faster.

Our first class is math and our teacher, Mr. Kendall, seems really mean. He's super strict and has no sense of humor. He also doesn't seem to like kids very much which, *hello,* why is he even a teacher then?

We're just getting settled in our seats, when he comes thundering into the room, shouting, "Who told you to sit where you want? *I* will tell you where to sit!"

We all jump up out of the desks we've just chosen. Everyone is rattled, even a troublemaker from my old school, Johnny Morgan. (Unfortunately, he's one of the few kids I *do* know. He's also in my homeroom.) Prudy's really flustered and as she starts to get up out of the desk, her books and notebooks fall on the floor in a big heap. Her face turns bright red just like mine does when I'm embarrassed. Her pencil case even comes apart, spilling pencils, erasers and pens all over the place. I feel so bad for her and stoop down to help her. I mean, I'd want someone to help me.

"And you are?" Mr. Kendall's voice booms across the room towards us.

We both look at him and then at each other. Who is he talking to? I guess it could have been either one of us. We aren't sure what to say, so we just remain silent.

"Let's see," the teacher says, his eyes scanning what must be a class list, "You, the pudgy one, you must be Leah Peterson and the klutzy one must be Prudence O'Brien.

Hmm—I guess the way you got out of that desk wasn't very *prudent.*" Once he starts laughing at his cruel joke, the other kids feel like they have permission to laugh along with him. I can hear Johnny snicker as he laughs the loudest. I want to punch him; either that or disappear.

"Well," continues Mr. Kendall, "it looks like you two ladies will be sitting in the same row anyway since it's alphabetical, so that's lucky, eh?" He raises his eyebrows in our direction.

Prudy and I just nod and slink to the back of the room, bonded by our shared humiliation. I hold my books tightly against my chest, fighting back tears that will only add to my embarrassment. I will *not* be caught crying on the first day of school, no matter what! Even though I'm only a kid, I know if I let a bully like Mr. Kendall know that he can make me cry, it will be a terrible year; he'll make sure of it. Just then, I feel a gentle nudge on my arm.

"You are *not* pudgy, but so what if you were?" Prudy whispers out of the corner of her mouth. "And I've heard that *prudent* joke at least a million times."

I don't dare turn my head to look at her; I'm not even sure if I should smile. Mr. Kendall will probably have a problem with that too.

After surviving math with Mr. Kendall, we walk down the crowded hall to our next class: English.

"How do you think he knew who we were?" says Prudy.

It's kind of hard to hear her. Have I mentioned that Prudy is really tall? My head barely comes up to her shoulder. Between the noise from all the kids in the hall and the distance between her mouth and my ears, well, like I said, it's hard to hear.

"I don't know. I sure wasn't going to ask him! I hate math as it is, so this year should be just great." My stomach is starting to ache a little bit; not like it does when I'm worried, but in a new and different way. It must be cramps. Perfect.

"Yeah, he was a jerk. I hope he gets nicer." Prudy talks a littler louder so I can hear her over the chaos.

"Does that ever happen?" I've never heard of such a thing.

"Well, I have an older sister who's in high school. She said that sometimes in middle school and high school teachers start out super strict and then get nicer once they know the kids respect them. So I guess it *could* happen." She smiles down at me.

"That would be nice. I'll keep my fingers crossed, but I won't hold my breath."

"What time do you have lunch?"

I look at my colored-coded, highlighted and page-protected schedule. "Eleven-thirty, so fourth hour, I guess. How about you?"

Prudy pulls her crumpled schedule from her pocket and glances at it. "Me too!"

"Awesome!" And together, we walk into English.

By the end of the day, the dull, achy feeling below my belly button is getting worse instead of better. I know I'm not dying or anything, but it sure isn't fun. I'm glad I wore two pads like Hope did because I ended up having to throw away the top one after lunch. I brought extras, like Mom suggested, but getting them out of my backpack is tricky. We have to keep our backpacks in our lockers all day which is really unfair. What are girls with their periods supposed to do? I'm not hemorrhaging or anything, but it still worries me. It's really depressing to think that this is going to happen to me every month until I'm an old lady. I don't even want to think about that!

As it turns out, Prudy takes the same bus that I do. How awesome is that? She got a ride from her sister this morning, so we didn't know until we got on the bus after school. Her stop is near mine, so she lives sort of close to me. I sure hope we turn out to be friends.

We choose a seat sort of in the middle of the bus where most of the kids usually sit. The back of the bus is where the troublemakers hang out, and the front is for the goody-goodies, so the middle is for everyone else. Because I saw Johnny on this bus this morning, I slide into a row closer to the goody-goodies than the troublemakers. The last thing we need is to be harassed by Johnny Morgan.

"Do you think you'll like it here?" I ask Prudy as the bus continues to fill up with rowdy kids.

Prudy wrinkles her nose and squints as she looks out the window. "Yeah, so far it's okay. I'm *really* glad I met you! This is the first time we've moved, so I was really nervous."

"We've moved a lot, but not in the past few years. I was nervous too, since my two BFFs are going to Rolling Hills." I fiddle with the strap on my backpack.

Then we hear, "Hey, look! There's Pudge and Prude!" followed by snorts of laughter. It's Johnny and his minions. What do they get out of being so mean?

"Ignore them," Prudy whispers. "Morons like that just do mean stuff to get attention. If we let them know it bugs us, they'll do it even more."

I slide down in the seat, wishing I was invisible. No one has ever been this mean to me before. Why did stupid Mr. Kendall have to go and say those things about us? If this keeps up, it's going to be a very long year. Prudy's stop is the one right before mine, and I hate to see her leave.

"Bye, Leah! I'm riding the bus tomorrow morning, so I'll see you then!"

"I'll save you a seat!" I give her a quiet wave.

As soon as the bus starts to slow down near my stop, I'm ready to bolt. My goal is to get off the bus before Johnny Morgan says anything else. I don't know where his stop is, and I don't really care. I just want to get home.

Now that I'm in middle school, I get home a lot earlier than Clara. Since she's only six, Mom decided that Clara should go to Kid's Club, the before and after school program at her school. She knows I'd be fine babysitting until she gets home from work but wants me to have time to myself to get my homework done. I thought it would make me feel grown up but letting myself into an empty house makes me feel lonely. It's also a tiny bit scary.

As soon as I'm in the door with it locked securely behind me, the tears I've been holding in most of the day make their escape. It feels good to just sob my heart out with no one around to hear me. Usually, I keep it super quiet when I cry so Mom can't hear, but now I can be as loud and dramatic as I want.

I carry my backpack up to my room setting the usual beginning of the year forms for my mom to fill out on my desk. There's no homework on the first day; even evil Mr. Kendall didn't assign any. I've decided to review some of the stuff in the first chapter anyway, just to be prepared for tomorrow. The last thing I want is to not know the answer for Mr. Kendall. He'd probably call me *moron* or something —then I'd have a new awful nickname.

I go to the bathroom before I do anything else to check my pad. It's not too bad, but I get a new one just the same. I'm not exactly sure what to do with it—Mom forgot to cover that little detail—so I roll it up and wrap it in toilet paper, just like I did at school. At school, they have neat little boxes attached to the wall of each bathroom stall for these things. I felt ashamed putting it in there, like the custodian would know it was mine, but didn't know what else to do. I sure didn't want to carry it out with me to put it in the main trash can in the bathroom!

I change my clothes and go downstairs to have a snack before tackling the math review. Mom, Clara and I made peanut butter cookies yesterday, and I've been looking forward to having one or two of them with a cold glass of milk all day long. They were the bright spot at the end of a very stressful day. The second I reach for the cookie jar, however, I hear Mr. Kendall's voice in my head whispering *pudgy, pudgy, pudgy.* Steering myself away from the cookies, I go to the fridge and peer inside for a healthier snack. I spy some baby carrots in a Tupperware container and decide to eat some of those instead. I'm still longing for a cookie after eating the carrots, but I must stay strong. Maybe I'll have a cookie tomorrow if I don't feel too pudgy.

Back in my room, I pull my dictionary from the bookshelf. I know I can look up words on the computer, but there's something comforting about the physical book. I bring it over to my comfy chair and settle in, quickly finding the words beginning with "p". It's not long before it's glaring offensively in my face: **pudgy: slightly fat**. My cheeks burn and my stomach flips. *Slightly fat?* The other day not too long ago Mom said I had *baby fat.* Is that the same thing?

The heavy book tumbles from my lap with a loud bang, as I hurry over to the full-length mirror on my closet door. I turn to the right and scrutinize my profile. What is it about me that looks *slightly fat?* Does my stomach stick out too much? Placing my hand on it, I suck it in and hold it there, studying the difference. I definitely look thinner doing that, but how long can I keep it in? Facing the mirror, I examine my reflection. There are tiny bumps on my chest under my nipples that weren't there before or did I just not notice them? A mortified blush sneaks across my face as I realize that those bumps will only get bigger. From what I see online and on television, it seems like big breasts are something women want because men like them, but I don't see what's so good about them. I haven't noticed bumps on other girls' chests, but I haven't exactly been looking for them. Do those bumps make me look pudgy? I move on from my chest to my lower half. It looks like it always has from what I can tell which helps me feel a little better. Turning around, I try to get a good view of my behind. I've never paid this much attention to it before, so I don't know if it looks pudgy or not. All I know, is that sort of like after I ate the carrots, I have a growing sense of dissatisfaction as I look at the girl in the mirror. I used to recognize her, but now it seems like she's turning into a stranger, one I don't like very much.

Hope

April 1, 1966

Dear Daisy,

I should say Happy April Fool's Day, but I don't feel very happy. Why did Mom and Dad think that *today* would be a good day to tell us they're getting a divorce? Now I'll always think of *that* when it's April 1st. If they had picked April 2nd, I'm pretty sure I wouldn't remember that date, but April Fool's Day has always been one of my favorites. I've always had fun playing pranks on my family, especially Pete. Part of the fun is that he's always played pranks on me too. Every year we try to outdo ourselves from the year before. Now it's ruined forever.

They sat us down after dinner and were acting all nervous. I knew they were going to tell us something bad, but I never guessed it would be this. My first thought was that they were joking. They had to be, right?

"But you guys never even fight!" Pete shouted. He even had tears in his eyes. I can't remember the last time I saw that. "Mark's parents argue all the time, but they're not getting divorced!"

Mom and Dad sat in chairs on opposite sides of the living room, looking awkward. Mom chewed on a hangnail as Dad's knee bounced up and down at a very rapid speed. No one said anything for minutes that felt like hours.

"We love you both very, very much," Mom said, trying not to cry. "This wasn't an easy decision."

"Then don't make it!" snapped Pete. I couldn't tell if he was more angry or more sad.

"We haven't argued in front of you kids, but believe me, we argue plenty," my dad said. He almost sounded proud of it.

I looked at Pete, who was sitting next to me on the couch, because I didn't want to look at either of my parents. My mom looked really, really sad and my dad looked mortified. I felt like crying, and unlike my brother, I didn't hold it in. Pete saw I was crying and reached over to hold onto my hand. That helped me feel a little better. It was the nicest he's been to me in a long time.

"Are we gonna have to move? Sam's parents got divorced and had to sell their house and move into crappy apartments."

"No, you won't have to move," said Dad. "I'll be moving out, but you kids and your mom will stay here."

"And every other weekend you kids will stay at your dad's new place," added Mom. "Unless we work it out differently." She looked at my dad out of the corner of her eye.

"Will we have our own rooms there?" Pete glared at them.

I hadn't thought about it, but it was an important question. Who wants to share a room with their annoying little sister? I sure didn't want to share one with my stinky big brother!

Dad ran his hands back through his crewcut. "There's a lot to figure out, guys. Your mom and I will work it all out."

"Hope, honey," my mom said at last, "you've been awfully quiet. Is there anything you want to say or ask?" I've never seen her look so unhappy.

I didn't want to make anyone feel worse, so all I said was, "Are you *sure* this isn't an April Fool's joke?"

Mom and Dad looked at each other for the first time since we all sat down. They didn't laugh, but they didn't cry either. They just shrugged and kinda smiled.

"You know what, peanut?" (My dad always calls me that.) "We didn't even think of that, but no, I'm afraid it's not a joke."

"We'd never joke about something like this," Mom said, sadly. "But if either of you have any questions or want to talk, just say the word, okay?"

Pete and I just sat there like bumps on a pickle. I knew I should have questions but couldn't think of any. Pete had asked about moving, and at the moment, that was the most important thing. I was pretty sure I'd think of more later on.

"Is one of you having an affair?" Pete's question dropped into the silence like a giant brick.

Mom and Dad looked shocked that he'd ask that, and to be honest, so was I. It was a logical question, even though I'm pretty sure Pete didn't want to know the answer.

"No, of course not. It's nothing like that," said Dad. "We're just not happy anymore."

"But *we* were," snarled Pete. And with that, he stood up and stomped out of the room.

Everything seemed kinda normal after that, but it wasn't. Mom hid in the basement doing laundry and Dad— well, Dad just left. I thought he went to run an errand or something, but he didn't come back. At least he wasn't back by the time I had to go to bed. I tried to stay awake until I heard his car pull into the garage but couldn't hold my eyes open. They must've been too tired from all the crying.

Sorry this was so depressing, Daisy. I'll try to be more cheerful next time.

Love,
Hope

Leah

There's a huge lump in my throat when I finish reading the diary entry from April 1, 1966. I didn't know people got divorced in those days. From the television shows I've seen on Nickelodeon from back then, everyone is married and happy, like The Brady Bunch. If they aren't married, their husband or wife has died, like on Full House. I've always felt sorry for myself because my dad died, but it seems like having divorced parents would be way worse since they had a choice. Dad didn't have a choice; he just died. I can feel my cheeks burn as I realize that I'm lying to myself again. Dad *did* have a choice—he drank and drove. It's the people in the other car who didn't have a choice.

Here I've been thinking that Hope had a happy, normal family; I've even been jealous of her. Now I find this out and don't know what to do with it. I feel angry, like I've been lied to, but that's not true. She's just telling Daisy things as they happen. She never promised her family was happy or that she had a perfect life. That was something I told myself. Well, at least I don't feel jealous anymore—not too much anyway.

I hear the back door open and close and my little sister chattering downstairs. Clara has obviously had a good first day of school because she's bouncing all over the place and talking a mile a minute. She does that when she's happy and excited. I put Daisy back in her hiding place and hurry downstairs to hear all about it.

"Hey, Clare-bear!" I say as I enter the kitchen. "How was the first day of school?" I lean against the counter next to the sink.

"It was *great!* I love my teacher, and I made six new friends!" She holds up her right hand and the thumb of the left to show me. "And the lunchroom is so awesome, and the playground is epic!"

I suppress a giggle at the adjectives she uses. Mom and I share a quiet smile over her head.

"Well, that's good!" I'm happy for her in spite of my day not being great, awesome *or* epic.

"How was your first day, Leah-loo?" Mom asks as she takes some chicken out of the freezer. "Did you make six new friends too?"

I know my mom is sort of kidding, but it stings to know that I'll never make six new friends in one day. I'm just not like Clara in that way.

"No, but I made *one!*" I try to sound as enthused as Clara did, but it sounds fake when I try to be that bubbly. "Her name is Prudy, *and* she takes my bus."

"That's wonderful, sweetie!" She takes the chicken out of it's plastic wrapper and throws the plastic and the styrofoam tray into the trash. "I always say it's better to have one good friend than a hundred bad ones."

I try to find the comfort in this, when Clara tugs on the hem of my t-shirt.

"Look at my Take Home folder, Leah! I actually have *homework!*" Clara is positively glowing.

"Wow!" I look at the folder she's shoving at me. "So tell me about your homework." I want to see how much she's actually listening in class.

"Mommy has to sign this, and this, and this one too. And I have to bring this one back with money in it!" She dangles the school picture form and envelope in front of my nose.

"Good job remembering, kiddo! You'll do great in school if you always listen that well." I tousle her hair and wink. "You better give those to Mom right now so you don't forget."

"Okay! Here, Mommy—here's my homework!" She scampers across the kitchen to where Mom is opening the cookbook.

"Thank you, Clare-bear! Let me wash my hands, and I'll sign those right now." She glances at the due date on the school picture form. "We have a week before this is due, but let's return it tomorrow. It's best to do things sooner rather than later, right?" Her eyes avoid me as she retrieves the checkbook from her purse.

I wonder if she's remembering all the times my school picture forms weren't returned because we didn't have enough money to buy the pictures. At April's house, there were picture frames for her and her sisters that had the school picture for each grade arranged in an oval. April always thought it was dorky, but I thought it was amazing. I would have loved to have something like that. As it is, we have no school pictures of me from first through fourth grade.

There was also the field trip to the Science Museum I couldn't go on because we never returned the permission slip. I had to stay back at school and help in one of the kindergarten classrooms. It had been so humiliating! Some of the other kids, Johnny Morgan being one of them, had teased me about being poor. It wasn't about being poor that time; it was because my dad had knocked over a beer and ruined it. I'd set the permission slip on the kitchen counter for one of my parents to sign, so I figured it was my own fault. I was too embarrassed to ask for another one and just decided I wouldn't go. Mom never knew about it and Dad had forgotten, probably because of all the beer he drank afterwards.

"Are there any forms you need me to sign as long as I'm at it?" Mom looks up at me from where she's bent over the counter.

"Yep, I'll go get them."

I'm thankful for an excuse to leave the room. It was getting stifling in there with all those bad memories haunting me. As I climb the stairs two at a time to my room, I remind myself that that was then and this is now. Things are better now.

On my way back to the kitchen, I see that Clara has settled herself in front of the TV, thumb in mouth, to watch her favorite afternoon cartoons. It's the best way for her to unwind.

"How did everything go with *you-know-what?*" Mom whispers even though Clara is no longer in the room.

"You mean my period?" Mom blushes a little to hear me being so open about it. "It's still here!" I try to make her smile because I already feel guilty for being sassy.

She rolls her eyes. "Everything worked out okay with supplies and stuff?"

"Yeah, I wore two pads and that worked out okay. They even have a little box in the bathroom stalls to put them in. I just rolled it up in toilet paper and put it in there."

"Good thinking, sweetie! I forgot to tell you about that part. Is your tummy feeling okay?"

"I've got some cramps, but it's okay."

She smiles. "Let's get you some Advil for those. How was the rest of your day?" She hands me all the forms she's just signed, including the one for school pictures.

I pause for a second, not knowing if I should tell her about my horrible math teacher and what he said in front of the whole class. My mom tends to be my crusader. That's nice and all, but it can also be embarrassing.

"It was fine. I missed April and Nora, but Prudy is really nice. Her name is short for Prudence."

"That's a pretty name—sort of old-fashioned. And you like her?"

"Yes, I do! Her family just moved here from New York. We sit next to each other in homeroom and have three classes together. And we have the same lunch."

"Well, that's wonderful! I bet you made her feel a lot less scared."

"I hope so." I watch her get the Instant Pot out of the cupboard and know that we're having Instant Pot chicken *again*.

"How was *your* day?" It's just occurred to me that I should ask. Who else will, if I don't?

A smile blooms on her face, and I'm immediately glad I've asked.

"It was good! I found out I'm definitely in the running for the promotion I applied for." Her eyes sparkle with possibilities.

"Awesome!" I say, not remembering her mentioning this before. "When will you find out?"

"Not for a week or so. It would mean more responsibility and more money."

"Well, I hope you get it, Mom. You'll be great." I mimic the words she says to me when I need encouragement.

"Thank you, sweetie. I hope I get it too. At least I think I do. I'm not sure if I'm qualified, but my boss urged me to apply, so I must be."

"Do you need any help getting dinner ready?"

"No thanks—you go and relax. If I get this promotion, you might get plenty of chances to get dinner started, so enjoy it now while you can." She gives me a wink.

I join Clara on the couch in front of the television and she snuggles into my side. It feels good to pretend I'm only six years old again. Being the age I am right now suddenly feels like a lot to handle.

Hope

April 26, 1966

Dear Daisy,

It's been strange not having my dad around anymore. He was always here before, doing the things that fathers usually do. Now Pete has to do that stuff, like mow the lawn and take out the trash. Dad had been teaching him how to do those chores for a while, so it's not like he doesn't know *anything*. Now that I think about it, I wonder if my dad knew he was going to be leaving us. That thought makes my heart hurt, so I don't think about it very much. Luckily, Pete has a good attitude about it. He got kinda crabby about it once because he wanted to hang out with his friends instead of raking the lawn, and Mom started crying. He felt really bad about it and hasn't complained since. That's a good thing because when Pete is crabby, it's hard for everyone! I also try to help him sometimes, but he gets really bossy, so it's not always the best idea.

This our weekend to go to our dad's new apartment. The way it worked out is that we spend every other weekend with Dad. I haven't decided if I like going to his apartment or not; it's too soon to tell. It's really neat because there's a pool there, but it's too cold outside to swim in it yet. Maybe it will be more fun in the summer. There's also a game room that has pinball machines, a pool table, *and* a ping pong table. Pete and I went down there a couple of times but there were older teenagers and a bunch of adults, so we've never gone back. Dad said that next time he'll go with us. I was wondering why he didn't go there with us in the first place but didn't say anything.

One thing I like about going to Dad's, is that we get away from Mom. I feel bad saying that, but it's true. Ever since Dad moved out, Mom's been acting kinda weird. She got her hair frosted and wears more makeup than she ever did before. She also went shopping and bought some mini-skirts! I think that's super weird. I want to ask Dad about it, but Pete told me to stay out of it. It makes me think about how she doesn't seem like my mom anymore and that makes me feel awful. I guess she loves me, but I feel like more of a bother these days. What's the deal with that?

That's it for now!

Love,
Hope

Leah

Thank goodness the first week of school is over, and so is my period! I've never been so happy to say *good-bye* to something in my life. I'm hoping that since it's over (for this month anyway), school will be better. Having all that to worry about made everything more stressful. Maybe by the time it comes around again, I'll feel more settled in at school. Fingers crossed!

I'm so excited because April and Nora are coming for a sleepover tonight! I've never hosted a sleepover because there wasn't room in the garage apartment. Before that, it was because we never knew if Dad was going to be drunk or hungover. In our new house, there's no reason why I can't have one, and Mom agrees. She even suggested it! I've been to sleepovers at each of their houses, so I'm excited to have a turn. I know they're going to think my new room is amazing, and I can't wait to show it to them!

"What will *I* do while April and Nora are here?" says Clara in a semi-whiny voice. "Mommy says I can't be at the party."

Clara is lying on my bed on her stomach, her feet buried in the pillow shams. I don't tell her to please get her smelly feet away from my pillows, even though I wish she would.

"I bet Mom will have something fun for you to do. Maybe you two can have your own sleepover," I say, hoping to cheer her up.

"How can we have a sleepover if we already sleep here every night?" She rolls her eyes dramatically, making me want to laugh.

"Then call it a slumber party. It'll be boring for you with us. We'll be talking about stuff you're not interested in." I recross my feet on the ottoman.

"You mean like boys?" Clara bats her eyelashes at me and giggles.

I shrug, feeling a little stupid. I've been so preoccupied all week, I haven't even noticed any boys worth talking about except Johnny Morgan, and he's just a big loser.

"No, not boys!" I launch a throw pillow in her direction. "Middle school and stuff like that." I watch the frown slide across Clara's little face. "But they'll want to hear about kindergarten, so you better be ready to tell them all about it, okay?"

Clara considers this, her frown flipping into a grin. "Okay! I'm gonna go and ask Mommy what we're gonna do!" She exits the room like she's been shot out of a cannon. I guess that's why Momo calls her a firecracker sometimes.

It's finally sleepover night! I haven't seen April or Nora for about nearly a month, although it feels more like a year. I've decided to serve the same things we've always eaten at sleepovers: pizza, pop, ice cream and chips. Mom is even letting us eat in my room if we want. She's strict about not taking food out of the kitchen, so I'm really happy she's relaxing that rule tonight. It's going to be so fun!

It's nearly six o'clock, and I'm nervously waiting for them to arrive. The plan is for April's mom to drive them here, and Nora's mom will pick them up tomorrow sometime. I hope they can stay and hang out for a while and not hurry home first thing in the morning. I'm straightening the pillows on the sofa and checking for dust on the end tables when Mom peeks into the room.

"Leah-loo, everything looks great. Stop worrying, okay?"

"I just want everything to be perfect. I haven't seen them for *so* long." My stomach is full of butterflies banging into each other.

"I know, but just try to enjoy yourself. It doesn't have to be perfect. They're your BFFs, right?" She plants a kiss on my cheek.

When the doorbell rings, I jump about three feet in the air. Instead of racing to the door, however, I walk as though I have two-ton weights on my feet. It's weird to feel so shy and uncertain about hanging out with my two besties, but I can't shake the feeling.

"Hi!" I say as I swing the door open.

April, her mom, and Nora are all standing on the top step, checking out their surroundings: the front porch, the small yard, the house on the corner with peeling paint and overgrown weeds. Their neighborhood, which is close to where my aunt lives, is much fancier than this one, meaning the people who live there seem to have a *lot* more money. (I mean, my aunt has a house with a detached garage big enough to have an apartment in it, for Pete's sake!). Our new neighborhood is nice and clean and *most* of the homes are well-kept, but it's clearly not on the same level that my friends are used to. This idea makes me feel uneasy for a second, but I decide to ignore it. I'm just imagining things, putting thoughts in their heads. For all I know, they're looking around thinking how great our neighborhood is. I also notice that both April and Nora are wearing eye make-up. My heart sinks even lower; I can't wear makeup until I'm in high school.

"Hi, Leah!" says Lisa, April's mom, before either of my friends can speak, "It's so good to see you!" She must see my mom over my shoulder because she adds, "Diane! I just love your new house! It's adorable!"

"Thanks!" Mom says, smiling. "And it's so good to see all of you! It's been much too long."

April and Nora grimace and fidget. It looks like I'm not the only shy one.

"Well, come on in, girls! Lisa, you too!" Mom motions for them to enter.

"Oh, thanks, but I've got to run. I need to pick up Amanda at dance. Maybe another time, okay?" She talks as she moves backwards down the front walk.

"Okay! Another time!" my mom calls after her.

April, Nora and I are standing in the middle of the living room as though we've just met for the first time. Nobody says a word. They're each holding onto their sleeping bags with one hand and their cell phones with the other. It would be funny if it weren't so strange. We smile each time eye contact is made, but it's not very often.

"Leah, why don't you show the girls your new room? They can bring their things up there." Mom smiles at us, expectantly.

"Okay." I motion to the girls to follow me.

I'm very proud of my room and excited to show it off. Momo did a great job on the curtains and window seat cushions and even bought a new comforter for my bed that ties everything together. She also got me fun throw pillows and a purple fake fur area rug for the middle of the floor; they're the coolest things ever!

"Ta-da!" I say when we reach the top of the steps and do a Vanna White arm gesture at the same time. "Here it is!"

I wait for a reaction—a *positive* reaction—because what other kind of reaction would you have to a best friend's new room, even if you think it's lame? Instead of them saying how cool it is or how much they like it, they're oddly quiet. That's just weird since those two are always chattering about *something.*

"Here—look at this!" I lead them over to the window seat. "Isn't this just the coolest? And it opens! How awesome is that?"

I turn around to find them not looking at my window seat but at their phones. The last time I saw them, they didn't have cell phones—they said their parents wouldn't let them. Now, here they are, paying attention to those instead of me. I guess my silence gets their attention because they suddenly look up at me and seem inconvenienced.

"Sorry, Leah," mumbles Nora, looking embarrassed.

"Yeah, cool," says April, barely looking up.

"You guys got cell phones!" I'm trying really, really hard to sound excited, as excited as I wish they'd be about my room.

There's the 'deer in the headlights' look again. Do they think I won't notice? That it's not obvious? The butterflies return to my stomach, and it feels like they've multiplied by thousands.

"Yeah, my parents got me one for a first day of middle school present, especially because I'm home alone after school every day. We don't have a landline anymore," says April.

"Same here," chimes Nora. "Once April got hers, my parents just caved. Besides, *all* the kids at Rolling Hills have them." She looks at April and giggles some more. "Aren't you home alone after school?"

Nora says this like it's just a given, that it's a good enough reason to get a cell phone.

"Um, yeah, but we still have a landline." The words feel heavy on my tongue.

They look at each other, smirk, and then go back to their phones. What could possibly be so interesting? Don't they know how rude they're being?

"Well, let's go downstairs and get the pizzas in the oven," I say, hoping to move the party along.

Nora shoots April a nervous look and then says, "We don't exactly eat pizza anymore."

"You don't?" I'm panicking inside because I don't know what else we'll eat.

They look at each other again. "We're on a diet."

The words drop to the floor and yet hang in the air between us like a big, sticky spiderweb.

"Why?"

"To lose weight, silly!" says April, scoffing a bit. "Everyone in dance is doing it."

"But you guys don't need to lose weight." As I say this, I think that if *they* need to lose weight, then I do for sure.

"It can't hurt to cut out all of the empty calories," added Nora. "Did you know that one slice of pepperoni pizza has like three hundred calories?"

"How do you know that?"

"We have this amazing app on our phones," said April. "See? It lists all these different foods and their calories, and it keeps track of how many calories we eat as we go through the day. It also keeps track of the calories we burn. It's so amazing! You should seriously get a phone so you can do this." Her eyes are drawn back to her phone. "And there are sites where people post *Before* and *After* pictures that are really motivating. Here, look!" She holds her phone in front of me, showing a teenage girl who looks normal in the *Before* picture and way skinnier in the *After*. "Doesn't she look great? She's my idol!"

"How many calories do you have in a day?" I think about Mr. Kendall's description of me as being pudgy. I was going to tell April and Nora about it but now I'm not so sure. They'll probably agree with him.

"We're trying to keep it below a thousand; closer to nine hundred, actually. That would be best, but it's not easy."

"Yeah, especially because my mom thinks it's unhealthy." Nora sounds thoroughly disgusted with her mom.

"How much do you want to lose?" I can't wait to hear how many pounds two obviously thin people think they need to get rid of.

"We don't know." Nora glances at April for reassurance.

"Yeah, we'll know when we get there. It's fun to see the number on the scale go down."

"Yeah," Nora adds, "it's addicting!" They both giggle and look back at their phones.

I feel like I'm going to be sick, but don't want to do that in my bathroom, so I decide to go downstairs instead. Before I go, I say, "If you don't want pizza, what *do* you want? We've got pizza because that's what we've always had."

They look at each other, at their phones and then shrug.

"I'm almost at my limit for today, so maybe just celery and carrots? And water? No pop," says April as Nora nods along, "unless it's diet."

"I'll see if we have any. Be right back." As I go down the stairs, I can hear them giggling and whispering.

Mom and Clara are in the kitchen, putting the finishing touches on the pizzas. Mom went all out in an effort to make things special and has made homemade pizzas—even the crust and the sauce. They'd look delicious if I didn't feel so awful.

"What's up?" Mom says, grinning at me. "Are you ladies ready to eat pretty soon?"

I stand there, not sure how I'll say anything without bursting into tears. "They don't want pizza. They're both on diets. Do we have any celery and carrots?" My throat aches from holding in so many tears.

"What? That's the craziest thing I've ever heard!" Mom says a little too loudly.

"Shh! They'll hear you!" I peek behind me to make sure they aren't standing there.

"And I've made enough for five." Mom looks at the pizzas, thinking. "Well, more for us, I guess. Leftover pizza is always good." She looks over at me. "You're still having some, right?"

I squirm a little under her laser-beam gaze. "I'm not really hungry right now. Maybe later? Do we have any celery and carrots?" I go to the fridge to look. "Oh, and water, no pop." I know for a fact that we don't have any diet pop, so I don't even ask.

"Wow," says Clara, "they don't wanna have *any* fun, do they?" She takes a big swig of her root bear, a special treat for tonight.

I shrug. "I guess not. Sorry, Mom—I know you've gone to a lot of trouble." My voice wavers as I struggle to maintain control.

She walks over and gives me a hug. "Are you okay, sweetie?"

Feeling safe in her arms, some of my tears leak out, and I try hard to make them stop. I don't want to look like a crybaby in front of April and Nora. She smooths my hair, something that always calms me down.

"I just wanted it to be perfect, you know? And now they're both on diets and they both have cell phones that they're looking at constantly. They seem so different! And they're wearing *makeup*." It feels good to share some of my disappointment.

"Hmm—I thought I saw some mascara and eye shadow."

We stand there a moment longer. I wish I could just hang out with Mom and Clara. The thought of going back upstairs suddenly feels overwhelming and not fun at all.

"What should I do? I feel like I'm going to barf!" I double-check my stomach to make sure I'm not exaggerating. Nope—I still feel icky.

"Well," Mom says as she brushes my hair out of my eyes, "I could go up and tell them you're not feeling well and they have to go home, or you can take some deep breaths and stick it out until tomorrow. Nora's mom is picking them up around nine, so they won't be here too long. Either option is valid."

I hate it when Mom gives me choices. She claims it builds confidence in my decision-making skills, but I'm not so sure. She always supports whatever I choose, but I still hate it.

"I guess I'll stick it out. Maybe it'll get better." My stomach stills feels queasy. "But I don't think I'll ever do this again."

"And you don't have to, at least not with those two. You're going to have lots of new friends, Leah. It's okay to leave some things behind." She kisses the tip of my nose. "Let's get some rabbit food on a tray, and I'll bring up some water. You can sneak down for your pizza whenever it works out—if you feel better, that is."

When I get back upstairs, April and Nora are now sitting on the floor, legs crossed, eyes glued to their cell phones. I want to scream.

"Well, here's some celery and carrots. My mom's bringing up some water."

The words have barely left my mouth, when I hear Mom bounding up the stairs.

"Here comes the Water Girl!" She chuckles at her own joke as she hands them each a bottle of water.

"Thanks, Mrs. Peterson," April and Nora say in unison, not even looking at her.

"If you change your minds about the pizza, there's plenty downstairs. *Homemade* pizza no less—I even made the sauce and crust from scratch!" She gives them a quick wink. "Well, bon appétit!"

I think I see a hint of yearning on their faces as my mom describes the pizza—especially Nora's. She's always been the follower, with April being the leader. I sort of balanced out the group by being some of each. When the three of us were together, I'd keep April from bossing us around too much, but it looks like without me, April calls the shots, and Nora follows her orders. It makes my stomach clench in a weird way.

We gather around the tray of vegetables, or rabbit food as my mom calls it. I know this won't be enough for me, especially since I threw away half my lunch and skipped my afternoon snack today, but eating pizza would make me feel like a pig whether they see me eat it or not. I'm torn about what to do. I want to be with my friends like we used to be, but *they* aren't like they used to be. It seems like they're trying to be older than they are. They think having cell phones and wearing makeup makes them so cool and in comparison, I'm not.

As we sit there doing more munching than talking, I notice a pattern emerging where they seem to take turns either giggling or typing into their phones with their thumbs. I might not be cool enough to have a cell phone, but suddenly it dawns on me that they're texting *each other*. I stomp down that idea in my head because it would be so rude and hurtful if it's true. It seems like I can't get a word in edgewise, even though nobody is saying a word. My mind wanders to the diary, and I wonder if Hope ever had problems like this. Of course she didn't; there were no cell phones in 1966. It sounds like it was a good time to be alive.

My stomach stills feels weird, but I can also feel it growling with hunger. I suspect my friends must be hungry as well, but I admire their willpower. To know there's yummy pizza and pop waiting for them and to resist it must make them feel so righteous and strong. They seem better than me as they delicately nibble on their celery sticks and sip their water. I find myself feeling like there's something wrong with me, simply because I want to eat more than just this.

Hope

May 3, 1966

Dear Daisy,

Last weekend at Dad's apartment was actually kinda fun. Pete was nice to me the whole time! How weird is that? Dad kept his promise and went to the game room with us this time, and we played ping pong until I thought my arms were going to fall off! It was super fun, especially because I won a couple of times. We went earlier in the day so the other adults wouldn't be there. After that, we went out for burgers and went to a movie. I wanted to see *The Singing Nun,* but Pete and Dad wanted to see *Batman,* so that's what we saw. I thought it was silly to waste money on something we can see on TV every week, but Pete said I was outnumbered. I told them that's just dumb because I'll always be outnumbered when we're at Dad's. Then Dad reminded me that at home with Mom, *Pete* is outnumbered. I guess he has a point, but Mom never takes us to movies, so there's that. I just wish it was like it used to be—even Steven—two boys and two girls. Dad said that next time I get to pick the movie. Yay! Pete didn't even argue, but I know he'll worm his way out of it somehow.

I'm so excited that we're in last month of school! We actually have a couple of days in June, but they don't really count since we don't do any schoolwork. All we do on those days is clean out our desks and help our teacher clean the classroom. I love doing that, even though I hate cleaning at home. I wonder why that is?

The other day, Mom measured me for my school uniform for next year. Seventh and eighth-graders get to wear skirts and vests and the same white blouses we've always worn under our jumpers. The vests are plaid and Sister Mary Edward calls them "weskits." What a weird name for a vest! Anyway, I'm super excited! The trick is to get it big enough so it lasts two years. I guess skirts are trickier than jumpers, since jumpers don't have much of a waistline.

Mom slipped the tape measure around my waist, looked at the number, shrugged, and wrote it down on the order form. Then she slid the tape measure around my hips and butt. She was going to write down the number, but then frowned and measured again.

"What's wrong?"

"Nothing—I just want to make sure I get it right. It will be a waste of money if we need to buy a new skirt next year when you outgrow this one."

Her answer satisfied me in the moment, but I kept thinking about it a lot after I saw the size she wrote down on the order form. I couldn't believe it! I looked at the tag on my jumper and saw that the skirt will be *three* sizes bigger. How will it ever fit? How big will I get over the summer? How big will I be in two years? I don't know why it bothered me so much, but it did.

After dinner, we were doing the dishes like always— Mom was washing and I was drying. Pete was shooting hoops in the driveway. He never has to help with dishes, but he mows the lawn, so I guess it's fair.

"Mom, if my uniform is too big for me in September, what will we do? Won't the skirt fall down?"

"Don't worry about it." Mom set another dinner plate in the dish drainer. "We can move the button over if it's too big, or I can take some tucks in the waistband. At the rate you're growing, though, I don't think it will be much of a problem." She looked at me in a weird way. "As long as you grow *up* and not *out*, right?" And then she smirked as she placed her hand on her ever-shrinking waistline.

I was kinda surprised she said that. She's never said anything about my growing in *any* direction before. She was surprised when I got my period kinda early, but she didn't say anything about how *much* I was growing. It made me feel scared and confused about getting older.

Maybe it's because my mom, for the first time I can remember, is on a diet. She joined a group that's supposed to help people lose weight. She goes to meetings on Tuesday nights where she gets weighed by a leader in front of everyone. That sounds horrible! There's a whole book that has all the rules in it, and there are *lots* of rules. She's being super careful about how much she eats and writes down every single thing she puts in her mouth, even if it's only one bite of a potato chip! (Just kidding—she never touches potato chips anymore!) She also has to weigh her food, especially the meat. She's also supposed to eat fish five times a week and liver once a week. Eww! It's crazy! She's never been that fussy about stuff like that before, and now I worry she wants me to lose weight too, just from what she said about not growing *out*.

Pete thinks it's because she found out that Dad has a girlfriend. He thinks all the stuff she's doing with her hair and makeup and dieting has something to do with that or her new part-time job. The thing is, Mom is perfect just the way she is. There's nothing she can do to make herself any better. In fact, I think all the things she's doing to change herself are changes for the worse. She doesn't seem like herself anymore. I just want my old mom back.

Love,
Hope

Leah

I'm startled to see the diary laying on the bed beside me when I wake up. Propping myself up on my elbows, I search the room for April and Nora, wondering how much of it they've read. As I yawn and rub my eyes, I try to remember even getting it out of the window seat. With the way things were going last night, there's no way I wanted to show them Hope's private thoughts. I lean back against my pillow and it hits me—my friends went home last night. A sigh of relief whooshes out of me.

Right after we'd feasted on the celery sticks and baby carrots, my mom came back upstairs. I thought she was either delivering more rabbit food or was going to bring the tray downstairs. She sure wasn't coming up to tell us to quiet down or anything because we weren't even talking. April and Nora were still futzing with their phones, and I was sitting there counting the sequins on my teal-colored throw pillow.

"Hey ladies, I've got bad news. Clara seems to have come down with a tummy bug. I called your moms to see what they want to do, and we all decided it's best if you don't spend the night after all. Your moms both said that with dance competitions coming soon, it's important you stay well. Nora's mom is coming to pick you both up in about ten minutes. I'm so sorry. We'll have to do it again another time." She smiled one of her 'sorry, not sorry' smiles and went back downstairs.

Since April and Nora hadn't unrolled their sleeping bags, it didn't take any time for them to be ready to leave. It made me sad in a way they didn't act more disappointed; they just popped up from the floor and said, "Okay!" It sort of surprised me that *I* wasn't more disappointed, but at least I had the good sense to pretend a little.

"Bummer," I said, standing to join them. "I guess there's something going around."

"Yeah, my little brother had it last week," said Nora. "I hope you don't get it." Nora has always been the kinder one of the two.

"Thanks, Nora. I hope you don't either."

By the time we reached the living room, Nora's mom was already waiting at the curb, honking her horn. I was relieved they wouldn't need to stay any longer. This whole evening had been awkward enough.

"Well, thanks for coming, ladies," my mom said, ushering them to the door.

"Yeah, thanks for coming," I repeated. Neither of them said much of anything since their heads were down, glued again to their phones. Nora sort of gave a little wave. I guess it was better than nothing.

After they were out the door, I said, "How's Clara? It's strange that *she* got sick when *I* was the one who felt icky."

Mom grinned and winked at me. "Clara's fine—she's in her room playing with her Barbies."

I was confused. My mom never lies; at least I hadn't thought so until right then. "But you said—"

"Yes, sweetie, I said she's sick. I did that to rescue you from what seemed to be a terrible evening. It was all I could do not to give their moms a piece of my mind about how rude those girls were being *and* to alert them about the diets they're on. It's not healthy for eleven-year-olds to be dieting. Your brain is still developing along with the rest of you! Those girls are headed for trouble."

Her smile was long gone, replaced by the look she has when she's upset or angry about something.

"I'm sorry about lying, Leah. I know I said both choices were valid, but after I saw them ignoring you and acting like they were *all that* I couldn't stand by and let you be treated that way." She smoothed my hair back, and the tears dribbled out. She caught them with her thumb on one side of my face but on the other side, the tears slid down to my chin and then dripped onto my shirt.

"Why did they come over if they were just going to be mean to me?" I couldn't seem to stop the words from pouring out. "I thought they were my friends."

Mom led me over to the couch. We sat down, and she held me while I cried. It felt so good; I hadn't realized how many tears I'd been bottling up.

"Lots of things can change at your age, sweetie. Many of them are supposed to but many of them aren't; they just happen. Leah, if I had known the school boundaries were going to change, I never would've chosen this house. I hope you know that."

"Yeah, but maybe it's better not being at Rolling Hills."

"Why do you say that?"

"Well, if April and Nora would treat me like they did tonight, it'd be worse than not having any friends." I played with the fringe on the afghan bunched up next to me.

"I hadn't thought of that. "

"And there's something else about Rolling Hills—or the people in that neighborhood. They have *lots* of money. No offense, Mom, but it's a *lot* more than we have. I mean Aunt Kathy and Uncle Jim are sort of rich, aren't they?"

She sat very still and didn't say anything for what felt like a long time.

"I'm sorry, Mom, I don't mean to hurt your feelings. I know how hard you've worked for us. Clara and I are really lucky, and I love this house."

She reached over and squeezed my hands in hers. "It's okay. I know you didn't mean anything by it. It's been rough for all of us, even before the accident. You've been a trooper, Leah. You never complain, and that's amazing to me. I feel bad that I can't afford to get you a cell phone yet, but you know that money isn't the only reason, right?"

I nodded; we've had this conversation multiple times. The other reason she doesn't want me to have a cell phone is because of exactly what happened with April and Nora. She also thinks I'm too young to be on the internet unless I'm doing homework and then she supervises me very closely.

"April and Nora were basically bullying you in plain sight. Can you imagine what they'd do if they could text you?"

Mom's words made me flinch. She had just said what I'd been too afraid to even think but knew deep inside: my BFFs weren't my BFFs anymore.

Hope

May 30, 1966 (Memorial Day!)

Dear Daisy,

Happy Memorial Day! I'm excited about Memorial Day for a couple of reasons: we don't have school today *and* we're going out on a boat on Lake Minnetonka with some people from Mom's work! It's her boss's boat, and he invited everyone from the office. After the divorce, Mom got a part-time job as a receptionist in an insurance office for extra spending money. Dad gives her money every month for Pete and me and money for her, but she said she wants to have her *own* money. I don't get it—money is money. It works out for Pete and me because not only do we get to be home alone after school on the days she works, but now we get to spend the day on a boat!

I have to go and get ready, but I'll tell you all about it later! Toodle-loo!

Later....

I know I said I'd tell you about the boat ride, but I don't even want to think about it right now, so writing about it would be impossible. Sorry, Daisy.

Hope

Leah

It's the Monday after the sleepover disaster. I'm determined to become better friends with Prudy; maybe even branch out and see who else might want a new friend. I'm really bad at talking to strangers, but I'm going to make an effort. It's obvious I need some new friends not only because I'm at a new school, but because my old friends aren't exactly friends anymore.

Every morning, I save a seat for Prudy since her stop is the one right after mine. It's usually not a big deal since everyone sits in the same seats every day. They aren't assigned, it's just how it works out. Sort of like in the lunchroom—everyone has their favorite spot. It's a big deal if you sit in the "wrong" spot, but no one really lets that happen.

After everyone has gotten on the bus and Fred, the bus driver, has closed the doors, he opens them again and says, "Good morning, young lady! We almost left without you! Welcome aboard!"

A girl I've never seen before climbs onto the bus.

"Welcome to Bus 30!" Fred welcomes new kids with an extra big greeting.

The new girl smiles at Fred but hesitates before going any further. I can relate since I was new to so many schools, so many times. She's searching the bus with her eyes for a friendly place to sit. Everyone ignores her and looks down in their laps to avoid making eye contact, which is just rude. I feel bad for her, so I wave her over to me. Prudy won't mind; she knows what it's like to be new.

Besides, there's an empty seat right across the aisle and in front of me for Prudy.

"Hi! Do you want to sit here?" I say, smiling. "I'm Leah."

Her face breaks into a huge smile. "Thank you!" She sits down and swings her backpack onto her lap. "I'm Tabinda."

"That's a pretty name."

"Thanks! I like your name too." She wiggles in the seat to get comfortable and then adjusts the scarf thingy she has on her head.

"My friend is getting on at the next stop. We both just moved here too, so we know how hard it is." I feel stupid after I say this and hope Tabinda doesn't take it the wrong way. Maybe it's not as hard for her as it is for us. I also feel sort of bold calling Prudy my friend. "The more the merrier, right?" I smile.

"What a relief! I was worried about meeting people, and now I've met two before I even get to school! Almost two, that is." She grins and chuckles a little.

The bus is already at the next stop, and I see Prudy make her way up the steps. There's a confused look on her face when she sees the new girl sitting next to me. I send her a big smile and motion to the seat in front of us.

"Hi Prudy! This is Tabinda. It's her first day."

"Hi, Tabinda! I'm Prudy—but Leah already told you that, didn't she? It's nice to meet you. I love your hijab!" She plops herself down, turning around to face us.

For a moment, I'm horrified that Prudy has drawn so much attention to Tabinda's scarf thingy, but I'm also grateful because I didn't know what to call it.

"Thanks! My mom made it. She makes a bunch of them for my sister and me—and herself, of course. She likes us to be color-coordinated."

"It must really cut down on your getting ready time in the morning, huh?" says Prudy. "This disaster takes forever to tame!" She gestures to the tangle of curls jutting out all over her head. "They have a mind of their own most of the time!"

Tabinda laughs and doesn't appear to be offended at all. I just laugh along like I get the joke. My hair is as straight as a stick, but it's never given me any problems. It's actually one thing I like about myself—that and my eyes—but I'd never tell anyone that because it would be conceited.

"The thing I'm the most nervous about is being the only one like me in the school," Tabinda says as the bus bumps along. "In Chicago, there were lots of kids like me. I don't know about here."

I'm not sure what she means by that, but guess she must mean being Black and wearing the hijab. I think back to the first days at Shady Creek and remember seeing Black kids, but none of them wore hijabs. Suddenly, my worries about fitting in seem like less of a big deal.

"Who do you have for homeroom?" I ask, hoping she's with Prudy and me.

"Mrs. Donnelly. Is she nice?"

"I've heard she's super nice," Prudy says.

"My mom told me to go to the office as soon as I get to school. Can you guys show me where it is?"

"Of course!" we say at the same time and then laugh.

"We don't always say the same thing at the same time," we say at the same time again.

"Good, cuz that would be creepy!" laughs Tabinda.

The bus slows to a stop, taking its place in line with the other buses. As we all file past Fred, he waves and wishes us all a good day.

"Have a good first day, dear," he says to Tabinda. "You've got two good ones here." He smiles at the three of us.

And the day begins!

We bring Tabinda to the office right away. Mrs. Wilson, the office manager, asks Prudy and me if we'll show Tabinda where her locker and home room are. It feels good to be helpful because I know how overwhelming first days can be. Tabinda seems less shy than I am, but still. Change can be scary.

As we walk down the hall to our lockers, I notice that kids are going out of their way to walk around us as they whisper to whoever they're walking with. Whatever their reason is for doing that, it's just mean. Prudy and I walk on either side of our new friend, almost daring someone to challenge us.

The rest of the day goes along as usual. Tabinda doesn't have Mr. Kendall for math, a blessing no matter how you look at it. She has the same lunch period as Prudy and me which is another blessing. Again, kids who are sitting at the table we always sit at, scoot away from us once we sit down. It's embarrassing that they're being so rude, but I don't know what to do about it. Kids have left me out before but never like this.

"I'm sorry, Tabinda," I say, as we open our milk cartons. "I don't know why they're being so rude."

She rolls her eyes and says, "It's because of me, Leah. It's been like this all morning. I should be the one apologizing to you."

"No, you shouldn't," says Prudy. "What's wrong with people?"

"They're just not used to seeing someone wearing a hijab," I add as I move the pasta around on my tray. My appetite has been missing since the sleepover.

Tabinda looks at me and frowns. "You seriously think they'd be different if I wasn't wearing it? And," she adds, gently, "it's just 'hijab.' Like 'wearing hijab' not *a* hijab."

I immediately feel stupid for saying what I did. "Sorry."

Tabinda shrugs and smiles. "How would you know? Don't worry about it."

"Do you have to? You know, wear it?" I decide I might as well learn more.

"All Muslim girls and women in the United States don't wear one, but it's the rule my family has." Tabinda munches on an apple slice.

"Do you like wearing it? It must get hot in the summertime, but I bet it's cozy warm during the winter."

Tabinda laughs. "I don't mind it. I'm proud of who I am and by wearing it, I'm letting people know that."

"That's so awesome!" I say before I realize I've said it out loud.

Prudy and Tabinda stop chewing their food and stare at me. It's clear I need to say more, even though I really don't want to. I'd rather give a speech in front of the whole school instead of explain my words right now.

"Well, it's just that I don't think I've ever felt proud of who I am." My cheeks burning, I look down at my lunch tray, afraid to meet their eyes.

"Why not?" Tabinda says. "You have a lot to be proud of! I can tell that, and I hardly even know you."

"Yeah," says Prudy. "You were so nice to me on the first day when I dropped everything all over the floor in math. No one else was that nice to me."

I think about this, my head still down. I'm embarrassed because I don't want them to think I was fishing for compliments. I'm also embarrassed to have been so honest with them. In my experience, once I'm honest with people, they usually use it against me somehow. It happened enough times in elementary school, but middle school has to be worse.

"Thanks," I mumble. "You guys are really nice too."

"Yes, we are," Prudy smiles and nudges me with her elbow. "And we're very proud of it!"

When we get on our bus to go home, I see that Fred isn't in the driver's seat. There's a different driver, a younger woman with a pony tail and aviator sunglasses. She seems friendly enough, but doesn't greet us like Fred does every day.

The three of us are already in our seats when Johnny Morgan's voice can be heard as he climbs onto the bus.

"Everyone hold your breath!" He makes a big production of holding his breath as he passes us on his way to the back of the bus. Once he's past us, he dissolves into laughter.

I can see tears begin to form in Tabinda's eyes, but her expression is as solid as granite. She sits up tall and stares straight ahead.

"Just ignore them," I whisper to her, much like Prudy whispered to me on the first day of school. "They're losers. They're mean to Prudy and me every chance they get. They don't do it if Fred is driving, though."

She nods and remains silent, something I understand all too well. Sometimes talking is the very thing that will make the tears escape. I know how important it is not to let bullies see you cry.

Luckily, they're too busy being obnoxious with each other to bother with us anymore until the bus comes to a stop at Prudy's corner. There's only about three kids at that stop and two of them are already sitting in the front. Prudy stands up to leave and that's Johnny's signal.

"There goes the big giant *Prude*!" He and his friends all laugh hysterically. "Fee, fi, fo, fum!"

Prudy completely ignores them, instead saying goodbye to Tabinda and me.

"See you two tomorrow!"

Tabinda and I manage to exit at the next stop without too much drama. Johnny calls out, "See ya tomorrow, Pudge!" but leaves Tabinda out of it—for now.

"Where do you live?" I ask once the bus drives away.

"Down that way." She points toward a newer development of homes about two blocks away. "How about you?"

"Over there." I point in the opposite direction. "Down one block and over two. It's not too far. Maybe you can come over after school someday. My mom works, so I don't know if she'll let me have friends over when she's not home, but I can ask."

"That sounds like fun," she says, smiling. "Thanks again for being so nice today."

"Why wouldn't I be? You're a nice person."

"It sure makes the day better, doesn't it? I always wonder about what it must be like to be inside one of those mean kids' heads. They must be very unhappy."

"I never thought of it like that, but I bet you're right. I don't like feeling angry *ever,* so I wouldn't want to feel that way all the time." I think of how mean April and Nora have become.

"My mom says that mean people are to be pitied because they're so unhappy."

I look at her, surprised. "And you actually do that?"

Tabinda shrugs and chuckles. "I try, but it's not always easy. It was easier in Chicago because there were lots of Muslims and Black kids, but this year might be harder."

All of a sudden, I feel ashamed of my classmates, my school, and my community. I don't know what to say.

"But," Tabinda continues, "my mom says that middle school is a tough time no matter what. She said it's like kids turn into aliens or something."

"Yeah, two friends from my old school came over for a sleepover on Friday night and they definitely seemed like aliens!" My heart sinks as I remember how sad it made me feel, but then I hear Tabinda laughing.

"That's hilarious!"

"Yeah, well, it wasn't so hilarious at the time. My mom actually faked that my little sister was sick so they had to go home!" Suddenly, I'm laughing along with her.

"Your mom sounds cool!" She gives me a sly smile.

"Yeah, she is, but not all the time, of course."

"No parents are cool *all* the time, right?"

We both nod, knowingly.

"Well, I'll see you tomorrow!"

"Okay! Bye!" Tabinda gives me a little wave and sets out toward her house.

As I walk home, I feel like I accomplished my goal of making a new friend today. Helping Tabinda helped me not think about myself so much, and it felt really, really good. I just hope it lasts!

Hope

May 31, 1966

Dear Daisy,

I better tell you about the boat ride before I forget too much, although I don't know how *that* could ever happen. What was supposed to be a fun day turned into a nightmare!

It started right away in the morning when I got my swimsuit out of the bottom drawer in my dresser. I haven't worn it since last summer—*obviously*. When I put it on, it was a little snug but nothing horrible. I mean, at least I could *get* it on. It was a suit that I loved last year, and I still love it. It's a two-piece, with bright yellow bottoms and a lime green and yellow flower print top. The bottoms also have strips of fabrics on the sides of them that match the top. The top also has ruffles on the bottom half of the top. It's so cute! When I put it on after so many months, I noticed a change in how the top fits. Now it fits like I have boobs, because, well, I guess I'm starting to get them. So the top's a little tighter than last year, and that makes me feel embarrassed. It also makes my tummy pooch out a little bit since the bottoms come up to my waist. It made me feel like it was too small or I was too big, so I decided to wear a t-shirt and shorts over it all day. The water's probably too cold to go swimming anyway.

It was a long drive from our house to the lake. Pete just got his license, so he's more than happy to drive every chance he gets. Mom has always been really nervous about him driving, but today she didn't put up a fuss. She was much too busy checking out her hair and makeup in her compact. I kept telling her she looked great, but she kept fussing over herself. She got a new swimsuit for the occasion, which I think is totally unfair, but whatever. She promised we can get me a new one after school is out.

The place where the boat is kept is called a marina. All the boats there were HUGE! I never even knew that boats like that existed in Minnesota! We brought our stuff down to the benches by the dock and waited for her boss and the other people from her office to show up.

After about ten minutes, her boss, Mr. Horton, came up from the dock, waving at us to come down to where he was. He's younger than I expected and kinda handsome, but not as handsome as Dad. He was wearing shorts and a shirt that buttons down the front, only it wasn't buttoned. It was weird to see his bare chest, but I figured that's just because it's not even summer yet. Once I've been to the beach a few times, seeing bare chests on guys is no biggie. The first thing he did was give my mom a long hug. That really creeped me out! He's her *boss!* I couldn't tell if she was creeped out or not, but I could tell that it bothered Pete big time. When she introduced us to him, he hugged me too which was super creepy. Then he shook Pete's hand, going on and on about how Mom doesn't look old enough to have a son who can drive. She blushed and acted all embarrassed, but I think she loved it.

I kept wondering when the other people were going to get there but then he was telling Pete how to untie to ropes that held the boat to the dock. That seemed odd.

"Aren't we going to wait for the others?" Mom asked.

"I'm afraid they all cancelled," he said. "It's just us!" He smiled and winked in a way that gave me the willies.

Mom seemed okay with it, but also seemed like she didn't know what to say or how to act. (I get it because I feel like that almost every day!) We were all sitting on the seats in the front of the boat as it skimmed over the water, making humongous waves behind us. It was super fun to go that fast, and the wind blew my hair around like crazy! I held on for dear life because he was going *so* fast.

Finally, we slowed down and stopped in a bay where a few other boats had done the same thing. Mr. Horton dropped the anchors so we didn't drift off.

"You kids can swim if you want to. There's ladder on the back."

"Isn't it too cold?" Mom said. She's really careful about water safety, probably because she can't swim at all.

"Nah—only going in and getting out. It's fine while you're in the water."

Pete and I looked at each other, not knowing if we should get in or not. Pete's a really good swimmer, but I'm not yet—and this was a very big, very deep lake.

"Okay, but Hope, you need to keep your life jacket on," said Mom.

I didn't argue because it would kill two birds with one stone—the life jacket would cover up the parts of me I didn't want anyone to see. Perfect!

Mr. Horton was right—once we got in the water, it was great. Pete and I splashed each other and played around, enjoying the feeling of summer being just around the corner. The sun was warm on my arms and my face as I floated on my back and closed my eyes to relax.

Suddenly, I heard lots of water splashing and Pete yelling, "Mom!"

I opened my eyes and paddled up near the front of the boat, where I saw Pete staring at mom and Mr. Horton. I craned my neck to see what Pete was looking at, but the water in my eyes made everything blurry.

"Pete, what's wrong?" I had *never* heard him yell like that before.

"Nothing! Just get back on the boat." His voice was really angry.

Not wanting to cause trouble or make him angrier, I kicked my way back to the ladder and got on the boat. Pete followed, and grabbing the towels on the bench, shoved one in my face. He took another one to Mom in the front of the boat.

"Here!" he said, forcing her to take it from him.

"I don't need a towel, Pete, I'm fine." She pushed the towel back at him.

"Yes, son, let your mom show off her great-looking figure," said Mr. Horton, looking mom up and down. That's when Pete tried to punch him, but Mr. Horton caught his arm.

"Peter Andrew McMillan!" yelled Mom. "That's enough!"

Wrapping my towel around me because my goosebumps had goosebumps, I went toward the front of the boat to see what was going on. There, in the front of the boat, was my mom in the tiniest bikini I've ever seen on *anyone*, not just my mom. She's been dieting, but I hadn't noticed how thin she's gotten until that moment. I guess Pete was shocked to see her like that too. Mr. Horton seemed to like it, standing there with his arm around Mom's waist. He was touching her bare skin, *and* he had taken his shirt completely off. Eww! Dad never even did that!

I also wanted Mom to cover up with the towel, but she didn't. She seemed to like showing off her new body. It made me feel really icky, like I'd done something wrong by just looking at her and Mr. Horton together like that. What's up with that, Daisy?

The drive home was super uncomfortable. Pete drove kinda fast the whole way, and Mom kept telling him to slow down, that getting us all killed wouldn't solve anything. I just sat in the backseat and prayed to St. Christopher, the Patron Saint of Travelers, to get us home safely. Once we got home, Mom sat us down and told us that she's dating Mr. Horton, so it's okay if he has his arm around her. *Dating!!!* That really made Pete lose it, and he went to his room and slammed the door really hard. After that, Mom started crying and went to her room, although she didn't slam the door. That left me sitting in the living room all by myself.

Mom and Dad haven't been apart that long, so the idea of Mom dating is weird enough (although Dad *is* dating Kelly), but the idea of her dating that creepy Mr. Horton, HER BOSS, is even worse! It was yucky to see someone besides Dad touch her, but once I thought about it, I never saw Dad touch Mom or even kiss or hug her very much. I always figured they did that in private, but maybe not. Is it normal for men and women to do that in public? I don't think I ever could. It's too gross and embarrassing! Eww!

Does this mean they're going to get married and that he'll live with us? I got a really bad feeling when he hugged me like that because I didn't know him at all! Or what if they stop dating and then Mom loses her job? She says she only works to get out of the house and be around adults, but what if we really need that money? What will happen to us then?

So you see, that's why I didn't feel like writing about it yesterday. I was just too upset and wanted to forget it ever happened. The trouble is, Pete isn't talking to Mom now, and Mom's being all crabby, even to me. I haven't done a thing to deserve it. That really stinks!

Today, I asked her when I can get a new swimsuit, and she just yelled at me and told me my old one is good enough. When I told her it was a little tight, she told me to follow her diet for a while and then it will fit just fine. Does that mean she thinks I'm fat? She wasn't even fat when she went on a diet, so she definitely must think I am. I guess she's decided for me because tonight my dinner was a small chicken breast and some plain green beans. Pete got to have a giant baked potato with butter and sour cream, along with a huge chicken breast and green beans with gobs of cheese sauce. He also got to have a big bowl of ice cream for dessert. When I asked about it, Mom just said that he's a growing boy, and that boys can eat more and not get fat.

I guess that answers my question, Daisy. I need to go on a diet.

Love,
Hope

Leah

I'm lying on my bedroom floor with my feet up on the ottoman. Setting the diary aside, I wrap the afghan more tightly around my shoulders. Poor Hope! Her mom is actually making her go on a diet. Thank goodness my mom isn't doing that to me. That would be awful! I wish I knew what Hope looked like—you know, like if she actually *needed* to lose weight or not. Apparently, sometimes the person who needs to lose weight doesn't know it. I heard Aunt Kathy talking about one of her friends and she said how Mona needed to lose weight but just didn't see it. How does that work? Wouldn't her clothes stop fitting? Aunt Kathy said that she'd rather be shot than gain weight. That made me think that staying a certain size, a *small* size, is a really important thing to do, and people might not want to be your friend anymore if you don't.

The other thing that freaks me out is how Hope's mom started dating her boss. I think she started dating him because Hope's dad had a girlfriend and she was jealous, but still. Gross! I think about my mom and wonder if she's ever wanted to date anyone since my dad died. He's been gone over three years and as far as I know, she isn't interested in dating at all. I feel lucky that my mom isn't like Hope's mom. Her mom sounds pretty awful, but I also feel kind of sorry for her.

"Leah! Telephone!" Mom calls up the stairs.

That's another other thing I need to talk to Mom about: getting a phone in my room. It doesn't have to be a separate line or anything—just another phone so I can talk to my friends in my room. I know Mom wants to have some control, but this is ridiculous. If I can't have a cell phone, I should at least have this. It's not too much to ask, is it?

"Coming!" I shout as I stand, leaving the afghan in a heap on the floor. I'll fold it later.

I hurry downstairs, curious as to who's calling me. I doubt that April or Nora would call, especially after how the sleepover went. Mom hands me the cordless phone with a puzzled expression. Knowing she's dying to hear my end of the conversation, I simply take the phone and return to my room. As far as I know, there's no rule about that.

"Hello?" I say as I climb the stairs.

"Hi, Leah." It's Nora. This is a surprise.

"Hi, Nora. How's it going?" My heart starts to pound which is really sad since we used to be BFFs and all. I used to talk to her every day, and my heart *never* pounded like this.

"Good, I guess." There's a very long, awkward silence. "I'm calling to apologize for how rude I was at your house. I'm really sorry."

I don't know what to say. As happy as I thought I'd be with an apology, I don't even care that much. I've actually been enjoying getting to know Prudy and Tabinda and like them way more than I ever liked my old friends.

"Thanks," I mutter, remembering not to say, 'That's okay,' mainly because it's not. (Momo has drilled that into my head.)

"How's Shady Creek? Do you like it?"

"It's okay. I'm liking it more now that I've made some new friends. Although Johnny Morgan's there, so there's that." Nora also hates Johnny Morgan—at least she used to.

"Really?" She sounds very surprised, and I can't help but wonder why. She must know that he's not at Rolling Hills.

"Yeah, he's been pretty awful to me on the bus. The bus driver keeps him in line, but when there's a different driver, Johnny's still a bully."

"Really?"

"Why do you sound so surprised? He was always in trouble last year."

"Well, it's just that—well, his sister's in April's and my dance class."

So? I want to say, but don't. There's another awkward silence.

"Well, the thing is, April *really* likes Johnny, you know, and, well, she wants you to ask him if he likes her."

My heart skips a beat as I realize the only reason Nora is calling is to help April. For all I know, April is standing right next to her, listening. I might even be on speakerphone. She only apologized to get to this part.

"You're kidding, right?" For a moment I forget that Nora is no longer my best friend, and I answer her as though it's old times.

"Um, no, I'm not kidding. April would text him, but she doesn't have his cell phone number."

"Well, I sure don't have it! Why doesn't she ask his sister for it? Wouldn't that be easier?" My heart is hammering.

"You know how sisters can be. His sister's kind of a brat, so she'd probably put it all over Instagram that April likes him." Nora's voice has taken on a defensive tone that makes me uncomfortable. "So you'll ask him?"

"No, I won't ask him. I don't even talk to Johnny Morgan. Tell April to figure out another way." I'm surprised at how brave I'm being to turn her down like this;

I'm usually a bit more cautious. Maybe I'm still upset about the sleepover disaster.

Suddenly, I hear a new voice on the phone: April.

"You think you're all that now, don't you, with your new house and your pathetic new room? Well, guess what, *Pudge*? You're *boring*, with your stupid window seat and dumb breakfast nook! Who'd even *want* to be your friend? You don't deserve to have *any*! And who's going to want to be friends with a fat girl anyway? I'll put it all over Instagram and Snapchat how fat you're getting and how tacky your new house is! Everyone already knows the reason you're not at Rolling Hills is because you're too poor to live in our neighborhood!"

Tears burn my eyes. I'm speechless.

"Are you still there, *Pudge*?" April snaps. "If you don't get Johnny's number or ask him if he likes me, I'll put all that out there! See how cool you are then!" The line goes dead.

I don't know how long I've been sitting there with the phone in my hand when Mom puts her hand on my shoulder, making me jump.

"Hey, sweetie."

I turn my head to look at her, tears streaming down my face and hand her the phone.

"What happened?" She sits down on the floor next to me, setting the phone on the floor. She rests a gentle hand on my back.

I don't know how to tell her what just happened. I'm not sure if she'll believe me because I hardly believe it myself. April, who used to be one of my best friends, just acted like a monster, and Nora let her.

"April wants me to ask Johnny Morgan if he *likes* her and said that if I don't, she'll put bad things about me on

Instagram and Snapchat," I say in a quiet voice. Saying it louder seems dangerous, like April will be able to hear me.

"*What?* I thought it was Nora who called."

"April was there with her. At first Nora apologized for being rude at the sleepover, but then she asked me about Johnny and all that. I said I wouldn't do it and then April got on and was really mean." I leave out the part about her calling me Pudge, which she had to have heard from someone who goes to my school, and the part about how poor we are. Mom would be so hurt by both of those things, and she doesn't deserve that. Nobody does. I also know that if I tell Mom those parts, she'll call April's mom and that would be the worst thing ever.

"Oh, sweetie, I'm so sorry!" She puts her arms around me and pulls me in for a hug. "What's happened to those girls? They didn't used to be like this, did they?" She wipes my tears away with her thumbs.

I shake my head. "No, they were my best friends." Saying that makes me sob even more.

"Well, I'm proud of you for saying *no*. Even if Johnny was a nice kid, which he isn't, you don't have to do anything you don't want to—especially for someone who treats you so badly."

She has no idea.

We sit there like that for a while, and it's really, really nice, like it used to be when I was little.

"I've got an idea," she says, straightening up a little. "What do you say we invite Prudy and Tabinda over one day this coming weekend?" She brushes the hair out of my eyes.

My heart lifts for a second and then crashes again. What if it turns out like it did when I had April and Nora over? I don't even know these two that well yet.

"Well, maybe," I say, not wanting to disappoint her, "but not for a sleepover."

"Oh heavens no, not yet," Mom agrees. "Just for the afternoon."

"Okay, I'll ask them tomorrow."

"And please get their phone numbers so I can talk to their parents, okay?"

I roll my eyes. Here we go again.

"Seriously, Leah, it's the right thing to do. Their parents don't know me. I wouldn't let you go to their houses without chatting with their parents. Grandma Mo used to actually insist on meeting my friends' parents *in person*. Imagine how humiliating *that* was!"

"Yeah, that's pretty bad," I shiver at the thought.

"One time, she dropped me off at a new friend's house. My friend said her dad was home, but he didn't come to the door. Grandma got in the car to leave and started thinking about every bad thing that could happen, like if he had a gun or took drugs or whatever. She got out of her car and marched up to the house and asked to meet him. I wanted to die!"

It was funny to hear Mom talk about things that happened when she was my age. Fortunately, she learned what not to do when she had kids of her own. I guess just calling my new friends' parents isn't all that bad.

"Was your friend's dad upset about it?"

Mom shakes her head. "No, he was very nice, but your grandma had a few misgivings about him anyway. He looked pretty disheveled and tired. It turns out he worked nights as a paramedic and was waiting for my friend's mom to get home from the store so he could get some sleep. After that, we usually hung out at my house so we didn't have to be so quiet."

We sit in silence then, lost in our own thoughts. I wonder if Mom's feeling sad about never having my friends over to our house because we never knew what Dad would be like. When we lived in the garage apartment, I never had friends over because, well, it was a *garage* apartment. All of my friends at school lived in super nice houses, sort of like Aunt Kathy's, and it made me feel bad to let them know where we lived. Now I'm ashamed for feeling that way, especially after seeing what April and Nora are really like.

Mom gives me another quick hug. "Well, kiddo, I'm going to make a cup of tea and then get ready for bed. It's been a long day."

"I think I'll read for a little while," I say, my hand on the diary where I've hidden it under the afghan.

"Don't stay up too late, okay?"

"Okay, Mom."

"Sweet dreams, Leah-loo. I love you."

"Love you back, Mom."

I wait to hear her close the door at the bottom of the stairs before I begin reading again.

Hope

June 3, 1966

Dear Daisy,

Today was the last day of school! Yippee! I'm really
looking forward to summer vacation! Mom says she's going
to give me and Pete chores to do on the days she works to
keep us out of mischief. Like I'm going to get into so much
mischief! I can see where Pete might, with him having his
driver's license and all, but he has no car, so, yeah. He keeps
saying if he had a car he could get a summer job, but Mom
told him his summer job is watching me. Can you believe
that? She doesn't even pay him!

Since Mom said she won't get me a new swimsuit, I'm
being really serious about following her diet. One of the
things my friends and I like to do in the summer is go to
the beach at Lake Hiawatha, and I don't want to be bursting
out of my swimsuit. All of the cool kids hang out there, so
it's super important to look good. It's been nearly a week,
and I haven't noticed that I'm any thinner yet. I've kept my
swimsuit handy and try it on every day to check. Mom's
more preoccupied with getting herself ready these days, so
it's been easy to skip breakfast. I pack my own lunch for
school and have just been bringing celery sticks and an
apple. I've been super hungry every day, ALL day, but I've
managed not to snack when I get home. I just drink *lots* of
water. Mom said I could drink one bottle of Tab a day, that
it helps her feel fuller so she eats less. It really works! I
don't really like the taste of it, but if it helps me lose

weight, it's worth it. I've been eating whatever Mom makes for dinner which for her and me is smaller portions of diet food. In a way, it's fun to be on a diet with my mom—it's the one thing we do together. Pete gets to eat whatever he wants and that's so unfair. I hate that part!

We only had a half-day of school today. Mom said I could stop at the Dairy Queen on the way home from school with Reenie and Jill to celebrate, but said I have to get either a small cone or a small Mr. Misty. When I complained about that, she threatened not to let me go at all, so I shut up. We don't go to the Dairy Queen hardly ever, and I really wanted to get a Buster Bar, my all-time favorite. Oh well, once I'm done dieting, I'll be able to have one of those again, right? I won't be on a diet all summer —just until my swimsuit fits better. I can't wait!

Love,
Hope

Leah

Hope seems really serious about being on a diet. Her mom even let her drink diet pop to fill her up! My mom never lets us have pop unless we go to Subway or a movie or something and then it can never be the diet kind. She says sugar is better for us than all the chemicals they put in that stuff. I'm reminded again of how lucky I am to have the mom that I do!

It's also lucky for me that dieting isn't on her radar because it makes it easier for me to eat less without her noticing too much. I'm happy my mom isn't making me diet, but I want to eat less anyway. Weird. Ever since the sleepover with April and Nora, I've felt more unhappy about my body. The bumps I'm getting on my chest are so ugly and embarrassing. I usually wear sweatshirts to school since it's getting colder outside, but what will I do when spring gets here? I'm guessing the bumps will only get bigger if they're supposed to grow into breasts, and I'm too young for that. I hate this! I've also been looking at some websites online about dieting and finding more of those *Before* and *After* pictures April showed me. It's weird because most of the people looked perfectly fine before they lost weight, but they seem so much happier when they're thinner. I have to remember to clear my browsing history each time so that Mom doesn't see what I'm doing.

It's almost two months since I got my period. I'm dreading it happening again, but I don't have much choice. It came on the first day of school on September 8th. Today is November 5th, so where is it? I was worried about it, so I asked Mom if I'm dying or something. She told me that it's not always regular at first, so I shouldn't worry about it. The thing is, I *do* worry about it *all* the time! What if it starts at school, and I leak all over? That would be awful! Mom bought me some pantiliners and told me to wear one in my undies just to be on the safe side and to keep some pads in my backpack. I hope my backpack never spills or anything so that no one finds out. It's terrifying to even think about.

The good news is that Prudy and Tabinda are going to come over on Saturday afternoon. I'm so excited! Mom had the great idea that we can make jewelry. She bought a bunch of beads and supplies at Michael's, so we can make bracelets or necklaces or whatever we want. I asked Prudy and Tabinda if they like doing that sort of thing and they both said yes, so that's a relief. It's going to be so much fun!

I hope having my new friends over will take my mind off my old friends being so awful to me. Nora has called back every day, asking me to find out if Johnny likes April. Every day I tell her I won't do it and to please stop asking. Mom wants to talk to her mom about it, but that would be *so* humiliating. I finally asked if I could just not answer when her number comes up on Caller-ID. She said I could do that for a while, but that it's really better to confront problems instead of hiding from them. I know she's right, but I'm just so scared of what might happen.

The other day at school, Johnny walked by me when I was at my locker and knocked my backpack off my shoulder and onto the floor. That's exactly why I'm worried about stuff falling out of it. I keep it zipped all the way shut all the time, but it still makes me nervous. Prudy says he's just doing it to get a reaction out of me; she even says he probably *likes* me. Yuck! That's so gross! Tabinda says that her brother said that sometimes boys act annoying around girls they like because they're too shy to do anything else. If I didn't know how mean Johnny has been as long as I've known him, I might believe that, but I *do* know how mean he is. Even if he did like me, I'd never like him back. *Never.*

After he knocked my backpack on the floor, he said, "Aww, sorry Pudge. Are you too *pudgy* to bend over and pick it up?"

I wanted to evaporate; either that or die. All the kids around me laughed, except for Prudy. She just looked at Johnny with dagger-eyes until he stopped cackling. She's at least a head taller than Johnny, and I think he knows she could level him if she wanted to, so yeah, he's a little scared of her. Hey—it works for me! I gracefully picked my backpack up off the floor and ignored him. Ms. Wilcox, our homeroom teacher, is almost too nice. I don't see how she can't see and hear what's going on while she's standing out in the hall; she acts like she doesn't have a clue. I guess she doesn't want to start out her day yelling at kids.

Math with Mr. Kendall is always awful. He still calls me *Pudgy* and Prudy, *Prudent.* I wonder if he knows that Johnny uses these names to bully us every chance he gets? The only sort of good thing is that since the first day of school, he's made up embarrassing nicknames for the rest of the class as well. He thinks he's hilarious. His nickname for Johnny is *Morgan Horse.* Johnny acts like he thinks it's cool, but I don't know if he actually feels that way. The thing is, kids would never dare bully him about it, and he knows it.

The only thing that gets me through the day is to look forward to the end of it. Unfortunately, now I dread going home because I'm afraid Nora and April will call again. The times I've let it go to voice mail, April has been the one to leave a nasty message, always calling me Pudge. *Always.* Sometimes she says extra mean things about different parts of my body. She's even given me some new things to hate about myself—like I need that! I always make sure to delete the messages so Mom doesn't listen to them.

The bus ride home isn't too bad today because Fred is on duty. I think it's cool how all the kids respect him so much. Johnny and his evil friends don't dare bully us when Fred's there. I wish Fred could be our bodyguard so that we'd always feel safe. If only there was some way to have a bodyguard at home when Nora calls and April leaves her nasty messages.

Today, when Tabinda and I get off the bus, Johnny hops down the steps after us. This is strange because I have no idea where his stop is, but I know it's not here. My heart starts pounding in a bad way, pummeling more fear into me with every beat. Tabinda and I try to act normal, but I can tell that's she's nervous about it too. We walk to the corner where Tabinda and I go our separate ways, saying goodbye like we do every day. Tabinda quietly adds, "Good luck."

I walk along, minding my own business, when out of the corner of my eye I see Johnny appear beside me.

"Hey, Pudge, how's it going?"

I keep my eyes forward and quicken my pace. Unfortunately, Johnny also speeds up.

"Did you forget this isn't your stop, Morgan Horse?" He's not the only one who can use nicknames.

"No, I didn't forget. My sister tells me that you have a question for me."

I can feel him looking at me but keep my eyes straight ahead. "What are you talking about?" I hate to prolong this conversation but don't know what else to do.

"I don't know. She came home from dance and said that."

"Well, I don't know what she's talking about." I wish he'd leave me alone because I'm a bad liar. I always cave.

"How do you like Shady Creek?" he asks, suddenly sounding sort of friendly.

"It's okay. How do you like it?"

"Okay, I guess. I'm kind of glad I'm not at Rolling Hills. There's a lot of stuck-up people at that school."

I want to say *Tell me about it!* Instead, I say, "Did you move?"

"Yeah, my dad lost his job, and we had to sell our house. We live in an apartment over by the fire station." He's looking down at the ground as he talks.

I'm surprised to feel a little sorry for him; his life hasn't been perfect either. I'm not sure what to say, partly because I'm surprised he's actually being nice to me but also because I don't know if I should trust him. This could be a trap.

"Apartments aren't so bad. We lived in one for a few years after my dad died. It got a little crowded sometimes, but it was okay."

"At least I have two parents, so I guess I shouldn't complain, huh?"

I sneak a peek at him and can't decide if that was a cruel thing for him to say. I'm pretty sure I'd never say that to anyone, not even him. "Yeah, I guess."

We're almost to my house and even though I'm very proud of it, I don't want him to know where I live. For all I know, he and his stupid friends will t.p. it sometime. I stop at the corner and turn to face him.

"Look, Johnny, I don't know what your sister's talking about. Maybe just ask her."

He looks at me as if he's trying to think of what to say. Maybe he's trying to think of something mean, so I'm surprised when he shrugs and says, "Yeah, maybe. Well, bye, Leah," and then turns and walks away.

I stand there for a few minutes to make sure he keeps going and then start walking toward my house. The fact that he called me by my name instead of Pudge leaves me feeling very unsettled. In a way, I wish he'd been mean. At least that's what's normal for him. This is just weird.

Hope

June 14, 1966

Dear Daisy,

Hi there! Last weekend was crazy busy so I didn't have a chance to write to you. Sorry about that! I have so much to tell you!

First of all, I've lost enough weight to fit into my swimsuit more like I did last summer! That makes me VERY happy! It even seems a little loose. That could be a problem because I wouldn't want it to fall off or anything. That would be super embarrassing! My shorts and stuff from last summer also still fit. The only bad thing about that is that Mom says we don't need to buy me *any* new clothes now. She was actually really happy about that and has celebrated by buying *herself* a bunch of new clothes—more mini-skirts and things like that. Now she's wearing frosted lipstick to go with her frosted hair. She looks like the models in my *Seventeen* and *Teen* magazines which feels kinda weird. She's supposed to look like a mom, not a model.

Last weekend, we were at Dad's. It was going to be fun because the pool is open, and Pete and I were really looking forward to swimming in it. I hoped Dad would come to the pool with us just in case the rowdy adults were there. He came, but brought his girlfriend, Kelly, who also lives in the building. I don't know if Mom has seen her, but it kinda makes sense why Mom is on a diet and stuff because Kelly is thin and beautiful. I mean, *movie star* thin and beautiful.

All the men at the pool just stared at her every time Dad wasn't looking. Pete told me that he thinks it's pathetic that Dad has girlfriend like that because he's a dad. Kelly has to be a lot younger than Dad, mostly because she acts that way. She also flirted with Pete. It was *super* creepy. Pete said he thought it was creepy too, but I think he liked it.

Seeing how much attention Kelly got from everyone made me start thinking about how important looks must be, especially when you're an adult or at least old enough to date. I noticed that some of the bigger ladies and girls around the pool didn't get as much attention from the men *or* from the thin girls. It made being thin seem so much better and very important. Like, why would you ever want to be anything else?

I was super proud of myself for how much my swimming has improved from last summer and was excited for Dad to notice, but he only noticed Kelly. It made me really sad. It also made me even more serious about sticking to my diet. Maybe if I lose more weight, Dad will notice me more.

When we got home on Sunday afternoon, Mr. Horton was over. (We're supposed to call him *Neil* now. Eww!) I hate him. He acts all nice—*too* nice. He always gives me a really long hug when he sees me which makes me feel icky inside. I've tried to tell Mom that I don't like it, but she just says that's how he is, that it's fine and I shouldn't be rude.

Anyhow, he gave me a hug like always, and said, "You're not as curvy and cuddly as you used to be, Hopey."

Hopey? I wriggled away, shrugged and hurried to my room. I didn't know what else to do. I saw that Pete heard what he'd said and that he had that same angry look on his face that he's had every time Neil's around. That look is scary, but it also makes me feel safe. How's that for strange?

All I know, is that if Neil likes me 'curvy and cuddly,' I'm going to make darn sure I get even thinner!

Love,
Hope

Leah

I'm not home more than five minutes when the phone rings. Glancing at Caller ID, I see that it's Nora again. The girl just can't take a hint—and I haven't been exactly subtle. I've been telling her to stop asking me about Johnny liking April, but she just keeps at it. For a nanosecond, I wonder if I should say I talked to Johnny yesterday and that he didn't say that he likes April, but decide against it. It wouldn't technically be lying, but it wouldn't be honest either. I hate this! It doesn't even feel like Nora and April are my friends anymore, as April keeps reminding me when I refuse to ask Johnny for his cell phone number and all that. I didn't pick up the phone yesterday or the day before that, so I figure I better do it now.

"Hello?"

"Hi, Leah," says Nora.

"Hi, Nora." I don't say more because she's the one calling me.

"What have you been doing after school? You didn't answer the past two times I called." Nora's voice sounds kind of strange, like I can hear the stress in it.

"I've just been busy."

"Busy talking to Johnny!" It's April.

I don't know what to say. I *was* talking to Johnny yesterday, but not about if he likes April. I didn't even *want* to talk to him, but I have a sick feeling that April won't believe me. She doesn't know I talked to him and that's how I'm going to keep it.

"No," I say, my heart thumping.

"You're lying! I know you talked to him!" April shrieks into the phone so loudly, I nearly drop it. "Why are you lying?"

Again, I don't know what to say. I feel like she's backed me into a corner and there's nowhere to go.

"I meant that I didn't talk to him about you. I've told you I'm not going to ask him that." *There.* That should settle it.

"Why not? Because *you* like him?"

Her accusation is ridiculous and a giggle escapes before I can stop it.

"What's so funny, *Pudge?* You won't think *anything* is funny after everyone sees what I put on Snapchat!" The phone goes dead.

Hanging up the phone, I sit down in the breakfast nook, dumbfounded. How does April know I talked to Johnny yesterday? Does she have spies hiding in the bushes somewhere? It's weird because today Johnny *was* nicer to Prudy, Tabinda and me, but I thought it was just a fluke. Collin was absent today, so maybe he wasn't feeling brave enough to be a bully on his own.

The gnawing hunger I was feeling as I walked home from the bus stop has been replaced by queasiness. I make myself take a few deep breaths, hoping that will help me feel better. The thought of eating a snack makes me feel even worse which isn't all bad; maybe I'll be even less pudgy by tomorrow if I don't eat.

Unzipping my backpack, I hope that distracting myself with homework will make me stop worrying about what April's going to do. I don't have a cell phone and have never even seen Snapchat, so it's hard to imagine what might happen. I pull my math book out and open it to today's assignment. While flipping back through the chapter to refresh my memory about the lesson, I see a small piece of notebook paper with ragged edges nestled between two pages. That's strange—I hadn't seen it there during class. I smile as I begin to open it, thinking that Prudy must have snuck it in there to be funny. My hand flies to my mouth when I see what it says: **Johnny M. 555-555-5231**

I drop the note as though it's on fire, my heart beating wildly. It must be Johnny Morgan's cell phone number! What should I do? I turn it over to see if there's any more writing on it, but there's not. I hate this feeling of not being in control, of not knowing what to do. I also feel really nervous and afraid. What will April do if she finds out I really did lie to her?

Hope

June 30, 1966

Dear Daisy,

There's a saying that Sister Mary Patricia said all the time last year: 'Be careful what you wish for.' I'm finding out she was right about that in so many ways.

One of the things I've wished for was to not get my period anymore, and I haven't! You'd think that would make me happy, but it sort of makes me worried. I got the first one in March and now it's nearly July. That's 4 months! My biggest worry is that I'm going to have a baby. I can't talk to Reenie and Jill about it because I'm not supposed to tell *anyone* I got my period. I haven't had s-e-x with anyone —I don't even understand how that all works. What I'm really worried about is that I somehow got something from the toilet seat, either from Dad, Pete or Neil. My stomach hurts like crazy every time I think about it. Would Mom send me away to the home for unwed mothers? What will people think? Will my life be ruined? And what would Dad say? It's so scary to think about, and I don't know what to do.

The other thing I've wished for is to lose weight, and guess what? I have, so maybe I'm not expecting a baby after all! I'm super excited to be shrinking, except for now my swim suit from last year is way too big. I tried it on this morning because I'm going to the beach with Reenie and Jill tomorrow, and the bottoms are super loose. Since Mom has been all for me dieting, I decided to ask her if we can finally go shopping for a new one. It went something like this…

"Hi Mom," I said, sitting on the bed behind her as she was putting on her makeup. She has a really cool vanity dresser, with a special makeup mirror that she sits in front of, just like my Barbie doll had.

"Hi, honey." She was concentrating on drawing on her eyeliner with a teeny tiny brush.

"Can I get a new swimsuit soon? My old one has gotten really loose on me, and I'm afraid it will fall off when it gets wet. I'm going to the beach with Reenie and Jill tomorrow, so it's kind of important."

She looked at me in the mirror, a frown on her pale pink frosted lips. "I'm sure it will be fine, Hope. I have a date with Neil after work tonight so there's no time to go shopping. You should have asked me sooner."

This made me mad because I *have* been asking her sooner. For weeks! At first I asked because it seemed too small and now, because *she* wanted me to lose weight, it's too big. I feel like Alice in Wonderland or something.

My first mistake was that I said all of that out loud in sort of a snotty voice. My second mistake was that I said more.

"Well, young lady, if it's such a problem and because you've been so sassy, you're grounded. No beach for you tomorrow! You can stay home and think about how disrespectful you've been!"

"That's not fair! I've only lost weight because *you* wanted me to! And you don't have time because you're *always* with *Neil!* All you care about is yourself and him!" Yep—that was my second mistake.

Her face got so red, I thought she was going to explode.

"That's it! Go to your room and stay there the rest of the day! Now you're grounded for the rest of the week—not just tomorrow!"

"But—"

"Keep it up and you'll be grounded from the beach for the rest of the summer! Then you won't even need a swimsuit! Now go!"

My mom has never yelled at me that way, not ever. I didn't know what to do or what to say. She's never grounded me before, so that was something new and exciting. Pete must have heard her yelling at me and came racing downstairs from his room. He looked like he was ready for a fight.

"Mom! What's going on?"

She looked taken by surprise and a little embarrassed, but then she said, "Hope is being disrespectful. She's grounded for the rest of the week and that means *you* have to stay home and keep an eye on her."

"But Mom—"

"Uh-uh-uh! Watch it, Pete, or you'll be grounded longer than she is! Now leave me alone so I can get ready in peace." She turned back to her mirror and her makeup.

"Sorry, Pete," I mumbled, as we walked into the living room. He looked more shocked than mad, but I knew the anger would eventually resurface.

"I've never heard her yell like that before," he said, "especially at you. What did you do to make her so mad?"

"I just asked if I could get a new swimsuit because my old one doesn't fit anymore since I've gotten thinner."

Pete squinted at me. "I guess you have, haven't you? I'd almost say you're *too* thin. Besides—why would that make her mad? It was her idea, wasn't it?"

I felt self-conscious knowing that my big brother was looking at my body. Shrugging, I said, "I might've said something about how she's *always* with Neil."

"Well, she *is* always with Neil."

"Yeah, well, I might've said it kinda snotty." I could feel my face get hot.

An expression of understanding appeared on his face. "That explains it. I've gotta hand it to you, sis. That took guts. I'm proud of you—even if I'm sort of grounded with you." He gave me a high five and a wink.

"Sorry again, Pete." I really was.

"Why won't she buy you a new swimsuit?"

I shrugged. "I don't know. I even have birthday money that I could use, but she didn't give me a chance to say that."

"You don't need to use that, sis. Dad gives her money for us every month. You don't even need many clothes since you wear a uniform to school, so what's she doing with all of it?"

Our eyes met and grew wide. "Are you thinking what I'm thinking?" I whispered. "She's spending it on her new clothes?"

"And everything else?" muttered Pete. "Well, don't worry. When you're not grounded anymore, *I'll* take you shopping if you want. I have money saved too."

"You'd really do that?" I couldn't believe how nice he was being to me!

He turned sort of pink. "Yeah, I would. We've gotta stick together, right?"

"Right." I felt like I was going to cry, but I didn't. That might've pushed him over the edge. "Thanks."

I followed Pete up the steps to our bedrooms.

"I wonder if she'll let me come out for dinner or if I'll have to eat bread and water," I said, as I plopped down on my bed. "Or maybe just water, since bread is too fattening."

Pete didn't hear me. He'd already closed the door to his room. I guess he'd had enough togetherness for one day.

Love,
Hope

Leah

As upset as I am about what April said on the phone, I'm even more upset for Hope. I read Daisy whenever I want to escape from my own life, only today it isn't much of an escape. Hope's mom is getting stranger and stranger all the time. Why is she being so mean to Hope? It makes me really, really angry, but I have no one to tell. I wish I had a big brother like Pete to look out for me. I love Clara, but it'd be nice to be taken care of once in a while. If I had a diary of my own, I could write about how this makes me feel, but instead I have to keep it all inside.

My stomach growls with hunger, and I hug myself to make it stop. I'm really, really hungry, but I'm *not* going to eat. If only there was some way to eat but not gain weight. That's when I remembered something April said at the sleepover about 'eating without swallowing.' When I asked her what she meant, she explained that sometimes she'll chew something but then spit it out in a napkin or paper towel instead of swallowing it. She claimed it was the perfect solution to craving cookies or cakes or whatever but not eating any of them. She said she had to hide it from her family, but it helped her stay thin. I shudder at the thought, since ABC food (Already Been Chewed) is disgusting and gross and my mom would *kill* me if she found out I was wasting food like that. Nope—I just need to wait out the hunger pangs until they go away. Once that happens, I can go hours without feeling hungry again. At that point, I almost have to force myself to eat. It makes me feel so strong and better than people who need eat every meal.

As soon as I get on the bus, I can hear snickers and giggles from some of the kids in my grade and even some of the seventh and eighth graders. A couple of girls I recognize from the lunchroom look at me and then whisper to each other, their hands hiding their mouths. What's going on? Do I have toilet paper stuck to my shoe or something? I peek to make sure everything is exactly how it looked when I left the house. Luckily, it is.

Before I can even get comfortable in my usual seat, I feel a tap on my shoulder. Turning around, I see Johnny sitting there. Oh great—what a way to start the day. I give him a puzzled look and say nothing.

"Hey, Leah," Johnny says, smiling a little bit. "I need to tell you something."

It's encouraging that he's used my real name again, but I can't imagine what he'd need to tell me. I'm also afraid to ask since he doesn't have the best track record. Before he can speak, Tabinda is walking down the aisle toward me. Thank goodness! Maybe Johnny will mind his own business now.

"Hi, Tabinda!" I beam at her as she sits down next to me.

"Hey, Leah!" She glances over her shoulder toward Johnny, who is now slinking back to his seat. "What did *he* want?"

"I don't know. It's weird."

"I know, right?"

By now the bus has stopped at Prudy's corner, and she's marching down the aisle. She plops into the seat in front of us and immediately turns to face us. The look on her face is not her usual smiley one.

"Leah, did you hear what happened?" she whispers. "Have you, Tabinda?"

We both shake our heads. "Well, a kid at my stop said that there was a bunch of bad stuff on Snapchat last night."

Tabinda shrugs. "There's bad stuff on there all the time. My sister says it's awful because the stuff disappears, so no one can ever prove anything."

"Yeah, well, this time it was about *you*, Leah!" Prudy's eyes have become huge.

"*Me?*" I feel my face turn red, and my stomach instantly feels nauseous. I remember what April said and begin to feel even worse.

"What was it?" Tabinda asks because I'm just sitting there, speechless.

Now Prudy's face turns pink. "I don't even want to say it out loud. Let's just say it's not nice at all."

It's all beginning to make sense now—the kids laughing at me, Johnny "needing" to tell me something—it must be about whatever was on Snapchat. What's really hard to believe is that my once BFF is doing this to me over Johnny Morgan of all people, a boy she used to hate.

"Please at least give me an idea," I say, trying to sound brave. "Then I'll at least know what everyone's laughing about all day."

Prudy looks at me and Tabinda with sad eyes. "I don't want to hurt your feelings, Leah. And it *will* hurt your feelings."

Before she can tell me, we arrive at school. As always, as soon as the bus lurches to a stop, kids start jumping up from their seats and clogging the aisle. Prudy instantly clams up; there's no way she'll tell me now with so many ears close by.

Collin walks by us and shouts," Have a nice day, *Fat Ass*!"

Johnny is behind him and sort of kicks him, all the while keeping his eyes straight ahead. *Fat Ass?* I look at Prudy and she just sort of nods. So that's what April put on Snapchat about me. What a mean thing to do! I can feel my eyes fill with tears, but I'm determined not to cry. I'll wait until I get home for that.

Hope

July 6, 1966

Dear Daisy,

Happy belated 4th of July! It's sort of a joke because on Independence Day, I was grounded. It's so unfair! Mom decided to stick to her guns and kept me grounded for the whole day. Can you believe that? We were supposed to be with her on the 4th, but she made Pete and me stay home while she went out on Neil's stupid boat. I felt bad for Pete, but he said he was glad not to have to go on that boat again. (He hates Neil even more than I do.) Mom said she'd be home late but not to even *think* about sneaking out to watch any fireworks. I love fireworks and she knows it! It really hurts my feelings. I didn't even do anything that bad —I was just a little sassy is all. Dad would unground me for the fireworks if we were with him, but he wouldn't have grounded me in the first place!

Pete and I were asleep upstairs in our rooms when we heard Mom come home. I looked at my alarm clock and saw that it was 1:00 a.m.—much later than she's ever come home before. I could also hear Neil's voice booming and Mom shushing him. There was giggling and some silence and then he was loud again. He sounded like he was drunk.

One handy thing about our rooms is that there's a clothes chute in the wall in the hallway. The little door on the clothes chute on the first floor is in the hallway right outside the bathroom. (The door on it is missing, which is okay, since it makes throwing stuff in it even easier.) One good and bad thing about it has always been that I could listen to what goes on downstairs. That meant hearing Mom and Dad arguing. Pete thought they never argued, but I knew better; I'd been listening to them for years. Even though I was sad when they got divorced, it was a relief not to have to listen to Mom crying anymore or Dad pleading with her to stop. She cried a lot after Dad left too, but eventually that stopped—especially after Neil came into the picture.

The only way to describe what I heard that night is horrible. There was Neil's voice booming, Mom shushing, silence and then suddenly I heard Mom saying, "No, Neil! Stop it! Not here!" Then I heard something crash. What was happening down there?

I ran into Pete's room and shook his shoulder hard to wake him up. Dad always says that Pete sleeps like the dead now that he's a teenager. I don't usually dare wake Pete since he's so grouchy if he wakes up before he's ready, but this was an emergency.

"Pete! Come and listen!" I grabbed his hand, dragged him into the hall and pointed to the clothes chute. "Listen!"

He yawned and rubbed his eyes as he knelt down and stuck his head half-way into the metal chute. The sounds of Mom shouting and more disturbing noises made Pete leap into action. He bolted downstairs, ordering me to stay put, but of course, I didn't listen.

I'll never, *ever* forget what I saw. There, on the couch, was Neil on top of Mom, sort of wrestling with her and grabbing her. Mom was telling him "No!" and "Stop!" but he wasn't; it looked like he was holding her down. It was kinda dark, so Pete turned on the ceiling light. He told me to go upstairs and not come back down. That time I did listen and ran back to my room. I felt really scared and wished Dad was here to keep Mom safe, but then realized that if Dad was here, none of this would be happening. I curled up in a ball on my bed and waited.

The clothes chute door was still open, so the sounds of what was happening downstairs drifted up and found me on my bed. I tried putting my hands over my ears, but I could still hear loud voices, mostly Pete's and Neil's; Mom just cried.

"Get out of here!" Pete yelled. I heard the front door slam and Neil's noisy little sports car speed away into the night.

I decided it was safe to go back downstairs. Even though I wasn't supposed to, I quietly snuck downstairs and sat on the bottom step. I needed to figure out what was going on.

There, I saw Pete sitting next to Mom on the couch. She had the afghan that's always folded up on the back of the couch wrapped around her and she was just sobbing and sobbing. Pete sat there looking really angry and really awkward at the same time.

Mom must have seen me out of the corner of her eye because suddenly she said, "Hope, go to your room right now!" I did as she said because I didn't want to get grounded even longer than I already am.

In a little while, I heard Pete and Mom arguing. Would this night ever get better? I crawled back over to the clothes chute because I needed to know what was going on.

"Mom, we need to call the police. He attacked you!"

"Shh, Petey!" Mom was shushing again. "He just got a little carried away is all!"

"Mom—you've always told me *No* means *No*, and *Stop* means *Stop*. That if I force myself on a girl it's called *rape*." He whispered that last word, but I heard it anyway.

"Yes, but this is different!" she hissed.

"How? I heard you telling him *No* and *Stop* and he didn't! He kept on going! How is that okay?"

"I am *not* having this conversation with my sixteen year old son! Neil is my boss—"

"That makes it even worse!" Pete shouted.

Then Mom started crying even louder. "I'll be fired for sure after the way you talked to him!"

"So what? You can get another job if you want one. Maybe Dad will give you more money every month if—"

"Petey, there's no way your father can *ever* know this happened. You have to promise me you won't tell him; that you won't tell anybody!"

It got really quiet for a minute and then I heard Pete say, "*Mom*." He wasn't shouting and didn't sound mad like before. Then I heard Mom say, "It's okay, it's nothing, sweetie. I'm fine."

Since I was only listening, I had no idea what that was all about but sort of figured it out the next morning, when Mom was wearing a long-sleeved shirt on one of the hottest days of the summer. When I went to give her a hug like I do every morning, she sort of winced and moved away from me. Pete was eating a bowl of Wheaties and when I looked at him, he just shook his head—his signal to stop asking so many questions. We both knew I'd be asking later, which I did

I'll tell you about that later, Daisy. I'm sort of written out right now.

Love,
Hope

Leah

It's perfect timing that Prudy and Tabinda are coming over today. It's the day after all the Snapchat stuff, and I really want to talk to them about it without anyone listening in. I also want to tell them about Hope and Daisy. There's been some things in the diary I don't exactly understand, and I'm hoping they do. They both have older sisters, so they might know more about stuff like that. We won't be by ourselves the whole time, since Mom has all the beading stuff for us to do, and Clara will want to join us for that. That's okay because I want Mom and Clara to get to know them. I told both of them that I'm not telling my mom about the bullying just yet. I hope they remember!

Each of their moms drops them off around one o'clock, although not at the exact same time. Mom chats with each mom about school stuff and about our house rules. It's nice to see that both of my new friends' moms are just like mine—they *love* rules—but now Mom will feel okay about me going to their houses too, so it's a win-win-win!

Clara is on her best behavior and is being downright adorable. We sit in the breakfast nook with the beading supplies and tools in the middle of the table. Everyone decides, even Clara, to make matching bracelets, sort of like friendship bracelets with beads instead of thread. Mom sits with us for a little while to help with the crimping part, but before long we know what we're doing well enough to do it on our own. Tabinda is sitting next to Clara and is being so sweet to her. She claims she's always wanted a little sister, so she's excited to see what it's like.

Once we're done beading, we head up to my room to hang out. Mom made popcorn for us to take up there, along with whatever we want to drink, either water, pop or juice. We all choose water so that we don't have to worry about spills.

"This is amazing!" Tabinda says as we reach the top of the stairs. "It's so big! I have to share a room with my sister, and it's already kind of small."

"Thanks!" I say, beaming on the inside but not too much on the outside. "I used to share a room with Clara when we lived in the garage apartment. I love this, but I still miss her sometimes. I never thought I'd say that!"

"Yeah, I know what you mean. It can be fun, but also annoying. My sister's a slob and I'm not." Tabinda wrinkles her nose at the thought.

"You even have your own bathroom!" Prudy is peeking inside the bathroom door. "You're so lucky!"

"I do feel lucky. I still have to shower in the other bathroom, but it's really nice not to have to go downstairs in the middle of the night."

I suddenly realize that the package of sanitary pads is still sitting on the shelf next to the sink. How did I forget to put that away? It's not like I need them right now. What will they think? What will they say?

Tabinda's eyes grow big and she says, "You too?"

It takes a second for what she just said to sink in. "Did you say *too*?"

She nods. "First one last week."

I can't even find words for the feeling of relief that washes over me. I've been feeling so embarrassed and alone about it and now I don't have to feel that way anymore!

"The week before that for me," adds Prudy from over by the window seat.

Now my eyes grow big. "Seriously? This is great!" Now I *am* beaming on the outside! "I got it on the first day of school. I haven't gotten it again, but my mom says that's normal."

"The first day of school?! That's awful! I remember when my sister got hers the first time. She's quite the drama queen, so that's all we heard about for months and months. She didn't get hers regularly at first either, so she was worried she was pregnant. Can you believe that?" Prudy laughs and so does Tabinda. I think of Hope wondering the same thing and feel relieved for her that she wasn't the only one.

"But she wasn't, of course, and now that she gets it every month, she complains about it like she's literally *dying*."

"Did you get cramps?" Tabinda asks, her voice a little quieter.

"Yeah, but not too bad," I say. "My mom didn't want to tell me too much about them, like that would make me have them or something. She says it shouldn't slow me down, and it's not a reason to miss school."

"My sister gets *horrible* cramps," says Tabinda. "I feel bad for her. Sometimes she can't even sit up straight. I sure hope I don't get them that bad."

We all plop down on the fuzzy purple rug, the popcorn bowl in the center and our bottles of water next to us.

"I'm so worried about when I'll get it again—like if it happens at school, and I'm not ready. My mom told me to keep some pads in my backpack, but what if they fall out or something? Remember how Johnny knocked my backpack off my shoulder the other day?"

"That would be *so* embarrassing," groans Prudy.

"I'd cover for you," Tabinda assures me. "No one would ever know."

"And if they did, I'd let 'em have it! Johnny's such a little pipsqueak! I don't know why he thinks he's so cool," says Prudy, punching her fists in the air.

That brings the conversation to the whole Johnny subject. I've already told them about my former friends harassing me for his cell phone number and all that, so at least we don't have to go over that again.

"Well, if you ask me," Tabinda says as she stretches out her legs and crosses her ankles over the cutest red and white polka-dot socks I've ever seen, "I think he likes you, and your friend April found out and is jealous. She must have a spy on the bus or something." She drops several pieces of popcorn into her mouth.

"Yeah, she knows that he talked to you after school that day, right? She knew before you told her?" Prudy shifts onto her stomach and props herself up with her elbows.

"Yeah, but it was no big deal. I don't even like Johnny."

Tabinda gives me a knowing look. "But he called you Leah, didn't he? Not Pudge like he usually does?" I nod. "Well, that's proof. He likes you, Leah! *And* he stuck his phone number in your math book!"

"But I don't *want* him to like me! Even if I did, it's not worth getting bullied over, is it?"

"Definitely not!" Prudy goes back to sitting up again. "And cyber-bullying is the worst!" She takes a big drink of water and wipes her mouth with the back of her hand.

"Have you told your mom?" asks Tabinda. "She seems really cool. She'd do something about it, right?"

I shrug. "I haven't told her everything yet. As it is, she already wants to call Nora's mom. I'd die if she did that! It would just make it worse."

The three of us sit in silence as we mull this over. We're only in sixth grade, but we've all seen what happens when the victim tells—it gets worse, *much* worse. If April is putting mean things online now, what will she do if she gets in trouble because I tell? Chills run through me just thinking about it.

"Well, no matter what happens," says Prudy as she grabs a handful of popcorn, "you *don't* have a fat ass. I mean, who decides what that even is? And anyway—even if you did, I'd still be your friend. *You* are not your ass!"

Even though she said it in all seriousness, Tabinda and I look at each other and burst into laughter, rolling around on the floor as we try to catch our breath. Prudy just sits there, confused. "What did I say? What's so funny, guys?"

That makes us laugh even harder! Being called *Fat Ass* isn't funny, but for some reason, imagining Prudy defending me over it, is. Maybe it's just the happiness of having new friends who truly seem to be friends that's bubbling out of me. Whatever it is, it feels so good to belly laugh and be silly again. I hope it never ends.

Hope

July 7, 1966

Dear Daisy,

It seems like I'm getting into the habit of waiting a while to tell you everything after it happens. I hope you don't mind. It's just that sometimes I need to turn my brain off and not think about it so much even though telling you about it usually makes me feel better. Does that make sense?

I left off where my mom acted strange when I hugged her the morning after all the excitement with Mr. Horton— I mean *Neil*. Pete seems to know more about this stuff than I do, so I was counting on him to explain it to me when it was a good time.

After we finished eating breakfast—he had two big bowls of Wheaties with lots of sugar on top; I had half a grapefruit with no sugar on it—I whispered to him, asking when we could talk. I know he didn't want to talk about it, but I can be *really* stubborn when I need to be. Dad calls it 'persistent.' I get the feeling it's not always a good thing, but I'm not going to worry about that right now.

Mom had disappeared into her bedroom, so we could've talked in the kitchen, but Pete thought we should go for a walk instead. I guess he didn't want to take any chances. We left Mom a note on the kitchen counter and slipped on our shoes to go outside.

I can't remember the last time I went for a walk with my brother. Maybe it was when I was a baby and he was five or so, holding onto the stroller as Mom pushed me along. It's a nice memory to think about. Even though Pete and I were going on a walk to talk about something bad, it still felt good to spend time with just him.

"So, sis, what happened with Neil has to be kept secret. Mom doesn't want anyone to know, especially Dad." We crossed the street at the corner and headed toward the park. "I don't think she's right, but I don't want her to feel worse or get more upset. You got that?"

I gave him a firm nod.

"Okay, well, I don't know how much you saw or heard, but it looked like Neil was forcing himself on Mom." He turned his head to look at me. "Do you know what that means?"

I felt a big lump form in my throat, and my eyes started to sting. "He was trying to make her do something she didn't want to do?"

Pete nodded. "Yep—that's right. Do you know what that something was?" He shoved his hands in his pockets and kept his eyes on the ground.

"Not really—I *am* only eleven, you know." Mom barely told me about my period, talking mostly about birds and bees and plants and stuff. I guess she thought I needed to be older to understand anything about actual humans.

"I know. Okay, well, here's the deal: Neil was trying to make Mom have sex with him." Pete's face turned a soft shade of pink. "And that's wrong, Hope. Guys should never, ever do that. You understand?"

I shrugged. "Well, I heard Mom telling him *no* and *stop,* so it sounded like he didn't know he was doing something wrong. And she was sort of giggling before the shouting started, so it sounded like she was having fun at first." I looked up at my brother. "Did she do something wrong?"

"No, not at all!" We had reached the park and were waiting until it was safe to cross the street.

The park is really cool with all sorts of trees and hills and walking paths. It's fun to go there and pretend you're in some faraway place instead of a few blocks from home in the middle of the city. Reenie, Jill and I have spent hours and hours there playing Swiss Family Robinson. That day we just walked, though. I guess Pete needed to concentrate on talking.

I wanted to ask him more about s-e-x, but he was so uncomfortable, I didn't think he'd want to tell me. It all seemed very sinful to me, so I could see why Pete felt that way. Instead, we just walked without talking for a while. Is just *talking* about it a sin that he'd have to tell the priest during confession? That would be awkward!

"Why did Mom act so weird when I hugged her today?" I figured that was a pretty safe question. At least it wasn't about you-know-what. "And why was she wearing a long-sleeved shirt? It's super hot today."

Pete let out a long, slow sigh. He stopped walking and turned to face me, sort of stooping down so his face was even with mine.

"Well, it looks like he hurt Mom. Last night, I saw marks on her arms where he must've squeezed her hard or something. She feels really embarrassed about that too."

"Why did he do that? Why did she let him?"

I could tell that Pete was having a hard time knowing what to say. I could also tell that he felt really, really sad for Mom.

"She didn't *let* him, Hope. He's a lot bigger and stronger than she is and sometimes when a guy wants to have sex, if he gets told *no*, he sort of freaks out."

That sounds awful! I *never* want to have sex if that's what it's like.

"We have to be extra nice to Mom for a while. She might lose her job and if that happens, we just roll with it, okay?" He straightened up, and we started walking again. "Do you have any questions about anything?"

We walked a little longer when I said, "Mom and Dad never did stuff like that, did they? And if Neil was just trying to kiss Mom, why did he freak out when she didn't want to?"

"Geez, sis! Weren't you listening to me? Sex isn't the same as kissing!" Pete seemed totally frustrated with me.

I felt my eyes sting again. "Sorry! You asked if I had any questions. You don't have to yell at me!"

Pete stopped walking again. "I'm sorry, Hope. This stuff is just weird to talk about. Didn't Mom ever explain all of this to you?"

"Not really." There was no way I was going to tell him about my period, especially if I thought I might be pregnant from the toilet seat.

"And she's sure not going to want to tell you now," he said, under his breath. "Okay, sis, this is the deal: kissing is not sex…"

As we made our way back home, Pete told me all about sex (and I mean ALL about it!), and kissing and stuff like that. He also told me that he thinks Neil is a pervert and then explained what that is. He said that it had always bugged him how Neil gave me hugs at all, let alone hugs that were so long. He said that good guys don't do stuff like that. Then he confused me even more by telling me that nice people can kiss and even have sex, but it's only okay when they *both* want to and when they're adults. I was confused because it all seems really naughty and gross to me. Like I said, I never want to do that! And if kissing makes a person want to have sex, why would I ever do that? He also didn't say anything about *having* to be married and that's probably a really big commandment. I sure hope he never breaks it.

I wanted to ask Pete those questions, but by the time I thought of them we were at our back door. I also thought he'd had enough talking for one day; he looked really worn out.

"Thanks for telling me all that, Pete," I said right before we walked into the house. I gave him a little smile.

"You're welcome, sis. Just remember: Don't tell *anyone*."

So I'm telling *you*, Daisy, because I know *you* won't tell anybody. I just have to find a really, really safe place to hide you so that nobody ever finds out.

Love,
Hope

Leah

It was so much fun having Prudy and Tabinda come over yesterday! I had more fun with them than I ever did with April or Nora. That must mean something, huh? I'm also glad I accidentally left the package of pads out in my bathroom since that got us to talking about all that stuff. It's so great to not feel all alone anymore! I didn't tell them about Hope and Daisy after all because we ran out of time. Now that I've just finished reading the entry from July 7, 1966, I'm sort of glad I didn't.

Some really bad things happened to Hope's mom on the Fourth of July—*really* bad things. It sounds like Neil might have tried to rape Hope's mom. Rape her! I don't know what I'd do if that happened to my mom. I'd want to die and kill the guy all at the same time. Hope was lucky to have Pete to help her understand it all. I feel kind of panicky when I think how I'd be the one to help Clara through something like that. After all, I *am* the big sister. Again, I'm glad that Mom hasn't dated anyone yet so that I don't have to worry about bad things like that happening to her. That would be awful!

It's also sad that Hope didn't seem to know anything about sex—she didn't even know what her period was when she got it. It also seems like she doesn't have anyone to talk to about that stuff. Her friends seem nice enough, but I don't think they're allowed to talk about things like that. I wonder if that's because she goes to a school with nuns. It seems really strict and is so different from my school. Hope would freak out if she saw what goes at

Shady Creek! Kids probably got bullied back in 1966, but they didn't have super sneaky ways like Snapchat to do it.

Even though Prudy and Tabinda were really nice to me about the whole Snapchat deal and we even managed to laugh about it, I still can't shake the idea that I'm fat. I find myself comparing myself to other girls all the time now. It doesn't really bother me if they're bigger than me because then I feel skinny, but if they're thinner, I feel jealous and not good enough. That's when I resolve to eat less and exercise more. Why do I think about this so much all of a sudden? It's like there's an alien in my head. It's exhausting! I'm just glad it's getting colder outside, so I can cover myself up with sweatshirts, sweaters and jeans. Since I haven't been putting that much in my school lunches and not eating anything after school, I feel a little less pudgy, as Mr. K. would say, which makes me feel better. I might not be able to control the bullying, but I *can* control this.

Momo, Aunt Kathy and Uncle Jim are coming over for dinner tonight. Mom says it's sort of a 'thank you' for all the help they've given us the past few years. It seems like we should give them more than just a dinner, but it's a start. Aunt Kathy's kids, Emily and Austin, are away at college, so it will just be the grown-ups. That's fine with me. I like my cousins well enough, but they're like adults now, so we don't have much in common. Back when we lived in the garage apartment, Emily used to babysit us and so did Austin sometimes. It had been a lot of fun, something we didn't have too much of at the time.

I pull on jeans and an oversized sweater and go downstairs to help Mom get ready. I helped clean the whole house before Prudy and Tabinda came over yesterday, so not much else needs to be done cleaning-wise.

"Do you need any help, Mom?"

I find her and Clara in the kitchen where she's assembling the lasagna. A pang of panic shoots through me at the thought of having to eat my all-time favorite dinner. Nora said there's like three-hundred calories in a slice of pizza, so lasagna must be even worse. I hate that I think about things like calories so much of the time now.

"Thanks, sweetie!' Mom pushes a lock of hair out of her face with the back of her hand."How about you get the garlic bread ready? I already made the garlic butter and sliced the bread, so you just have to butter it and wrap it in foil. That would be a big help!"

Garlic bread is also one of my favorites, and I don't know if I'll be able to resist it. With my back to Mom and Clara, I take the long loaf of french bread out of its plastic bag. It's already cut into thick, uniform slices, just the way Mom always does it. Darn. If I'd done it, I would've made the slices thinner to literally cut out some of the calories, but it's too late for that now. Instead, I decide not to slather the garlic butter on one slice on the end of the loaf. No one usually wants the end anyway, so this way it can be mine. Bread is bad, but surely it's better without the butter.

"Can I help?" Clara nudges my elbow.

"Sure," I say, scooting over a bit to let her get at the bread.

She immediately grabs the knife out of my hand and plops a large dollop of butter on the slice of bread that I had reserved for me. "You forgot this one. Good thing I'm helping!"

Clara's so proud of herself, I hate to burst her bubble. "Thanks, Clare-bear. How did I miss that one?"

Another wave of panic hits me as I realize I'll have to take, if not eat, a slice of bread that has butter on it—

delicious, melted garlic butter. Taking a deep breath, I tell myself it won't kill me. No one will even notice.

Once the bread is buttered and I've wrapped it securely in foil, I ask Mom for another task. "Should I make the salad?"

Mom shakes her head. "Nope, Kathy's bringing a salad, and Grandma Mo is bringing dessert—your favorite—her homemade French silk pie!"

"Why is she bringing that? It's not my birthday or anything."

Mom glances at me as she covers the lasagna pan with foil. "Well, you're not the only one who likes it, you know. I thought you'd be thrilled."

My face feels hot, and it feel like she's reading my mind. How can that be?

"I *am* thrilled. Just surprised."

Maybe I can pretend I don't feel well when it's time for dessert, but I don't want to hurt Momo's feelings. Her French silk pie is fabulous, and I know it's a lot of work to make. I'll just have to eat even less tomorrow. Thank goodness it's a school day, so I can go back to my routine. Just knowing that makes some of the anxiety go away.

Hope

July 9, 1966

Dear Daisy,

It's been a long week, with having to be so careful and nice around Mom and all. It's also been the hottest week *ever,* and she's *still* wearing long sleeves. She doesn't know that I know why she's doing that. You'd think that would make her realize it's even stranger, but I've been keeping my mouth shut like Pete instructed. She only had to work one day this week because of the holiday, so she hasn't been fired yet. That makes me worry too. Will it happen next week?

It's our weekend to go to Dad's and I'm not grounded anymore. We're at his apartment now, since he picked us up last night. We're going to go to Excelsior Amusement Park today! He wants to get an early start which is why he picked us up early. I'm SO excited! I love the rollercoaster there!

"Is Kelly coming with us?" I asked before we climbed into his car.

"Nope," he said after he put the cooler and picnic basket into the trunk.

"Why not?" It was hard not to sound overjoyed.

"Well, peanut, Kelly and I aren't seeing each other anymore." He didn't sound very sad about it. It made me want to jump up and down, but I controlled myself.

"How come?"

Dad laughed and said, "You're just full of questions, aren't you?"

"It's none of our business, sis," Pete said, out of the corner of his mouth.

"That's okay, son—it *is* your business, in a way. I decided that Kelly isn't exactly mother material. I know you already have a mom and no one will ever replace her, but Kelly's just too immature. She's pretty and all, but looks aren't the most important thing. You two remember that, okay? She's also very jealous."

"What about?" I asked. Pete rolled his eyes and elbowed me at my never-ending list of questions.

"She'd get upset if I wanted to spend time with just the two of you. She always wanted to tag along and be the center of attention. It got old quickly."

My heart was singing! Kelly was better than Neil, but not much. Suddenly, the weekend looked a whole lot better. I was the only girl, but I didn't mind a bit. Whenever I had to go to the bathroom, Dad and Pete stood right outside the ladies room and waited for me. I never felt like I wasn't safe by myself but was used to having Mom with me on these family outings—or Kelly. The problem with Kelly was that she always acted all inconvenienced if Dad asked her to go with me to a public restroom. She'd stand there with her arms folded across her chest and pout the whole time. Once there wasn't any toilet paper in my stall, and she wouldn't even get some for me. She told me that I should be more *observant* when choosing a stall. Really? It had been the only one available, and I really had to go! Luckily, the lady in the stall next to me handed me some toilet paper under the partition. That was nice of her, not mean like Kelly had been. I never told Dad about it because I figured he'd get mad at me. Maybe he would've been upset with *her,* instead, if he had known.

It makes me feel safe to know that Dad chose Pete and me over his girlfriend. If only Mom would do the same thing. If I say anything bad about Neil, I get grounded. I just can't believe she's still going out with him after, you know…what he did to her.

Something else happened before we went to the amusement park. Dad said we should wear our swimsuits under our clothes because there's a lake with a beach near the park, and we could go swimming since it was so hot. That sounded super fun, but I was worried about my now too big swimsuit. Even though I was worried, I tried to act excited.

"Get a move on, kiddo! Time's a-wasting!" Dad said when he noticed I wasn't hurrying to get ready.

"Okay," I mumbled and went to my room to change. I felt like crying the whole way.

I yanked the suit out of my suitcase and pulled it on. It was bigger than it had been the last time I tried it on which meant *I* was smaller. That thrilled me, but there was no way the suit was going to work. It would come off when it got wet for sure. I decided to pretend I had forgotten to bring it. I was super impressed with how fast I came up with that idea! I took the suit off and stuffed it at the bottom of my suitcase and then went out to the living room, still in my shorts and my favorite rib-tickler top.

"All set?" said Dad, looking at Pete and me.

"Yup!" we said at the same time and headed out to the car.

I wasn't going to say anything about "forgetting" my suit until we got to the lake. That way, I'd make the best of it by sitting on the beach and watching Dad and Pete swim. I'd get hot, but it was better than losing my suit in the water.

Before I knew it, we were pulling into the parking lot at Sears. That was odd. I'm not great with directions, but I didn't think Sears was anywhere near the amusement park.

"What are we doing here?" Yep, I was still full of questions.

Dad turned around in the front seat to face me. "I thought it would be fun for you to get new swimsuit. I know you love that lime green and yellow one, but that's so last year, right?" He gave me a quick wink. "Pete and I will hang around outside the fitting room in case you need our opinion, but I'm sure you can handle it on your own."

I was so excited for the second time that day! How did Dad know I needed a new suit? Pete might have told him, but that was okay with me. It was unusual to shop with Dad and Pete, but it went okay. The sales lady was really nice to me and *really* nice to Dad. That was kinda funny to watch. Anyhow, I ended up getting not one, but *two* suits because I couldn't decide. Dad said I could keep one at his place which was a great idea. He didn't even notice that the suits I got were smaller than my old one which was a huge relief. Good thing he doesn't pay attention to that type of thing. It was turning out to be a great day!

Excelsior was great! We went on every ride two times and the roller coaster *three* times. It was so much fun! We brought a picnic lunch, but Dad said we could get whatever treat we wanted for dessert. I panicked at the idea of eating too much. As it was, I picked at my peanut butter and banana sandwich and managed to throw most of it away when Dad wasn't looking. Mom would freak out if she knew I'd even eaten *any* of something with so many calories. Peanut butter is at the top of our list of forbidden foods.

"What are you going to get for your treat?" Dad asked, as we wandered through the food stands. "Cotton candy?"

Cotton candy has always been my favorite thing, and it's not easy to find just anywhere. I wanted some more than anything but didn't dare get any. Way too much sugar and too many "empty" calories, as Mom calls them.

"I'm not that hungry right now. Maybe later."

Dad looked at me funny and then shrugged and looked at Pete, who was wolfing down a foot long hot dog with chili and cheese on it. He can be such a pig!

"She's been on a diet with Mom," Pete said with a full mouth. I couldn't believe Pete snitched on me like that! It was supposed to be a secret.

I didn't like how Dad was looking at me, all serious-like. I've gotten used to dieting with Mom and didn't want him to ruin it. I also like not being the size I was when I got measured for my school uniform. The other day Mom said something about my uniform probably being too big when school starts, and she was so happy about it. She tells me how proud she is of me *all* the time now—whenever she takes the time to notice, that is.

"I'm guessing cotton candy's not on your diet?"

I laughed a little bit. "Nope—things like fruit and carrot sticks are."

"Yeah," said Pete as he swallowed a large gulp of pop, "Hope and Mom eat plain chicken or fish and vegetables. They even have *liver* once a week! That means I get all the potatoes and bread and stuff. I get to eat all I want—even junk food! Since Mom and Hope don't eat it, there's more for me!" He took another huge bite of his hot dog. All he cares about is eating these days—and girls and cars. We didn't talk about it anymore while we were at the park. Instead, we went on the roller coaster one more time.

The saleslady at Sears had let me put one of the suits on under my clothes, so when we got to the lake we were ready to swim. I slipped my shorts and top off quickly and was ready to run down to the water as fast as I could. At least that was my plan after I figured out that Dad seemed worried about my dieting. I knew I'd lost weight since the last time he saw me in a swimsuit. We'd gone swimming at his apartment pool, but he'd been all distracted by Kelly, so he didn't really notice.

Just when I was all set to follow Pete into the water, Dad put a hand on my shoulder. "Wait a sec, peanut."

I turned and looked at him, not sure why he wanted me to wait. The suit I was wearing had a blouson top, and the sales lady said it looked very nice on me. I'm keeping this one at Dad's place because it covers more of me so my ribs don't show like they do in a regular two-piece. The trouble was I couldn't hide my legs or arms. They stuck out for all to see. I still think they're a little too big, but he might have a different opinion.

"How much weight have you lost on this diet?"

My heart started racing. What if he didn't let me diet anymore? We only saw him two weekends a month, but I was still worried.

"Not that much—it just looks that way because I've gotten taller. Shooting up like a weed and all that, you know." I felt bad lying to him, but he didn't need to know the truth right now. "Gotta run!"

The rest of the weekend was super fun, except for mealtimes. Dad would watch me more carefully than he ever had before which was really annoying. It makes me look forward to when the weather gets cooler, and I can cover up more.

See you next time!

Love
Hope

Leah

"Hey there!" Tabinda sits down next to me on the bus.

"Hi! How was your weekend?" I skooch myself over to give her more room and immediately wonder if I have to do that because I really do have the fat ass everyone keeps talking about. I vow to not eat anything for the rest of the day.

"I wish it wasn't so cold already," she says, adjusting her blue down jacket. "It's not even Halloween yet."

"I know, right? Clara's all worried that she'll have to wear a coat over her costume." I'm excited for colder weather, so I can hide my body more.

Just then, a crumpled up ball of paper comes flying between our shoulders from the back of the bus and lands on the floor by Tabinda's feet. We both look down at it, afraid to pick it up. The floor is sort of dirty and so is the paper ball. We look at each other, wondering what to do. I have a sick feeling in the pit of my stomach.

"Should we look at it?" she whispers out of the corner of her mouth.

I shrug. "I don't know. I have a bad feeling about it."

Before we can do anything, the bus rolls to a stop to pick up more kids, Prudy being one of them. She smiles when she sees us, but then her smile fades and she looks confused.

"You guys look like you've seen a ghost or something. What's going on?"

Pointing to the floor, Tabinda whispers to Prudy about the crumpled paper ball.

"Well, I'll look at it if you guys don't want to. Give it here." Prudy holds out her gloved hand. "My mom made me wear these today. It's so dorky. It's not even that cold out yet."

I push the ball with the toe of my shoe under Prudy's seat so that it's within her reach. In the process of taking off her gloves, she "accidentally" drops one on the floor and then bends down to grab the ball at the same time she picks up her glove. (She's a clever one, that Prudy. I never would've come up with that idea!)

Tabinda and I watch Prudy as she opens the paper ball and studies it. Then she quickly crumples it back up and shoves it in her pocket.

"What is it?" I ask her, keeping my voice a whisper.

"Nothing," she says, focusing on the scenery as the bus lumbers along.

"Then why won't you tell us?" Tabinda hisses.

"Later," is all Prudy says.

Whoever threw the ball from behind us remains a mystery as we file off the bus at school. I would think that someone would say something or act strange, but everyone seems normal; even Johnny. What's really weird is that he's acting less obnoxious and is even nicer to us three than he's ever been before. That alone makes my stomach twist into a tight knot.

The morning drags on and on, and Prudy refuses to show me the paper. I have a feeling she's at least told Tabinda what's on it because Tabinda doesn't seem as desperate as I do. It makes me feel more worried and paranoid than ever.

It's finally lunchtime, and we're at our usual table in the far corner of the cafeteria, closest to the door. One time, at

6

the beginning of the year, we tried to sit more in the middle of everyone, and it didn't go so well. We had actually been told we couldn't sit there, not by a lunchroom supervisor, but by some kids. It was so humiliating. After that, we found our current spot and it's been much better. Today, however, lots of kids are purposely walking by our table and gawking at us. Prudy and Tabinda seem to know why, but I'm still in the dark. Kids aren't saying or doing anything that mean, but the gawking and then the whispering when they sit down at their tables worries me.

"Prudy, will you please tell me what's going on?" I haven't even taken the apple out of my lunch bag and don't intend to; my stomach is still feeling pretty awful.

Prudy and Tabinda look at each other and then at me.

"Well, it was really nasty, Leah. I told Tabinda because I needed some advice." Prudy's cheeks are turning a bright shade of pink, the way they did on the first day of school when her pencil box spilled all over the floor.

"Is it about me?" If they want to play 20 Questions, I'm up for it.

"Yes," says Prudy, quietly.

"Is it about my fat butt?" I can't bring myself to say the word *ass* when I'm in public.

They glance at each other and then Tabinda shrugs. "Not directly, I guess. And FYI, your butt is just fine."

"What kind of advice did you need from Tabinda?"

"Geez, you ask a lot of questions!" Tabinda straightens up as she adjusts her hijab.

"Well, you can't blame me for being curious."

"Good point," Prudy says. "Here's the deal—we brought it to the assistant principal, who then brought us to the social worker."

My heart starts pounding in my ears, and I think I might start crying. "Why did you do that?"

Tabinda squirms a little and then puts a gentle hand on my arm. "That was my idea. Look, Leah, last year I had something like this happen to me and that was how it got better."

"What happened to you?" I ask, although I don't really even know what's happened to *me* yet.

"Some kids were teasing me about wearing hijab and being Muslim. They were drawing all kinds of nasty pictures and putting mean notes in my locker. At first, I tried to ignore it, thinking they'd give up if they didn't get a reaction from me. Instead, it got worse and worse. I don't want that to happen to you, so Prudy and I went to the office with it. I'm sorry if we made a mistake."

"I don't know if it was a mistake because I don't know what's on the paper. All I know is that lots of kids are staring at me today. They're not exactly laughing at me or saying anything, but still." My throat hurts from holding the tears in.

Prudy sighs. "Ok, but promise you won't freak out. We have the rest of the day to get through, so freaking out right now is *not* an option. You promise?"

I nod quickly, knowing there's no way I'll be able to keep my promise if it's something really bad, but what's really bad?

Prudy goes on to tell me what was on the crumpled sheet of paper. Her voice is so quiet, I can barely hear her. My mind is racing as she talks, and I hear her say some things I don't understand—things about sex. I don't know enough about what she's saying to know how bad it must be; I'll just have to take her word for it.

"How do you know about this stuff?" I whisper, keeping my eyes on the table in front of me.

"I have an older sister, remember? I also do *lots* of eavesdropping when she has friends over. She'd kill me if she knew how much I listen. Anyhow, I thought it was better to go to the office with it than to get your mom involved just yet."

"My *mom*? Why would she have to get involved?" As soon as I say it, I realize that I want nothing more than to have my mom take care of me, to tell me it will all be okay.

Tabinda and Prudy share an uncomfortable look.

"Well, Leah," says Tabinda, "the social worker might have questions for your mom—like if you've ever seen anything like that before or whatever."

"We told them we don't even know who threw the ball of paper or who drew it," adds Prudy, "but they want to know, so if it happens again they can do something about it."

The tears that have filled my eyes spill over. This is just horrible! Some kids I don't know drew a really nasty picture of me doing something I've never even heard of, and now I have to worry about them doing it again and the assistant principal and the social worker thinking I'm a bad person.

"Please don't cry," Tabinda says softly as she hands me a tissue.

"Yeah," says Prudy, "we didn't mean to make you sad. We did it because you're our friend."

I wipe my tears and then blow my nose. "I know. It's just so unfair. I've never done anything mean to anybody."

The three of us suddenly make eye contact and gasp. April has to have something to do with this and maybe Nora too. Someone on the bus must know them, maybe from their dance studio. I've always felt bad that my mom couldn't afford for me to be in dance, but now I'm relieved. In fact, they said that dance is one of the reasons they went on their stupid diet. If being in dance makes you feel bad about yourself, I'm glad I'm not in it, although I feel pretty bad about myself anyway, thanks to all of their diet talk and Mr. K.'s insults.

The afternoon drags on. I'm trying to ignore my hunger and concentrate during social studies, when Mrs. Wilson from the office comes into the classroom and whispers to the teacher. Nearly everyone is reading the chapter on ancient Egypt like they're supposed to. I remember learning about Egypt in third grade and being fascinated. Maybe everyone thinks the same thing now because their noses are buried in their books. Ms. Simpson, the teacher, glides over to my desk and taps me on the shoulder.

"They need you in the office, dear," she whispers and gives me a kind smile.

Without saying a word, I get up and leave the room with Mrs. Wilson. I'm sure everyone is peeking over the tops of their books, silently laughing at me. Once we're in the hall, I figure it's safe to talk.

"What's wrong? Is my mom okay? Is my sister okay?" My voice sounds panicky even to me.

Three years ago, when my dad died, the same thing happened. I was called to the office during school, where Momo was waiting for me with the awful news. Naturally, my mind has gone right back there.

"Oh, it's nothing like that, hon. Your mom and sister are just fine."

By now we're at the office door, and I'm terrified to go in. I know I haven't done anything wrong, but do they know that? Stopping outside the door, I freeze.

"The only time I've ever had to go to the principal's office is when my dad died in a car accident."

She puts a gentle arm around my shoulders. "No wonder you're so worried! I promise it's nothing like that. And I don't think you're in trouble, so no worries about that either, okay?"

I take in a deep breath and let it out in a whoosh. "Okay."

She leads me into an office labeled Ms. Winters, Social Worker. I don't even know what a social worker *is*, let alone what they *do*.

"Hi, Leah! Please have a seat."

A gray-haired woman around Momo's age gestures towards a chair at a round table. There are several chairs there and she sits down on one of them. Her gray hair is super short, and she's wearing a really pretty turquoise and brown top and a long, brown skirt. Brown boots peek out from the bottom of her skirt as she crosses her legs. She's also wearing beautiful dangly turquoise and silver earrings.

"I'm Ms. Winters. It's nice to meet you, Leah." Her cat-eye glasses magnify deep blue eyes that have lots of wrinkles around them, I'm guessing from smiling a lot. "You must be wondering why you're here."

All I do is nod. I wish I could disappear into the floor.

"Well, Prudy and Tabinda came to see me this morning. Did they tell you?"

I nod again, not knowing what to say.

"You're lucky to have friends who care about you so much, Leah. It's not easy for kids to come and tell me things."

I sense it's my turn to talk, but I just sit there. The clock on the wall, the same type of clock that must be in every school in the world, ticks loudly and makes my silence even more obvious. Ms. Winters is very patient and just sits and waits.

"The thing is, I don't know exactly what they told you because they wouldn't tell me—not exactly, anyway." I sniffle as quietly as I can to keep the tears in.

"They didn't show you the drawing before they brought it to me?"

I shake my head. "Prudy sort of told me what it was, but I don't really get it. All I know is that it's really bad." I look up at her as the tears spill over. "It's not fair! I haven't done anything wrong! Why are kids being so mean?"

Ms. Winters shakes her head, which makes her earrings sound like tiny wind chimes. "I don't know, Leah. If I had the answer to that, I'd be out of a job." She leans toward me. "I believe you, Leah. I know you've done nothing to deserve this. I have a question for you and then you can ask me anything you want. Sound like a deal?"

I nod and sniffle, this time a little louder.

"Is it okay if I call your mom to tell her about this?"

My heart starts beating at top speed, as though someone flipped a switch.

"Why do you want to tell my mom?"

"It just seems like something she'd like to know about so she can help you. I have a daughter and if she'd had something like this happen to her, I'd want to know. You don't agree?"

I look down at the hangnail on my right thumb and shake my head.

"Can I ask why?" Ms. Winters' voice feels like a soft blanket.

"I don't want her to worry. She's finally happy, and I don't want to ruin it."

Ms. Winters pauses and looks as though she's trying to find the perfect thing to say. She doesn't know about my dad dying and our living in the garage apartment for the past three years and everything else that's been hard for my mom. Is it my job to tell her? Would my mom be upset if I told this person I just met all that personal stuff about our family? I now know where that saying, 'Stuck between a rock and a hard place' comes from. It's exactly how I feel.

"You know, Leah, parents just want their kids to be happy. I think it's very commendable that you want your mom to be happy, but believe me, dear, she wants that even more for you."

I pick at the hangnail until I manage to rip it off. I hold my thumb against it to keep it from bleeding.

"That's why I don't want her to know about this; not yet anyway. If you tell her, she'll want to talk to the other parents or whatever and then it will just get worse. Maybe if we ignore it, it will stop." I suggest a plan of inaction, just like my mom did about my dad's drinking all those years. It didn't work then, so I don't know why I think it will work now, but it's all I've got.

Ms. Winters looks at me with the kindest eyes I've ever seen.

"Okay, Leah—you're a smart girl, so we'll try it your way. I won't call your mom right now, but if it happens again or anything like it happens again, I want you to promise you'll tell me. At that point, we'll decide together how to proceed. How does that sound?"

"Okay," I say, hoping against hope there won't be a next time.

"And you'll promise to come to me if anything else happens? Because here's the thing: it's my mission in life to keep kids safe and to try to help them be happy. Your safety and happiness are really important to me, Leah, and I'm not just saying that. You can trust me to keep up my end of the bargain, but I have to be able to trust you. Can I?"

Wow. So much pressure and from a social worker at that. I really like her, so I agree.

"Great! Do you want to ask me about anything else while we're here?"

I really want to, but don't know for sure if she'll give me an honest answer. Taking a deep breath, I decide to go for it.

"Just one thing: can you show me the picture and explain it to me? I feel like I should know for sure what it was about." My face is on fire by the time I complete my request.

Ms. Winters takes a deep breath and then goes over to a file cabinet, unlocks a drawer and retrieves a folded up, wrinkled piece of notebook paper. She walks back to where I'm sitting and moves her chair a little closer to mine.

"Okay, Leah. Let's take a look at this together."

Hope

August 1, 1966

Dear Daisy,

Sorry it's been a while since I've written to you. Things have been crazy around here. I almost can't wait for school to start! (That's something I never thought I'd say!)

Since the incident with Neil last month, Mom has been acting really strange. She still works for him, and I think that's even stranger. How can she stand to be around him? She seems less worried about dieting than she used to be— in fact, she seems less worried about lots of things—but she's still losing weight. She doesn't pay that much attention to Pete and me which is both good and bad. Good, because she doesn't bug me about how I look, but bad because I miss her caring about me the normal amount. Nothing feels normal anymore.

The only thing *I* really care about is staying thin. Since Mom doesn't pay much attention, it's been easy. I don't really eat breakfast anymore and for lunch I have a piece of Ry-Crisp and an apple. Dinner is hit or miss since Mom's usually with Neil somewhere, so Pete and I are on our own. He eats a can(or two!) of Spaghettios or a couple of frozen pizzas, and I eat Ry-Crisp and cottage cheese. I love how thin I'm getting and to make sure I stay this way, I measure my wrist every chance I get. I can get my index finger and thumb from one hand to overlap when I put them around the wrist of my other hand. Yesterday, I was able to *completely* cover up the thumb nail! That's how I need to stay

—at *least* that. You're the only one I've told about that because nobody else understands. Reenie and Jill don't get it. I haven't spent much time with them for the past month or so. All they want to do is sit around and eat potato chips, drink pop, listen to records and read teen magazines. Don't Jill and Reenie see that if they let themselves get fat, nobody will love them? No, it's much safer to spend time by myself; much easier to stay in control.

We haven't seen Dad for a few weeks because he had to go out of town for work—to Europe! That's the most exciting thing ever! Even though I've missed him, it's been a relief because he hasn't been able to look at me with worried eyes or urge me to eat more. He's sent me and Pete a few postcards from Paris and London that said he misses us a lot. He gets back next week, so we'll see him then. I hope it's not too hot outside so he doesn't ask why I'm wearing a sweatshirt and jeans. I have a feeling he won't think my thinner body is a very good thing. I'm not sure how I'll work around that, but I'll figure it out. Besides, I'm not *that* thin. My ankles are actually looking kinda thick these days.

Another reason I miss Dad so much is because being with Mom all the time is getting more and more unpredictable. She's really crabby to both Pete and me, usually for no reason. We think it's because of Neil but don't know what to do about it. She doesn't need the job since Dad gives her enough money for her and for us each month, so why she keeps working for that creep *and* dating him is beyond me. At least they don't come to our house anymore if we're there. Pete said that if Neil ever does that to Mom again, he'll call the cops. He told Mom that once and she flipped out. She told him if he calls the cops on Neil, she'll kick *Pete* out. He said, 'Fine, kick me out!' That really upset me because I don't want to live here without him. (That's something else I never thought I'd say! Ha, ha!)

The only thing Mom ever says to me is about how much I eat or don't eat. It seems to make her happy that I'm 'thinning out' as she calls it, so at least I'm doing something right. I kinda worry that if I gain any weight she'll be mad at me and kick me out. I hope if that ever happens, I'll be able to be with Pete. I just have to make sure it doesn't, and the best way to do that is to lose more weight. Daisy, you're so lucky to be a diary!

Love,
Hope

Leah

It's really strange. The more I read Hope's diary and read about how much weight she's losing, the more I wonder if I should keep losing weight. Why is that? I keep hearing Collin's voice saying *Fat Ass* and believe it's true. I also keep remembering the drawing Ms. Winters showed me, the one that was being thrown around on the bus. She didn't want to show it to me, but I begged her. I need to know what's going on. I wish I'd never seen it. Mom can *never* find out about it because it would break her heart. I explained that to Ms. Winters and even though she said she understood, she's trusting me to tell her if it happens again. I pray to God it never does.

Another interesting thing that's sort of convenient, is that thinking about this stuff takes away my appetite, so it's easier to eat less. My jeans and leggings are getting looser which means that my butt is getting smaller. Mom has been so busy with her new job, she hasn't really noticed, and that's fantastic. She still pays attention to Clara and me, but she's not spending lots of time scrutinizing my body. It makes me happy, but I also feel sort of guilty about it, although I don't know why. Maybe because I'm sort of lying to her by hiding under baggy clothes? Reading Hope's diary makes me see how sick it is for Hope to starve herself like she did, but since it pleases her mom so much, it make me think it's a good thing to do. I don't really have anyone to talk to about all of this, so I'm just figuring it out as I go. I try not to think about it too much, but it's always on my mind. *Always.*

Today, Momo is taking me on our annual pre-Christmas shopping trip. It's only November, but she takes Clara and me on separate shopping trips right before Thanksgiving so that we can plan for what to get Mom and each other for Christmas. Momo also gives us money to add to our allowances for shopping. The other fun part of the day is that it includes a sleepover at Momo's house. She likes to put up her Christmas decorations early and lets us help. The bottom half of the tree is always saved for Clara to decorate since that's the only part she can reach. Every year, my part gets higher and higher as I grow taller and taller. Pretty soon, I'll be able to reach higher than Momo!

We're on our way to the Mall of America. I chose it because Mom never wants to go there. It's not that far from our house, but she always says it's so big. She's right—it's humongous—and that's the best part! It seems like each year the Christmas decorations go up in the stores earlier and earlier, almost right after Halloween. Mom thinks it's too early but Momo loves it just like I do. Christmas is our favorite holiday.

"Okay, kiddo, what's the plan? What should we do first?" Momo says as she maneuvers her car onto the exit ramp. "The usual?"

I gaze at the mall through the windshield. It's like the Emerald City from The Wizard of Oz, waiting for us in the distance. My heart speeds up just looking at it, and it's not because I'm excited about shopping. It's because *the usual* is the hot chocolate and big, gooey cinnamon rolls we get before we start shopping. It's been a tradition since I was little. My mouth begins to water just thinking about those yummy cinnamon rolls. I haven't had one since last year, and it's something I've always looked forward to—until now.

"Maybe we should do some shopping first, Momo. It's already almost ten o'clock." I hope she agrees with me. That would make life so much easier!

"Skip our tradition? No way! I've been dreaming about that cinnamon roll for days! Besides, have you got somewhere else you have to be? We've got all day *and* all night, kiddo! We can have a late lunch and an even later dinner if we want." She peeks at me out of the corner of her eye, but I pretend not to notice.

My heart starts pounding even more at the thought of lunch. Why didn't I think this through? I can't eat a cinnamon roll *and* lunch! Another part of the tradition is that we eat lunch at my favorite restaurant at the mall, an Italian restaurant that has the *best* garlic breadsticks I've ever tasted. And she wants us to eat dinner besides? All of my careful eating this week will be wasted if I eat so much today. I feel like crying just thinking about it.

"Are you okay, Loo-loo?" Momo glances at me. "You look upset about something." She places her hand on my leg. "I'll be fine if we skip the cinnamon rolls, if it's that important to you. No worries, okay?" She gives me a friendly wink and squeezes my leg.

The crisis is averted for now, but how will the rest of the day go? How will I be able to not eat like I have every other year? She'll probably expect me to eat even more at lunch now. I just smile at her and shrug as my stomach growls.

Shopping without our annual treat is going fairly well, except for the fact that I'm starving. I didn't eat breakfast, which seemed like a good idea at the time, but now I'm regretting it a little. I just keep telling myself that the hungrier I am, the thinner I'll be if I don't give in and eat.

It's fairly easy when it's just me but now that Momo is with me, it's much harder.

"You're finding some great ideas for Clara, aren't you?" Momo says as we browse in Barnes and Noble.

"Yeah, it'll be hard to decide what to get. She really wants to start her own book collection, so I should for sure get her a book."

"Good idea! Say, it's almost eleven-thirty. Let's head over to the restaurant to beat the lunch rush, okay? I don't know about you, but I'm ravenous, especially since we didn't have our cinnamon rolls." She looks at me, expectantly.

"Okay. I guess I'm getting hungry."

Momo wraps her arms around me and gives me a big hug. "You *guess*? I've been listening to your tummy growl since before we got out of the car! Did you eat breakfast?"

I squirm out of her arms and shrug. How embarrassing to be hugged in the middle of The Mall of America by my grandma! I try not to scowl, but it's not easy while she's questioning my eating habits and commenting on my tummy sounds. She takes a step back from me, her arms folded across her chest.

"Did you eat breakfast or not?"

Again, I shrug and look away.

"Leah Ann Peterson, answer me, please." She isn't yelling at me, but her voice is very stern. Momo only uses that voice when she means business.

"No," I whisper, staring at the floor.

"May I ask why not? If you were planning on the cinnamon rolls I could understand, but you didn't want one, so what's the deal, Leah? What's going on?"

"Can we please keep walking, Momo? Or sit down somewhere?" It was humiliating enough to be hugged in the middle of the mall, but having a discussion like this is even worse. She leads the way to a bench off to the side and sits, pulling me down with her.

"Okay, we're sitting down. Why don't you tell me what's going on with you, Loo-loo?" Her voice isn't as stern anymore, just concerned.

It's hard to know where to look. I know if I look at Momo, I'll start crying; it happens every time. My grandma seems to have a sixth sense about lots of things. Maybe because she raised two daughters, she knows what to expect.

"You have to promise not to tell Mom," I say, peeking at her out of the corner of my eye.

Her expression almost morphs into alarm, but she reins it back in. "Why?"

"Because she'll get all worried and protective and stuff, and I don't want her to feel that way."

Momo considers this for a second. "I can't promise anything until I know what it is; that's just a safety thing, Loo-loo."

I think about her comment. As much as I don't want my mom to worry about anything, the thought of telling Momo what's been going on is kind of appealing. It helps that Ms. Winters knows about some of it, but having someone who loves me know about it would help a lot. One downside, however, would be that she might figure out that I'm trying to lose weight, and I don't want anyone to make me stop doing that.

"While you think it over, can I at least ask you a question?" Momo recrosses her legs and unbuttons her coat.

"Sure."

"It's not my imagination that you've lost weight, is it?"

I feel like an insect under a magnifying glass. How does she know that? She squeezed my leg in the car and hugged me, but I didn't think she'd be able to tell anything from that. I've been so careful to hide it.

"Well, maybe a little. I don't really know." I avert my eyes. "How come you're asking me that?"

She smiles. "Loo-loo, I wasn't born yesterday. I'm a woman and have also raised two girls. Both your mom and your aunt went through phases when they were about your age or older when they went on diets. Unfortunately, so did I. So many fad diets! The stranger, the better it seemed. I know the classic signs: no cinnamon roll, for example, and no French silk pie the other night. You feel thinner when I hug you and your clothes are hanging on you."

"No, they aren't—that's the style! Besides, I'm getting taller." I can feel my cheeks grow hot as I sit up straighter.

"Hmph—it's not the style, my dear, and you haven't gotten that much taller. I'm not trying to catch you at anything, Loo-loo, I just care about you. You haven't been yourself lately. Is everything okay at your new school? Your mom says you've made some new friends."

I nod, still looking down at the floor. "Yeah, Prudy and Tabinda—they're really nice."

"Well, that's wonderful! Are there any mean girls? There always seems to be one or two of those around." She shakes her head at some invisible memory.

"Sort of." How much do I tell her about April and Nora and all that? I'm afraid that once I start, I won't be able to stop.

"Are Prudy and Tabinda on diets too? I remember doing that with friends once. It was supposed to make it more fun, but it just turned out to be a horrible competition. And the diets never worked. The weight always came back, plus some. That's how it works, so it's just not worth it."

At this moment, I realize that I haven't cared about the sizes of my new friends' bodies. They're nice and funny, and I like them because of that, not how they look. Maybe real friends don't care about that stuff. I try to imagine my new friends and all I can see is their faces and hear their voices and the happiness I feel when I'm with them.

"I don't know. We don't talk about it." I take a deep breath. "My old friends, April and Nora are, though. When they came over for a sleepover right after school started, all they talked about was the diet they're on and the app they use and it was awful." It feels kind of good to tell her this, so I keep going. "It made me feel like there was something wrong with me for *not* being on a diet. And then there's some kids at school."

Momo doesn't say anything right away, but I can tell by the look on her face that she's trying to choose just the right words.

"Tell me more. If you want to, that is."

I feel sort of squirmy and nervous because this is the part I don't want Mom to know about. The thing is, right now it feels so good to share this that I want to keep going in case it makes me feel better still.

"This is the part I don't want Mom to know about, Momo. She knows about April and Nora and also about how they keep calling me to get Johnny Morgan's phone number for April and to ask him if he likes her." I stop and wait for Momo to digest this new bit of information.

"Ah, so there's a boy involved. Of course."

I turn my body to face her. "What do you mean?"

She takes both of my hands in hers. "It's often about a boy, my dear. But go on."

"Well, even before all that happened with April and Nora, on the first day of school, my math teacher called me *pudgy*. Then some kids on the bus started calling me Pudge. The kid that started it is the boy April likes."

"Johnny, right?"

"Yep."

I go on to tell her everything about the note with the drawing that they threw at me and the meeting with Ms. Winters. I tell her all of it.

"Let me see if I understand," Momo says. "Because your math teacher bullied you, which, but the way, he has no business doing and should be dealt with, some kids on the bus started bullying you also?"

"They bully Prudy and Tabinda too, but not as much as me so far."

"Yes, but that doesn't make it okay, does it?" I shake my head. "Anyway, now it seems that since you won't do what April wants, the bullying has escalated to inappropriate drawings that they're throwing around on the bus. Your new friends were right to bring it to Ms. Winters, Loo-loo. Bullying is never okay, but what they're doing is horrendous! And you don't want your mother to know?"

"No! She's been so happy since we moved, Momo. She loves the house and her job. Everything is going good with Clara too. She loves school and Kid's Club. I don't want Mom to be sad like she was before. If she knows about the bullying, she'll want to get involved, and I'm afraid that'll only make it worse." Tears sting my eyes.

"Of course she'll want to get involved! She's your mother and she loves you very, very much. She wants you to be safe and happy; that's what parents do. It's not up to you to make sure she's happy, kiddo, it's the other way around."

"But if I can help make things easier, I should do that."

"Easier for who, Loo-loo? Are things easier for you right now?"

I shake my head and feel a teardrop slide down my nose.

"Exactly! Look, it's not easy being in middle school but it doesn't have to be this hard. You want your mom to be happy, but if she finds out that you've been keeping this from her, she'll be devastated."

I sniffle loudly, and Momo digs in her purse for a tissue. My grandma is always prepared for anything. She likes to say she has a 'kitchen sink' purse, whatever that is.

"Just think about it, okay?"

I nod. "Okay. Thanks for listening, Momo."

"Anytime, honeybunch! Now, what do you say we go eat lunch? Hey! That rhymes!" Her eyes are sparkling in anticipation of eating at our favorite restaurant. "I'm still starving, by the way."

"Okay!" I try extra hard to put my heart into it. It might've felt good to talk about things with Momo, but it hasn't solved my fear of being pudgy. She didn't tell me that I'm *not* pudgy, so the idea of eating pasta scares me all over again.

On our way to the restaurant, we walk by Abercrombie, one of the coolest stores at the mall. A mannequin in the window catches my eye. It's wearing the cutest outfit I've ever seen! The mannequin is freakishly thin, but I know they sell bigger sizes than what it's wearing. Who's *that* thin? Momo sees that I've slowed down because she doesn't miss a thing.

"Cute outfit!" she says, standing next to me outside the store. "Let's go in and you can try it on. My treat!"

I turn and stare at her. It's not only a cool store but an *expensive* store, one that Mom never lets me set foot in.

"I can't go in there, Momo."

"Why not?"

"Mom never lets me even go in there because it's so expensive. She doesn't want to take the chance that I'll find something I like. She says that Old Navy and H&M have stuff that's just as cute. Target, too. She'd freak if you bought me something from here."

"Well, she's got a point, but that doesn't mean we can't go in and look, right?"

I look at her, speechless. I love her for suggesting it but also hate her for wanting me to break one of my mom's rules. I don't know what to do and when that happens, I don't do anything. Momo has always been very patient with me, and she's being really patient right now, especially considering how hungry she is.

"Tell you what, kiddo. I'm going to zip down to the restaurant to put our names on the list and then I'll come right back. You don't need me breathing down your neck while you decide. Is that okay?"

My mom also has rules about always staying with an adult in stores and malls, and Momo knows that. Why is she wanting me to break so many rules in one day? I glance in the direction of the restaurant and can see it plainly from here, just two stores away. I'd feel like a baby if I say it's not okay, so I nod, and Momo almost sprints to the restaurant.

Looking at the outfit in the window, I consider the options. My grandma has basically offered to buy me an outfit from Abercrombie. I feel sort of guilty about it, but I know she'll do the same for Clara someday. She's very fair that way. She'll even write it down somewhere so she doesn't forget about it. I'd feel so cool if I had an outfit like that! None of the popular kids would tease me if I had an outfit from the coolest store ever, would they? For a minute or two, I imagine how awesome it would be and then I'm ashamed for wanting other kids to be jealous of me. Maybe it wouldn't be so great after all. I wouldn't want Prudy or Tabinda to feel bad or think I want to be one of the popular kids because I definitely don't.

I'm minding my own business when I hear a familiar voice say, "I don't know if they have *plus* sizes at Abercrombie. It's not really a store for pudgy girls with fat asses, is it?"

My heart plummets. Without looking, I know who it is: April. Standing next to her is Nora, looking mortified. What are they doing here? I know what they're doing here. They get most of their clothes at Abercrombie, American Eagle and Gap. My little secret is that the only items I have from any of those stores are from a thrift shop, but this isn't about whether I can afford it, it's about being able to fit into them. I feel about two inches tall and one hundred feet wide. My panicky heart is bouncing around like crazy.

"So," Momo says loudly, magically appearing at my side, "we have about a half-hour. Let's make the most of it and do some power-shopping!" Then she turns towards April and Nora. Momo knows April and Nora because they were my besties for the past three years. "Well, hello ladies! I hardly recognized you two!"

It's obvious that Momo is referring to the gobs of makeup they're both wearing, as well as their ripped jeans and crop tops. They're trying to look older and even sexy, but they don't. They look ridiculous and pathetic. I'm also alarmed to see how thin they've gotten; they look like skeletons. Cringing, I pray she doesn't mention any of it because how embarrassing would *that* be?

"Hi!" Nora squeaks out the greeting, keeping her eyes on the floor.

April just glares at Momo and doesn't say a word. How rude! She could at least smile or something. If we had run into Prudy or Tabinda, we'd be inviting them to join us for lunch, not be rudely ignored. I can't believe these two brats were ever my best friends, a thought that makes me sad and disgusted at the same time.

"Yes, well, we have to run! Good to see you!" Momo says in a hurry and then whisks me away. As we put some distance between them and us, she whispers, "Wouldn't want to *be* you!" She gives me a wink, and we both begin to giggle.

"Where are we going, Momo?"

"I have no idea. I just wanted to get out of there before I said something I'd regret. I wasn't lying when I said I almost didn't recognize them. They look terrible! So much makeup for young girls! And such tasteless outfits! I usually try not to judge too much, but it's totally inappropriate for girls their age to dress that way! Do their parents allow that? And where *are* their parents?" Momo is on a roll.

"At the sleepover, April mentioned that their moms drop them off at the mall and let them shop by themselves. They've never invited me, but I know Mom would never let me do that."

"You're darn right she wouldn't! I know that parents need to loosen the reins a little bit, but at a huge mall, alone and dressed like that? They're just asking for trouble! Where do they get all the makeup?"

"They're both in dance and wear makeup for that, so I guess that's where they get it. Or maybe they sneak it and put it on when they get here. Some girls at school do that.

They had some on when they came to the sleepover, but not *that* much."

"That makes me so sad. Why do they think they even *need* it? I know I wear makeup and have since I was in eighth grade, but I kind of wish I'd never started. It's a vicious cycle to get into—thinking you're not good enough the way you are." She goes quiet for a moment which is unusual for Momo when she gets on her soapbox, as she calls it.

"Are you okay, Momo?"

She inhales deeply and then smiles at me. "Yes, Loo-loo, I'm fine. I got a little carried away for a minute there. Look, if you want to go back and try on that outfit, we will. I didn't mean to spoil that for you."

We walk along in silence as I try to think of what to say. We pass other stores that also have cute clothes in their windows, all on stick-thin mannequins. I suck in my stomach as I glance at them, wondering if they have my size or if I'm cool enough to wear them. April and Nora are so much thinner than they were the last time I saw them. I bet they never have to suck their stomachs in.

Maureen

Okay, I just have to jump in here. I'm Leah's grandma or Momo, as she calls me. From the moment we first laid eyes on each other, about an hour after she was born, we had a special connection. At first, I analyzed it to death because I was so surprised by it. After all, my older daughter and her husband have two kids, Emily and Austin, who I adore. Perhaps it's because when they were born I wasn't as ready to be a grandmother as I was when Leah came along. Leah is also my baby's first baby, so that might have something to do with it. Whatever the reason, it doesn't really matter. Leah is my Loo-loo, and I'm her Momo—that's just the way it is.

Every year, I take each of my grandkids on a pre-Christmas shopping trip. Emily and Austin are in college now, so my trips with them fizzled out a few years back, but Leah and Clara still love the tradition. Frankly, I look forward to it every year as well. The time I spend with my grandkids without their parents hovering around is special indeed. It gives me a chance to get to know them as the people they are rather than my children's children.

This year's shopping trip with Leah was strange from the get-go. The first thing that caught my attention was her request to *not* get a cinnamon roll and hot chocolate before we started shopping. I nearly drove off the road when she said that! Since I didn't want our day together to get off on the wrong foot, I agreed to skip the treat. I've never believed in forcing things on people. When I reached over and patted her leg, I almost veered off the road again. She felt like a rail—it truly took me by surprise. In an instant, I remembered that she'd also turned down having a piece of the French silk pie I'd brought to their house for dessert recently. Leah has always loved my French silk pie, so for her to turn it down was very odd. Needless to say, I was on high alert from that moment on.

I've also never been one to tiptoe around issues. The proverbial elephant in the room doesn't stand a chance with me! When I got her to admit that she hadn't eaten breakfast, my granny radar spiked off the charts. Something wasn't right with my Loo-loo; in fact, something was very, very wrong.

I forgot myself for a second when I hugged her right outside of Old Navy. Good Lord, you would've thought I'd started skipping or something, she was so embarrassed! She wriggled out of my arms so fast I couldn't believe they were still attached to my shoulders. I felt extremely lucky when she agreed to talk to me, but only if we sat down on a bench that was almost out of sight. My little Loo-loo is becoming a teenager.

It was difficult to keep my expression neutral when she told me about the dieting and the bullying, but when she asked me not to share any of it with her mom, I had to really dial back my reaction. I've never been asked by any of my grandchildren to keep information from their parents. Of course there have been the typical agreements not to tell how many treats I let them have, but that's about it, and it's always been my idea. This was different; it felt strange and a little dangerous. I told her I couldn't agree to her request until I knew what it was she didn't want me to tell Diane. She told me Diane knew some of it but not all of it, so that helped me feel more comfortable with the idea. When she then proceeded to tell me about the obscene picture some awful child had drawn of her and had thrown around the bus, my blood began to boil. Who do they think they are? It seems that cruelty has risen to a whole new level with this generation, and it breaks my heart.

Once our little chat was over, (for the time being because I can't let things like that go) we began to make our way through the mall toward the restaurant. As we walked past Abercrombie and Fitch, I noticed that her eyes were drawn to the display in the window. Her gait slowed the tiniest bit, and I knew she saw something she liked. When I suggested we go in so she could try it on, her face lit up but then quickly flickered out. I knew what she was going to say before she said it: it was too expensive. She was right— that store *is* expensive, especially for growing kids, but I also know how important it is to feel like you fit in. It's everything when you're that age. When I was Loo-loo's age, I went to a Catholic school that required uniforms, so fitting in wasn't quite as difficult. I hated it at the time, but learned to appreciate it when I no longer had to wear one. Isn't that just the way? There were still mean girls, of course, who always found something to criticize. Unfortunately, some people never grow out of being cruel.

We were only a stone's throw from the restaurant, so I told her I was going to go and get our names on the list while she decided what she wanted to do about the outfit. I figured she'd have an easier time making a decision without me there. Diane would probably kill me if she knew I left Leah's side for a *moment* at the Mall of America, but the girl's got to build some confidence. Surely, she can handle a couple of minutes by herself.

Imagine my horror when I came back to find two very scantily dressed, overly made-up, skeletal girls talking to my granddaughter in what appeared to be a very hostile way. As I got closer, I saw that the girls were Leah's friends, April and Nora! I barely recognized them, both by their appearance and their behavior. Leah had told me about their dieting, but I had no idea they'd taken it so far. The last time I saw those girls was at a school program at Leah's elementary school. From what I was told then, they were BFFs. (Diane discretely explained what that meant, bless her heart.) The situation at the mall didn't look like they were treating Leah like a human being let alone a BFF. Little did these two young ladies know, they had activated Grandma Bear. You've heard of Mama Bear? Well, kick that up about ten notches and you've got Grandma Bear. No one treats my grand cubs the way they were treating my Loo-loo!

The last thing I wanted to do was embarrass Leah, so I had to maintain the utmost control. I'm not going to lie—it was nearly impossible. I decided the best strategy was to get out of there fast and to act as though nothing was wrong. If I stormed up to them demanding that they stop bullying my granddaughter, she'd be the one to pay the price. So I simply said hello and that I hardly recognized them (because I didn't). I also said we had to run, and we booked it in the opposite direction before Leah even knew what was happening. I didn't ask exactly what they'd said to her; I knew she'd tell me if she wanted to. I just wanted to spare her any more pain, the poor kid.

Lunch was an ordeal for her even though she tried to pretend otherwise. She didn't think I noticed her pushing her food around on her plate to make it look like she'd eaten more than she had. I know that trick. My own daughters went through phases like that which I did my best to promptly shut down. It was a delicate dance to not be too forbidding, which would make the dieting behavior more attractive, but to make sure they understood the consequences for their health.

"Breadstick?" I held the wicker basket of deletable bread in her direction. "They're still warm. Don't they smell scrumptious?"

Leah fidgeted like she had ants in her pants. "No thanks, Momo. I'm getting pretty full."

I glanced at her plate and simply set the basket down after taking another breadstick for myself. "Can you please pass the butter?"

She picked up the small dish of garlic butter as though it was the most disgusting thing she'd ever touched. It would've been comical if it hadn't been so heartbreaking. Leah has always loved the garlic butter at that restaurant. Slathering it on a soft, warm breadstick has always been one of her favorite parts of eating there.

After a very tense and unsatisfying lunch, (I mean, who wants to eat when the other person is barely nibbling?), we kept shopping. I worried that Leah wouldn't want to shop after eating, but she did. Maybe that was part of her reason for not eating very much. Who knows?

"Are we going back to Abercrombie? Those girls are probably gone by now."

"Can we go to H&M instead? Or maybe Old Navy?"

"Of course! Why the change of heart? That outfit was super cute."

She looked down and shook her head. "Yeah, but the stuff there is so expensive. I'd be afraid to wear it in case it got spilled on or something."

I wanted to say that a girl who barely eats shouldn't worry about spilling, but I bit my tongue. "Okay, that's fine with me. Then you get can get twice as many things!"

Her head whipped around, and she gave me a huge smile. "Really?"

"Yes, *really*, my dear! After the morning you've had, you deserve to get *lots* of new clothes! Unless, of course, you don't want to." I gave her a sly grin.

"Are you kidding? Of course I want to! Let's go!"

In years past, I always went into the fitting room with Leah, but this year she gently asked me to wait outside. It sort of made me sad, but I didn't make a peep. I just stood like a sentry outside her fitting room and fulfilled my duty as her personal shopper. It alarmed me when I had to go back not once, but twice to get smaller sizes. A girl Leah's age isn't supposed get smaller; it's just not right. When a smaller size was a little roomy, she was ecstatic. Her enthusiasm would've been contagious if it hadn't been for the dull, nagging ache in the pit of my stomach. My little Loo-loo was growing up and not in a good way. I had no idea how to save her.

Hope

August 12, 1966

Dear Daisy,

Dad's back home from Europe! I'm so excited to see him I can hardly stand it! Even Pete's excited and for him to actually admit that is a really big deal. He's picking us up this afternoon to spend the weekend with him. He said he gets some extra time off since he was away for so long, and he's hoping Mom will let us stay with him longer than just the weekend. I can't decide if I want that to happen or not. I have a feeling he's going to harp on me about how thin I am, and I do NOT want to hear about it! It's weird because Pete's even starting to bug me about it. I don't know what to do. It's almost 4:00, the time he's getting here, so I better get ready. I'll be back later!

Love,
Hope

Later....

Dear Daisy,

I told you I'd be back and here I am! When Dad got to the house, it was strange because he wanted to come inside and talk to Mom. They hardly ever do that. I thought it was because he wanted to ask if we could stay at his place longer. Why he couldn't have done that on the phone?

Anyhow, it was super awkward and uncomfortable. Pete and I stood there with our duffle bags, not knowing what to do or say. Finally, Pete signaled to me that we should wait on the porch. I followed him out there like an obedient puppy.

We sat down on the wicker furniture to wait. Before long—the minute we closed the front door behind us— Mom started yelling at Dad. He kept his voice quieter, but we could tell that he was getting frustrated and that he was upsetting Mom by whatever it was he was saying. He just kept saying, "Ellen, calm down. Please calm down."

Mom *hates* being told to calm down, so even *I* know it's going to make her even madder. Pete and I ended up playing I Spy With My Little Eye while we waited, trying not to eavesdrop. Finally, Dad emerged onto the porch with an odd expression on his face.

"Okay, kids, you ready?"

Pete and I looked at each other and shrugged. Of course we were ready; we'd *been* ready the whole time they were arguing. Without saying a word, we both stood up, grabbed our duffles and followed Dad out to his car.

It took a while, but we eventually figured out that Mom had given her permission for us to stay at Dad's for more than the weekend. That was a mixed blessing for both Pete and me because of how much more Dad pays attention. We'd gotten used to doing our own thing for the past few weeks.

We were sitting around the dinner table that night when Dad explained things to us.

"I know you kids heard your mom and me talking." He used his fingers like quotation marks when he said *talking*. "Part of it was about having a longer visit, but it was also about something else." He cleared his throat and looked away. "It was about your mom's boyfriend."

Now it was our turn to look away. What did Dad know about that? I knew I hadn't said anything and neither had Pete. I just sat there moving the spaghetti noodles around on my plate so it would look like I'd eaten something. Pete, on the other hand, reacted by shoveling food into his mouth.

"I don't know how much you two know, but Arlene Hartley called me with some concerns she has about him." He paused and looked at us, I guess to see how we reacted.

"What about him?" I asked, since I didn't have any food in my mouth.

Dad wriggled in his chair. "Well, Arlene said that she's seen some things happening with your mom and him."

"What kinds of things?" I asked, not to be annoying but because I really didn't know.

Dad's eyes met Pete's for a second and then he continued. "Well, she's worried about your mom being safe. She said she's seen him not being very nice to your mom."

Pete, who had a mouthful of milk almost spit it all over the table. Milk dribbled down his chin as Dad shoved a napkin toward him.

"What do you mean?" I asked. This was great as far as I was concerned because no one was paying any attention to how much I was or wasn't eating. Dad sighed and actually looked at Pete for help—at least that's how it seemed to me.

"You know that one night a while back?" Pete whispered. I nodded. "I think that's what he means."

"Anyhow, Arlene also said that your mom seems different lately. She said they used to chat over the fence all the time and get together for coffee, but they don't do that anymore. I asked your mom about what Arlene told me, and she got really upset."

"Well, Mom's working now, so maybe she's just busier," I said as I continued to rearrange my spaghetti. For some reason, I felt the need to defend her.

"Yes, Arlene mentioned that, but said it's more than that. She said your mom leaves you two home alone a lot. Is that true? I don't want to talk about your mom behind her back, but I want to make sure you two are okay."

Pete looked at me, and I looked at Pete. I could tell that he didn't know what to do or say and neither did I. We both *like* being left home alone because of how strange mom has been lately. We don't want to spoil it by tattling, although it sounded like Mrs. Hartley has already taken care of that. Does she think she's Mrs. Kravitz from "Bewitched" or something? It gave me an icky feeling to think about saying anything.

"Um, we're okay, Dad," Pete said before I could speak. "I'm nearly seventeen. I don't need a babysitter, and I can be there for Hope, you know. We do fine."

"Yeah," I added, trying to sound casual and proud at the same time, "I do my chores first thing every morning."

Dad sat there and seemed to be thinking about what we'd just said and then he took another deep breath, like he was leading up to something big.

"Okay, well, this is the deal. Your mom agreed to the longer visit, but I've been thinking about something else that I also ran by your mom today." He squirmed in his chair again. "While I was gone, I missed you guys like crazy —I always do but being so far away made it worse. I've been thinking about buying a house in your school district and having you two live with me. We'd sort of flip the way it is now; you'd visit Mom two weekends a month and live with me the rest of the time. What do you think?"

Then it was our turn to wriggle and squirm. What were we supposed to say to that? My stomach started to flip-flop, and I thought I was going to throw up.

"What did Mom say?" Pete asked, looking nervous.

"She got really angry, as you probably heard. She loves you guys and would miss you. She was also upset because she thought I was saying she's a bad mom. Now she's afraid the Hartleys think so too."

Pete spoke first. "Whatever we do, we want to stay together." He reached under the table and grabbed my hand. I almost fell off my chair at the kindness!

"Of course," said Dad. "I'd never let you be split up. I'm glad to hear you feel the same way, son."

Pete blushed a little under Dad's praise. It was nice to see that it still matters to him even though he's nearly seventeen and thinks he's all cool and stuff. All of this was nice and all, but it still didn't solve the problem.

"Mom wants us to stay with her?" I asked, afraid of the answer in so many ways.

Dad shrugged and sighed. (He was doing a *lot* of sighing during that conversation.) He was acting all strange again, like he knew something he didn't want to tell us.

"Your mom is struggling with some things right now and is easily upset. Actually, she's been struggling for a while, even before the divorce." He looked down at the floor.

The look on his face was so full of pain, I wanted to give him a hug, but I just sat there like a good girl and waited for him to continue. (Even though I'm only eleven, I'm not stupid.) When they told us they were getting divorced it was a huge shock, but once I thought about it for a while, one thing became obvious: they had both been unhappy for a long time. The trouble is, Mom doesn't seem any happier now, but Dad does, at least from what I can tell.

"What's the plan then?" I decided to get right to the big question. "Where will we live?"

"That's what I'm asking you," Dad said. "What do you guys want?"

Pete suddenly jumped up from his chair, his face all red and angry. "Does it matter what we want? Mike's parents got divorced and even though they asked him where he wanted to live and he told them, it didn't happen that way, so I'm asking: does it matter what we want?" He stayed standing and sort of paced around the room. That's what Pete does when he's upset.

"Of course it matters, Pete! We love you guys and want what's best for you. The problem lies with the judge and your mom's lawyer. I don't know what they're going to do or say. These things can get messy."

"Well, isn't that too bad!" Pete shouted. "Our lives are already messy because of the divorce, but no one seems to notice that!"

I could reach Pete from where I sat, so I grabbed his hand, giving it a squeeze. He looked at me, sort of smiled, and sat down again. I have a magic touch with him sometimes. (I know—it's hard to believe, right?)

"Can I ask you a question?" I said, still holding onto Pete. "If we live with you, what happens when you go on business trips and stuff?"

Dad thought for a minute. "That's a good question, peanut. For one thing, that trip to Europe was a one time deal. I'm not going to have to do that again. I guess if I did have to travel, you'd stay with your mom. We'd work it out ahead of time. Any other questions?"

Pete looked at me like I was the one to speak. I guess made sense since I'd started all this question-asking, but I didn't have a clue what to say next. No, that's not true—one thing I really wanted to know was if my dad would make me eat more if we lived with him. It might sound odd, but it's a really big deal to me.

Well, Daisy, I've got to go now, but I'll keep you posted! Wherever I live, don't worry—I'll bring you along!

Love,
Hope

Leah

Wow. Hope's last entry in Daisy is really disturbing. There are so many things I want to ask her, but obviously, I can't. I could keep reading but find there's only so much I can handle at a time; it makes me too uncomfortable. I have to admit that I'm liking her dad more than I did at first. At first, he seemed like kind of a jerk, but now I'm not so sure. He seems like the "good" parent and her mom just seems like a different person. I'm glad my mom isn't like that.

I'm excited because today I'm going to wear one of the new outfits Momo bought me! After lunch that day, we decided to go shopping at H&M because as Momo put it, I could get more bang for my buck—or *her* buck. She let me choose: one thing from an expensive store or more things from a less expensive store. I decided on H&M and got two pairs of jeans, two sweaters and three shirts! They're all so cute! Momo got a little irked when I wouldn't let her come into the fitting room with me, but I stood my ground. (I can be really stubborn sometimes!) I acted like I was all modest and stuff, and it worked! There's no way she needed to see how I look in my undies.

It was cool to see myself in the triple mirrors. I could see my front, back and sides way better than I can at home. When I turned sideways, my stomach was so flat, especially since I hadn't eaten much at lunch. I even took at big risk and let it hang out instead of sucking it in, and it *stayed* flat. I was so happy!

I pull on the new black jeans and zip and button them with ease. My hipbones are even sticking out a little more than they were the day Momo bought these for me. It's going to be such a good day! The animal-print sweater looks super cute with the jeans; I know that because the salesperson told me so. I also know that because I like it so much. It's amazing how much difference a new outfit can make!

After brushing my teeth and pulling my hair back into a messy bun, I go downstairs. Mom had to go to work early today, so she and Clara are already gone. That means that I can get away with skipping breakfast and that makes me even happier. Mom said if I do okay with getting myself ready for school, she might make the earlier start permanent. I'd love that because I could skip breakfast *and* make myself the kind of lunch I want every single day.

Grabbing a clean glass from the cupboard, I fill it with water and guzzle it all down. I've figured out that if I drink a lot of water sort of quickly, it makes me feel really full. I brush my teeth *before* I come downstairs so that I'm less likely to be tempted to eat anything; then I'd have to brush them all over again, and that would just be inconvenient. I also don't allow enough extra time to brush them again. It keeps me on the straight and narrow, so I can *be* straight and narrow!

I get a brown lunch bag and a baggie from the drawer and head to the fridge. Right away, I see a post-it note on the vegetable drawer that reads: *Sorry, sweetie —we're out of baby carrots. How about a sandwich today?* What's the deal with this? Obviously, my mom knows I like baby carrots for my lunches, but this note makes it sound like she knows that's *all* I'm eating. Damn it! All of a sudden, I feel my cheeks get hot. I'm blushing because I *thought* a swear word. Good grief! Why am I always such a goody-goody? I'm also angry that my carrots are gone—there were plenty of them here yesterday. Then a terrifying thought strikes me: maybe Mom isn't as distracted and clueless as I think she is. Maybe Momo tattled on me. This is *not* good!

There's no way I'm going to eat a sandwich for lunch, so I grab an apple, wash it and gently place it in the lunch bag along with a paper napkin. After that, I go into Mom's room and take four quarters out of the change bowl on her dresser for the pop machine at school. It's technically not stealing, but I feel guilty anyway since the rule has always been to ask first. The thing is, how can I ask if she's not here? I drop the coins into my pocket, even though my guilty conscience is screaming at me to put them back.

There are a few kids at my bus stop, but nobody talks to each other—we're all early morning zombies. Once the bus arrives, we file onto it in our usual order in silence. I find my usual seat and look forward to Tabinda getting on and then Prudy. I've told them about my shopping trip with Momo, but they haven't seen any of my new clothes yet. I've tried really hard not to brag to them, though; I don't want them to feel bad or anything. I don't think they will because their families both seem to have enough money for clothes and stuff. I'm the "poor" one of the group.

Tabinda makes her way down the aisle and sinks down next to me. "Good morning, Leah!"

"Hi, Tabinda!"

She looks at me, puzzled. "What are you so happy about?"

"I don't know. I'm just in a good mood." It's so hard not to brag about my new outfit.

"*Really.* You're never in this much of a good mood on the way to school. What's up?" Then she gives me a once-over. "You're wearing one of your new outfits, aren't you?"

I blush and nod. "I didn't want to brag."

Tabinda smiles and shakes her head. "It's not bragging to be excited about a new outfit, Leah. You're allowed—as long as you let me brag when I get one."

It's times like this when I'm glad I took the chance and told Prudy and Tabinda about my family. They know how hard it was for my mom, Clara and me even before my dad died. I feel really lucky to have them for friends. April and Nora never knew the whole story but had figured out most of it by listening to their moms gossip. They were always nice about it until now, when they clearly don't care if I'm their friend anymore. For whatever reason, I don't think Prudy and Tabinda will ever be mean to me or use my past against me, but it makes my stomach hurt to think about the possibility.

"Hey ladies!" Prudy plops down in the seat in front of us, a big grin on her face.

"Hi!" Tabinda and I say in unison.

"You're happy today too," says Tabinda. "What's up with you?"

"Have you got something against happiness?"

"Nope! Just not used to it so early in the morning, I guess. Leah has a new outfit; what's your reason?"

"My cousins from New York are thinking of moving here!" She's sparkling with excitement. "How cool is that?"

"Very cool," Tabinda and I say in unison again.

"I think so too," she says as she settles into her seat with satisfaction.

It looks like it's going to be a good day.

As soon as I step off the bus at school, I have a very ominous feeling. Unfortunately, the ominous feeling is stronger than my happy-new-outfit feeling, and my stomach starts churning. It's a good thing I didn't eat any breakfast.

Kids are acting strange and looking at the three of us out of the corners of their eyes. It's the same types of looks we got the day of the nasty drawing incident. I glance over at Prudy and Tabinda to see if they notice it too or if it's just my imagination. Prudy still looks like she's floating on sparkling rainbows and fluffy clouds. I hate to bring her down to earth, so I take a peek at Tabinda. Our eyes meet at the same split-second, and I know she sees it too. All she does is shrug, and we keep walking to our lockers.

Prudy's locker is close to mine since we're in the same homeroom, but Tabinda's locker is at the other end of the hall. I kind of hate to let her walk to it alone but can't think of a reason to make her wait with us. I'm so preoccupied worrying about Tabinda that I don't notice the look of shock on Prudy's face when about a dozen notes fall out of her locker when she opens it. That's partly because I'm busy watching my own waterfall of notes land in a pile at my feet. Kids going down the hall hide their giggles as they hurry by, laughing at some cruel inside joke.

Prudy and I scoop up the notes and shove them into our backpacks without looking at them. We seem to have the same idea: get to Tabinda ASAP. After stashing our coats in our lockers, we hurry to find Tabinda. She's standing at her locker, a single trickling down her face. There's a small pile of notes at her feet, and she's holding one in her trembling hand. Prudy and I walk up to her, one on each side, and each put an arm around her shoulders. I look at the note that's made her cry and feel sick.

I can't believe what I'm seeing! The note and the picture drawn on it is not only mean about Tabinda being Black and Muslim, but body-shames her too. It's gross and disgusting and actually calls Tabinda those things, which is ridiculous because she's the exact opposite. My heart is pounding so hard I can barely breathe. I feel dizzy and hold onto the locker to steady myself.

"We're going to the office," Prudy announces. "There's Mrs. Donnelly now. Let's tell her, then we'll stop and tell Ms. Wilcox."

She says it with such authority, neither Tabinda or I argue. There are so many reasons to be upset about this, I don't know which is worse. The three of us don't say another word as we march to the office together. I don't know what my friends are thinking, but I'm thinking about my deal with Ms. Winters. I'm going to have to tell my mom.

Luckily, Ms. Winters is available to see us. She doesn't seem very surprised, which is sort of disturbing. Did she expect the bullying to continue? The really disturbing part is that she's done nothing to prevent it in the first place. I have no idea how she'd do that, but she's the adult *and* the social worker, so she should know.

"Good morning, ladies," Ms. Winters says, rising from her chair. "How can I help?"

Ms. Winters has the round table as well as a small sofa and a couple of comfy chairs, I guess in case people need something cozier. She sort of waits for one of us to say something before she decides how comfortable we need to be. Prudy leads the way.

"It's happened again, and this time it's really, really bad." As Prudy reaches into her backpack for the notes, I take it as a signal for me to do the same. We hold out the handfuls of intricately folded notes for her to see. "We haven't even looked at these yet, but we *have* looked at one of Tabinda's." She drops it onto the table in front of Ms. Winters.

Ms. Winters picks up the note, barely touching the edges. For a second, I wonder if she's going to have it checked for fingerprints or something, or maybe she's as disgusted by it as we are. Her eyes grow big as she reads it. Her face turns red but not in an embarrassed way. Ms. Winters is *angry*.

"Please, sit down," she says, sinking into her chair at the table. I guess we're not going to be cozy. "First, let me say how truly sorry I am that this has happened to you, Tabinda. Obviously, I haven't looked at the rest of the notes, but this is horrendous. I hope you know that you are none of the things this note says you are."

Tabinda just looks down at her hands as more tears run down her face. I push a box of Kleenex over to her, and she gives me a grateful smile.

"This is very serious," Ms. Winters continues. "I know you girls are reluctant to hold these students accountable, but something has to be done. It's not acceptable for you to feel unsafe in any way while you're here or on the bus. Do you have any idea who's behind this?"

The three of us fidget for a couple of seconds before I clear my throat and sit up a tiny bit taller.

"We think so, but we're not exactly sure."

Ms. Winters waits for a moment and then says, "Go on, Leah."

Glancing at Prudy and Tabinda for support, I find myself not caring so much about what my notes might say but more about how hurt Tabinda is right now.

"I think that some friends—well, they used to be friends—from my old school might have something to do with it. They've been really mean to me lately, and one of them likes a boy at this school. She wants me to ask him if he likes her, but I told her I wouldn't do it. Ever since then, some kids here have been mean to me, and to Prudy and Tabinda because they're my friends." Suddenly, I'm crying. Tabinda pushes the box of tissues in my direction.

"That must feel awful," says Ms. Winters. "The boy-girl thing can get really ugly in middle school. Can you tell me who the boy is, Leah?"

My heart hammers, squeezing out more tears with every beat.

"Johnny Morgan," blurts Prudy.

"And his friend, Collin," adds Tabinda. "Leah said that Johnny went to her old school and was a bully there too." She inches the Kleenex box even closer to me. "Prudy and I don't know any of these kids."

For some reason, Ms. Winters doesn't seem surprised. "Are you ladies ready to let me do my job?"

The three of us look at each other, speechless. I know the bullying can't go on like this, but it's scary. I'm afraid it will only get worse if Johnny and Collin get in trouble because we reported them.

"Let me put it this way," Ms. Winters says, leaning forward, her elbows resting on the table. "There's a good chance you three aren't the only ones being bullied. I can't give you specifics, but there's any number of ways this information could have made its way to my office. No one will ever know you ladies said a word."

Again, we just look at each other. I glance up at the clock and see that homeroom will be over in about five minutes. Being late to Mr. K.'s class is never a good thing. Then a thought strikes me, and I can't let it go.

"There's one more thing, Ms. Winters, and you have to *promise* I won't get in trouble for saying it." I don't know where my new-found courage has come from, but I'm not stopping now.

"Everything you say to me is confidential, Leah."

"Yeah, but if you have to do something about it, then you'll have to tell someone, right?"

"Right, but no one will ever know the source. What is it, Leah?"

My face feels really hot, and my hands are clammy. "Well, Mr. Kendall kind of started some of the bullying."

Prudy and Tabinda stare at me like *What have you done?* I try my best to ignore their shocked expressions and forge ahead.

"On the first day of school, he called me *Pudgy* and called Prudy *Prudent.* The very same day on the bus ride home, Johnny was calling us Pudge and Prude. I mean, Mr. Kendall has nicknames for all the kids. He calls Johnny *Morgan Horse* since his last name is Morgan. It's supposed to be funny, but it's not, you know? Especially when it gives kids permission to bully other kids." Wow. That felt great!

Ms. Winters sort of rolls her eyes and sighs loudly as she shakes her head.

"She's not making this up, Ms. Winters," Prudy says, backing me up. "He really does that!"

"Yes, Prudy," says Ms. Winters. "I believe you, Leah. I'll handle it. It makes it hard for kids not to bully when teachers do it. Thank you for telling me this. No one will ever know that I heard it from you." She checks the time on her watch. "You girls better get to class. I'll check in with you later today, okay?"

We all stand up, hoisting our backpacks onto our shoulders. It's amazing how much lighter mine feels without all those hateful notes in it, notes I haven't even read yet.

"Thanks, Ms. Winters," we say and leave her office, hoping that we didn't just bring ourselves more trouble.

Hope

August 15, 1966

Dear Daisy,

Things have been kinda crazy around here. After Dad's suggestion that we live with him instead of Mom, I haven't been able to eat much of anything. Thinking about it makes me feel queasy, so it works out well that way, I guess. Don't they see what they're doing to me Pete and me? They're asking us to choose between them and that's just wrong! My friends don't understand because their parents aren't divorced. Hardly anyone's parents are divorced which makes me feel like a freak. Divorce is probably a mortal sin if you're Catholic, so it makes me feel ashamed all the time just being their kid. I hate it.

Spoiled brat that I can be, I threw a fit and said I didn't want to move. The *real* reason is so that Dad won't realize how much I don't eat, but the other reason is that I'm worried about Mom. I mean, if she's acting strange, is it a good idea to just abandon her? The day we came home from Dad's she acted all weepy and sad, like she was never going to see us again or something. Pete thought she was exaggerating a little, but I didn't. Even though Mom's been kinda weird since the divorce, I know she still loves us and wants to be our mom. The chance that we might not want to live with her anymore would have to hurt her a lot, and I don't want that on my conscience. I'd have to add that to my list of sins for confession every month, and I can't figure out which commandment that would be. The fourth

commandment, *Honor your father and your mother?* I usually
include disobeying them under that one, but would
breaking your mother's heart also be that one? It seems like
there should be a separate commandment for something as
hurtful as that.

Anyhow, since I was being so stubborn and since Dad
even said that he saw my point about Mom, they actually
worked out a compromise! Dad will still buy a house not
too far from Mom's, and we'll be able to spend more time
with him if we want to. They're even talking about an every
other week type of deal. I don't know if I'd like that, but
Dad said Pete and I could have duplicate things at his
house so we wouldn't have to pack our duffles to spend
time there. I like that idea! Since I wear a uniform to school
and don't have that many regular clothes, there's not a lot to
keep at Dad's house. The idea of him buying me some new
stuff is nice, but will he discover how much weight I've lost
then? I still think I look kinda chubby, but I can tell by how
loose my clothes are that I'm thinner even if I don't believe
it. The scale also says I am, but I don't really trust that
either. I mean, what if it's wrong?

One thing I don't know if I'll need is the supplies for
my period. I haven't gotten it after that first time, so maybe
not. I know that Dad would be SUPER embarrassed to buy
that stuff for me, so maybe I'll just sneak a few there and
hide them in my dresser. I like not getting it since my
friends don't have theirs yet—as far as I know. (We aren't
supposed to talk about it, as you know.) I don't care if I *ever*
get it again! I know I need it to have a baby someday, but I
don't care about that at all. If what I saw Neil trying to do
to Mom is what you have to do to have a baby, count me
out! That looked *horrible!*

The good news is that it takes time to buy a house. Dad's been living in an apartment, so he doesn't have a house to sell, but still. He said that people selling houses usually need time to find a new one and move out. The *other* good news is that Pete and I get to go house-hunting with him this weekend! I'm so excited!

I'll keep you posted, Daisy! I might even get a duplicate of YOU, but I have no idea how that would work!

Love,
Hope

Leah

I close Daisy and set her on the window seat. How sad for Hope and Pete, but also how exciting! I guess if I had a dad like hers, it would be cool to have another room of my own with duplicates of all my stuff and to live with him half the time. It makes my stomach hurt to realize that I wouldn't have wanted to live with my dad—not the way he was, anyway. I shake my head to reorganize my Etch-a-Sketch thoughts because it's pointless to think about. My dad is gone and is never coming back. I'd never want to leave Mom. Someday I'll have to, when I go to college or whatever, but I love her so much. I can't imagine being asked to choose. Poor Hope and Pete! I'm glad their parents worked out a compromise.

Reading Daisy usually makes me realize how nice my life is, but it's not working today. My stomach is all tied up in knots because I have to tell Mom about the bullying. I'm terrified to tell her, but Ms. Winters made it clear that if I don't, she will. I've decided to ask Momo to help me out, since I'm worried about how it will go. Momo can talk Mom down off the ledge about anything.

We've just finished cleaning up the kitchen after breakfast, when the doorbell rings. Clara races to the door before Mom and I can even react.

"Grandma Mo!" Clara squeals as Momo swoops her off her feet in a big hug. I miss the days when she greeted me that way.

"Happy Saturday, my little Clare-bear!" Momo says, planting a loud, sloppy kiss on my little sister's cheek. "How are you today?"

Clara giggles as she wipes it off. "I'm great! Mom and Leah are in the kitchen!" She grabs Momo's hand and drags her along as though Momo doesn't know the way.

"Hi, Mama," Mom says, giving her a hug. "Coffee?"

"Of course!" says Momo, digging in the over-sized purse she always carries. "Let's see what I have in here. Where did it go?" A huge smile slides across her face as she whips a DVD out and hands it to Clara. It's the Diary of a Wimpy Kid movie she's been wanting since forever. (Diaries are showing up everywhere!)

"Oh thank you, Grandma Mo!" Clara runs to give Momo a hug. "Can I watch it now? Please?" She looks to Mom for permission, batting her eyelashes for added effect.

"Yes, sweetie, go ahead." Mom smiles at her but then gives Momo the evil eye. She hates it when Momo spoils us. "What brings you by on a Saturday morning?" She gives Momo a mug of coffee and tops off her own.

Momo looks at me, smiling, and then gives me a small nod. I know what she's doing—she's making me talk first. I take a deep breath and wipe my sweaty palms on my pants.

"Actually, I asked Momo to come over," I say, walking over to the breakfast nook, hoping they'll join me. Once we're all seated, I continue. "I need to tell you something, Mom. Momo's here because she already knows about some of it."

Mom looks at us, thoroughly confused. She has that icky worried look on her face, the one I saw so much right after Dad died. It makes me want to run and lock myself in my room—if I had a lock, that is.

"Well, it's about the bullying. I told you about some of it, like when Nora kept calling and all that, but I haven't told you about all of it. The thing is, it's gotten worse. Now they're bullying Prudy and Tabinda too." My heart is galloping.

"Oh no," Mom reaches across the table and takes my hand. "I'm so sorry! How has it gotten worse?"

I squirm on the bench. This is the part I've been dreading. I glance at Momo, and she nods for me to continue. I take another really deep breath.

"A couple of weeks ago, someone on the bus threw a scrunched up ball of paper at me and Tabinda. Prudy picked it up, and she and Tabinda looked at it and brought it to the office. They wouldn't show it to me. Then the social worker, Ms. Winters, called me down to her office to talk about it. She wanted to call you, but I told her not to. I mean, if it never happened again, I would've upset you for nothing, and I didn't want to do that."

My mom's eyes are huge. "Leah-loo, you know you can always tell me anything." She squeezes my hand. "What was on the paper?"

I shift my gaze to Momo, hoping she'll pick up that it's her turn to talk.

"Well, Diane, apparently it was a very crude drawing of Leah doing something very inappropriate for her age. Whoever drew the awful thing also exaggerated the size of Loo-loo's body, especially her lower half. Some horrible things were written on it as well, calling her all sorts of terrible names. Leah told me Ms. Winters had to explain the drawing to her. Part of it, anyway." Momo stops for a second and looks at me . "And some kids at school are calling her Pudge, which makes her feel like she's fat. She's not, but even if she was, it's a fine way to be." She pats her own soft stomach for emphasis.

Mom's eyes fill with tears, exactly what I've been dreading. I *really* don't want to make her cry.

"I made a deal with Ms. Winters that if anything else happened I'd tell you about it. Well, something did. All three of our lockers, Prudy's, Tabinda's and mine, had nasty notes stuffed in them. Tabinda's notes were really, really awful. Ms. Winters said they were racist. They made fun of her hijab and said she should go back to where she came from and things like that. She's from Chicago, for Pete's sake! Prudy and I didn't even look at ours, but we gave them all to Ms. Winters." I feel tears filling my eyes.

Mom, who is sitting across from me, grabs both of my hands. If Momo wasn't sitting on the outside of the bench, she would've come over to hug me, I just know it.

"Oh, sweetie!" Tears run down her cheeks now. "I wish I had known. I could've done something!"

Momo straightens up and puts her arm around me. I feel so loved and safe snuggled next to her. Ever since I was tiny, Momo has felt that way to me.

"Diane, she's telling you *now*. This is exactly why Leah didn't tell you right away. She didn't want you to get upset and go charging in there to rescue her. That might only make matters worse. I know that as a mother that's your first impulse, but pull yourself together; for God's sake!"

Mom shrinks back into her seat. For a second, I can see what she must've looked like as a kid when she got scolded and have to hide my smile. I also feel like smiling because I love how Momo just stood up for me.

"It's just hard to hear that Leah and her friends are being bullied," Mom says, defiantly. "I won't apologize for

that." She redirects her gaze to me. "What's Ms. Winters'
plan once you've told me?"

"She said I should have you call her to set up a meeting.
She wants to keep you in the loop." I put air-quotes around
"in the loop" because that's what Ms. Winters had done.
"Prudy, Tabinda and I are just worried that since we told, it
will get worse—only sneakier."

"I have to say, tossing drawings like that around on the
school bus is pretty ballsy," Momo says and then looks
pretend-horrified. "Oops! Did I say that out loud?" Mom
gives her the evil eye again, and it's hard not to laugh.
"What? It's a perfectly valid word. It means *courageous*. Look
it up." She gently squeezes my leg under the table.

Mom rolls her eyes, crosses her arms tightly in front of
her and leans on the table. "Fine, but let's not add it to
Clara's vocabulary just yet. Okay, I'll call Ms. Winters first
thing Monday morning." She smiles at me.

I'm feeling relieved at how well that went, when Momo
clears her throat and straightens up a little more.

"As long as we're all here together, there's one more
thing I'd like to discuss, Diane." Mom looks in her
direction. "I'd like to discuss Leah's recent weight loss."

I shoot up in my seat, fiercely bouncing Momo's arm
off my shoulders. How dare she say anything about that!
I'm so angry I could scream, but I don't. Instead, I stare
down at the table, feeling my face turn redder and redder.

"Well, I've noticed she's thinned out a bit, but she's also
gotten taller since we moved." Mom looks at me with
squinty eyes, as though I'm some rare species she's seeing
for the first time. "*Have* you lost weight, Leah?"

"I think the question is: How *much* weight and *why*
should a sixth grader even be aware of a scale?" Momo

says, her voice firm. "It's not healthy for a growing girl to be losing weight."

"No, of course not!" says Mom, still staring me. "Is this about April and Nora and their dieting?"

Feeling ashamed and exposed, I just nod. This is so humiliating! Momo reaches over to hold my hand, but I yank it away, stuffing it in my lap. There's no way I'm going to let that traitor touch me.

"Leah-loo," Mom says, gently, "can you tell me how much weight you've lost?" She's using the soft and gentle approach, which is what works best when I'm shutting down. I can hear Momo sigh impatiently beside me. (Momo is *not* the 'soft and gentle approach' kind of gal.)

"I don't know. Maybe five pounds?" I try to act like I don't know, but I do. I weigh myself every morning when I get up, when I get home from school and before I go to bed. It's my goal to have the number stay the same or lower, from morning to night. It's actually closer to ten pounds, but there's no way I'm saying *that*.

"I only bring it up because when we went shopping, Leah passed on getting cinnamon rolls and hardly ate any lunch. We also saw her *former* friends, April and Nora, and they looked like death warmed over, they're so thin. They made rude comments to Leah about the store not having sizes big enough to fit her which is as ridiculous as it is mean. Leah told me about their dieting and about the bullying, which in my opinion, is at the bottom of *all* of this. And it seems to be over a boy named Johnny Morgan." She leans back against the nook bench, visibly exhausted. "I just thought it might help you to know that for your meeting with the guidance counselor."

It all sounds so simple when Momo explains it like that, except for the part about Mr. Kendall. I'm glad she didn't tell Mom that part; that's how it got started as far as I'm concerned. If Mr. K. hadn't called me *pudgy*, I really don't think Johnny and his loser friends would've called me Pudge. They might've called me something else, but not that. I've been really worried about tattling to Ms. Winters about Mr. K. and the nicknames he gives kids but don't know how much of that to tell Mom right now.

Mom slides out of the nook and says, "Come here, sweetie."

Crap. I gently nudge Momo to let me out and go to stand in front of Mom. She pulls me in for a long hug and actually feels for my ribs. It's embarrassing but at the same time it feels really nice. For a second, I feel like I did when I was a little girl. Then she pulls back, takes my face in her hands and examines my cheekbones. At least I *think* that's what she's doing. (I love my new cheekbones, by the way, almost as much as my hipbones and thigh gap!)

"Now I understand why you've avoided my hugs lately. I thought you were just outgrowing them. Now I know why you acted so reluctant to show me the new clothes Momo bought for you. You didn't want me to know the sizes, did you?" Her voice doesn't exactly sound sad, but it makes me sad to hear what she's saying.

"I'm sorry, Mom. I don't know what happened, but especially after April and Nora were here for the sleepover and talking about their diets and all that, I started thinking about what *I* looked like. I never really thought about it before. And because of what Mr. Kendall said—" *Oops.*

"What did Mr. Kendall say?"

"Well, he called me *pudgy* on the first day of school. And he called Prudy, *prudent*. Now those are our nicknames in his class. He gives nicknames to all the kids, though." My face is on fire, and I feel like crying again. "That's why some of the kids call me Pudge and Prudy, Prude."

"Oh, Leah-loo," Mom says, hugging me again. "I'm so sorry this is happening! Nicknames are one thing, but doesn't this Mr. Kendall know how much damage he's doing? This is *not* okay!" She holds me close, and I wish I could stay here forever.

"I told Ms. Winters about it, but I'm worried I'll get in trouble for telling on him."

Momo sort of snorts from the breakfast nook. "If you get in trouble for that, they'll have *me* to deal with!"

Now it's Mom's turn to tell Momo to calm down. It's kind of funny to watch them switch roles.

"I'll take care of this, Mama," she says, firmly. "It looks like Ms. Winters and I will have a lot to talk about." She leads me back to the nook to sit down next to her. "The bullying is horrible and has to stop, but I'm also concerned about this losing weight business, Leah. What are we going to do about that?"

I look at her and Momo and shrug. I have absolutely no idea what to do about it, except to keep losing weight—or at least not gain any. From the expressions on their faces, it doesn't look like they agree with me.

Momo sighs and reaches for my hand. "The thing is, Loo-loo, I had a friend when I was about your age who lost a *lot* of weight. I'd never heard of eating disorders and didn't really know that's what was going on, but it was very serious. I don't want you to have to go through what she did. That's why I ratted you out to your Mom." She pats my hand.

I get a scared, worried feeling in the pit of my stomach. Is Momo saying I have an eating disorder? That I'm crazy or something? I'm just trying not to look pudgy is all. I don't have any *disorder!*

"What happened to her?" I ask, even though I really don't want to know.

"In sixth grade, she started getting really, really thin. She'd been in my class since first grade and when she got so thin it was really disturbing. Then she started being absent a lot. It was as though she literally disappeared." Momo gets a far-away look in her eyes. "It was just really sad."

"What do you think happened?" Mom asks, clearly wanting more information to apply to my situation.

Momo shakes her head. "I don't know. Her family went through some hard times. Her parents got divorced that year, so that was a big deal. In those days, people didn't get divorced as much as they do now, especially Catholics."

"That must've been really hard," says Mom, her voice a sad whisper. I know she's thinking about Dad. Had she ever wanted to get a divorce?

"From what I remember, her mom had some issues after the divorce, but her dad seemed okay. Although at that age, how much do you pay attention to your friends' parents? You hardly pay any attention to your own."

My stomach clenches listening to Momo talk about her friend. It all sounds so similar to Hope's life, and I don't want it to be. Her life, or at least what she wrote in her diary, was so messed up. As compelling as it is, it scares me to know that families can fall apart like that or that moms can struggle like Hope's mom did. Our family went through a lot with my dad dying, but we're better now. At least I hope we are. What Momo said about not paying attention to your own parents—well, that's just not true. I've paid *lots* of attention.

"I need to go to the bathroom," I say even though I don't. I just want to be alone.

I race upstairs to my room and curl up on the window seat as though I'm protecting Hope. It feels dangerous to take the diary out of its hiding place because I know I'll want to read ahead. Momo didn't say exactly what happened to her friend, but she said it was like she disappeared. A chill runs down my back and then I shake it off, telling myself that Hope couldn't have been Momo's friend. If she was, wouldn't Momo have recognized this as Hope's house? She hasn't said a thing about that, so it's probably just a huge coincidence.

Before I go back to the kitchen, I flush the toilet and wash my hands so that it sounds like I really went to the bathroom. The last thing I need is for them to come looking for me.

"You're back!" Mom says, as I walk into the kitchen. She pats a spot on the bench next to her for me to sit down. "I've been talking to your grandma, sweetie, and we think it's a good idea to bring you to the doctor, just to make sure you're okay."

I stiffen and glare at her. "I don't need to go to the doctor! I'm fine!" *It's perfectly normal to feel dizzy most of the time, isn't it?*

"I'm sure you are, Leah, but it can't hurt to check. If Dr. Melton says you're healthy at this weight, then we're good to go. Besides, we never got around to scheduling your yearly check-up with moving and all, so you're overdue."

I slump back and fold my arms across my chest, assuming my best "stubborn brat" pose. I'm not a doctor, but I have a sneaking suspicion that losing this much weight at my age is *not* healthy. This is *not* good.

"Okay, *fine*," I say, grumbling, "but I'm not happy about it."

Mom winds her arms around me and pulls me in for a hug. "Oh, Leah-loo, no one expects you to be *happy* about it." And she plants a big kiss on my cheek.

Maureen

Befuddled is the only word to describe how I feel about the conversation Leah and I had in the car after our shopping trip. Leah had asked me not to tell her mother certain bits of information, but after I thought about it, I told her that I couldn't do that and live with myself.

"Please, Momo, *please!*" Leah begged as we drove home from the mall that day. "Please don't make me talk to Mom about this! She'll freak out and get all emotional."

I contemplated my response as I merged onto the freeway. Thankfully, there wasn't a lot of traffic. I had to choose my words very carefully, sort of how I had to drive very carefully.

"Loo-loo, listen—you'll feel so much better if you tell your mom everything. I know you will. Yes, she'll get emotional, but why is that a bad thing? It just proves that she loves you. She wants you to be happy."

Leah slumped down as much as she could without getting her airway obstructed by the shoulder belt. She also stuck out her chin as much as possible and folded defiant arms over her chest to let me know how annoyed she was with me. Lucky for me, I've raised two teenaged girls, so I can take whatever she dishes out. Being a grandmother also has the added perk of not having to live with the consequences 24/7.

We drove along quietly for several minutes. I knew not to say anything else even though it was killing me. I turned up the volume on the radio—the radio that was tuned to her favorite Top 40 station, I might add—in an attempt to fill the oppressive silence. It felt like I was trying to coax a skittish filly into letting me put a saddle on her, not that I have any experience with that type of thing. If I made one wrong move she'd shut down even more, and I couldn't take that risk. Sure, I was concerned about her being bullied, but it was the weight loss that had me really worried. It brought back a flood of bad memories.

Out of the corner of my eye I saw Leah's hand reach for the volume knob on the radio. She turned the volume down so much it was barely audible. I kept my eyes on the road.

"Will you be there with me?" Her voice was a whisper, only slightly louder than the imperceptible background music.

My heart soared. "Of course I will, Loo-loo! Anything you need."

"Because she's gonna freak," she added, her voice sounding a bit louder.

I glanced over at my granddaughter and smiled. "She's gonna freak all right, but we can handle it."

I was extremely nervous that morning on my way to Diane's house. The early morning yoga class I attended relieved some of my anxiety, but it raged back as I drove. I wasn't worried about Leah telling my daughter about the bullying. I knew she'd be upset for Leah, but I had no doubt that she'd handle it just fine. No, the part that made me so apprehensive was the part that Leah didn't know about because I hadn't told her. I hadn't told her that I was going to bring up her weight loss. Speaking of people freaking out, I knew Leah would freak out about that. She loves the new slimmer version of herself and in a way I understand. With so much pressure from the media and the world in general to be thin, of course she loves it. In her mind, she's succeeding. I feel ashamed for having bought her some new clothes to fit her new body because I don't want to encourage or enable her, but I also want her to feel confident. What's a grandma to do?

The reason I wanted to bring up her weight loss is because of what happened to a friend of mine, one of my best friends from when I was Leah's age. I've wanted to bring it up ever since they moved into their new house but have stopped myself because they were all so happy. Don't get me wrong, it's a great house, but it holds some very painful memories within its walls. It's become my mission to make sure history doesn't repeat itself at the expense of my dear, sweet Loo-loo and her family.

Everything went perfectly when Leah told Diane about the bullying, even the part about the inappropriate drawings. Diane did start to overreact a bit, but I quickly reeled her back in. I think Leah got a kick out of watching me scold her mother. It mildly annoyed me that I needed to, but I expected nothing less. Diane has had to put up with a lot with the way things have gone in her life. Because of that, she's very protective of her girls. She's evolved from a quiet, tolerant woman into a warrior who speaks her truth and doesn't put up with any shenanigans from anybody. I love that about her.

At one point, Leah escaped upstairs. Diane's first impulse was to run after her, but I placed my hand on her arm.

"Let her go, Di. She needs a moment. I sprang this on her as well as you."

Diane looked at me, confused. I sat back down across from her took both of her hands in mine.

"Let me tell you a little story…"

Hope

August 30, 1966

Dear Daisy.

I'm so excited! The house that Dad, Pete and I all liked
is the house he's going to buy! It's so cool! It's not super
close to Mom's, but it's inside the school boundaries and
that's all that matters. It's actually right on the edge. It will
be a longer walk to school, but I don't really care. The more
I walk, the more calories I'll burn!

It has three bedrooms, two on first floor and one big
one on the second floor. And guess what? *I* get the one on
the second floor! It's so cool! I thought Pete would want it,
but he doesn't. The ceiling is slanted and he says he'd hit
his head on it in some places, so he wants the bedroom on
the first floor. It also has a window seat under this really
neat window that the real estate guy called a *dormer.* The
window seat is like a storage bench in a way because the
top opens up and you can put things inside of it. That's
where you're going to stay when I'm at Dad's house, Daisy.
I hope you're not afraid of the dark! There's also *lots* of
built-in bookshelves which is good since I have *lots* of
books—not enough to split between two houses, but it's
still cool. Who knows? Maybe Pete and I will end up living
at Dad's more than we think. There's not a bathroom
upstairs—another reason Pete had for wanting the
downstairs bedroom—but I don't mind that a bit. Again,
more steps, more exercise!

Another super neat thing about this house is the breakfast nook that's in the kitchen. It's like the booths they have in restaurants, only in our very own kitchen! It's really cozy and there's a phone on the wall right by it. I can already see me sitting there talking to Reenie or Jill. It's so cool! The basement's kinda creepy, so I hope I don't need to go down there a lot. (The furnace reminds me of an octopus. Eww!) There's a washer and dryer down there, but Dad promised he'll do any laundry I need if I'm afraid. That's a relief!

Since the other people have already moved out, Dad can move in really soon—next week, actually—so he'll be there when school starts. He won't have much furniture at first since the apartment he rented was furnished, but he promised to get Pete and me beds right away—and him, of course! He said he wants it all set for when we stay there the next time. We've already bought bedspreads and sheets and stuff for our beds. We did that before we even found the house! I can't wait, Daisy! It's going to be so cool!

Love,
Hope

Leah

Wow. Momo's friend and Hope have so much in common. What if Hope was Momo's friend who got so thin? Did Hope actually sleep in this room and lived in this house? I pull the afghan tighter around my shoulders as I wonder if whoever it was, is somehow here with me. The thought makes me pull the afghan even tighter since ghosts and stuff like that scare me a lot. Momo just said her friend had an eating disorder; she didn't say she *died,* right? She also didn't say this was her house. It's just a weird coincidence I've imagined.

I get up from my comfy chair and go to the window seat to hide the diary. Running my hand over the cushion that Momo made, I wonder if she ever sat here. She couldn't have because one thing about Momo is that she's really bad at keeping secrets. She could never keep that to herself! I try to block these thoughts from my mind and walk away from the window seat. Like *that* will help.

The alarm clock on my nightstand says that it's nearly five o'clock. Mom should be home soon since she had the meeting with Ms. Winters at three-thirty. I got home at three, so I've had a long time to worry about how it's going. She'll stop at Kid's Club to pick up Clara, so she probably won't be able to talk much about what happened right away. Arrgghh! The suspense is killing me.

School was actually pretty good today for a change. For one thing, we had a sub in math who was awesome. She clearly *loves* teaching math and also seems to love kids. It was a welcome change from cranky Mr. K.! All the kids seemed happier all day as well. The bus ride home wasn't nearly as stressful as usual since Johnny and Collin weren't on it *or* in school today. It's amazing how much of a difference just two kids—and a teacher—being gone can make!

I hear the back door open and the pounding of Clara's feet as she runs through the kitchen to bathroom, something she always does the second she gets home. I can hear Mom shutting the back door and moving around as she hangs up her coat and purse. She also does the same things in the exact same order every day which gives me a surprising sense of security. I decide to do the same thing *I* do every day at this time and go downstairs to greet my family.

"Hi, Mom!" I try to sound upbeat and cheerful to hide my anxiety about the meeting.

"Hi, Leah-loo!" She comes over and gives me a big hug. (She's been giving me a *lot* more of those since our talk with Momo.) "How was your day?"

"Pretty good, actually," I say, leaning against the counter with my arms folded across my chest. "How was yours?"

"Thanks for asking! It was good. A typical Monday, but still good. Of course, leaving early was a plus." She smiles at me.

Just then, Clara comes barreling into the room.

"Hey, Clare-bear," I say as she throws her arms around me, something she does every day after she's done in the bathroom. She smells like lavender soap, so I know she's washed her hands. "How was your day?"

"Great!" she says with enthusiasm. (Oh, to be in kindergarten again!) "Mommy, can I watch TV?" Being home earlier than usual means that she can watch SpongeBob, one of her favorites.

"Do you have anything to show me from your Take Home folder?"

Clara thinks for a second and then runs to her backpack to retrieve her folder and then runs to show it to Mom. Mom opens it, takes out the papers that can stay at home and then gives it back to Clara.

"Okay, sweetie, put this in your backpack and then you can watch for a little while. By the way, I really like the colors you used in this picture," she adds before Clara dashes off.

"Thanks, Mommy!" Clara's voice fades as she scampers away.

"I bet you're curious about my meeting with Ms. Winters." She says as she attaches Clara's artwork to the refrigerator with magnets that look like ladybugs.

I nod, enthusiastically.

"Let's have a cup of tea, and I'll tell you all about it." Tea is Mom's go-to feel-good beverage. Is this a good sign or a bad omen?

"Okay. Need any help?"

"Why don't you get the tea out, and I'll get the water going?"

We go about our tea-making duties in calm, companionable silence. Maybe since I had a good day I feel less anxious in general. We agree on peppermint tea, my favorite. I put a teabag in only one mug so we don't waste an extra bag and sit in the nook to wait for the water to boil.

"Let's live a little and each have our own teabag," says Mom, when she sees what I've done.

"Okay." I get another teabag from the box and plop it into my mug.

Mom joins me in the nook after she's poured the boiling water into each of our mugs. We sit there, dunking our teabags up and down for a couple of minutes. The kitchen smells like Christmas.

"What was it about your day that made it good?" Mom asks, still dunking her teabag.

"Well, we had a really cool sub in math, and Johnny and Collin were both absent. *One* of those things would've been good, but *both* of them were awesome!" I transfer my teabag onto the saucer in the middle of the table.

"I'd like to be able to take some credit for either of those things, but Ms. Winters had already been busy after she met with you girls last week." She blows across her mug to cool off her tea. "This is between you and me, Leah, so please don't tell anyone else, and I mean *anyone,* not even Prudy and Tabinda. At least not yet, okay?"

"Okay." I take a tiny sip of tea. For some reason, it always seems to smell so much better than it tastes.

"Ms. Winters told me that she'd already met with some other parents and students last week and earlier today. The fact that Mr. Kendall, Johnny, and Collin were gone today isn't a coincidence. She confirmed that the boys were the ringleaders of the bullying, and they've been suspended for two weeks. She also told me that she looked into the nickname thing that Mr. Kendall does and found that lots of other kids have felt bad about the names he's given them. After meeting with the principal and assistant principal, they decided to suspend Mr. Kendall too. Apparently, they want to fire him, but the school board needs to approve that." She sits back in the nook, her eyes shining in triumph. "Like I said, I wish I could take some credit, but I had nothing to do with it. *You* did, Leah. Ms. Winters said that until you told her about Mr. Kendall and the nicknames, they had no idea how bad it was. Nobody was brave enough to speak up before you, Prudy and Tabinda did. Do you know how amazing that is?"

It's a lot take in all at once, so I just sit there speechless.

"I'm very proud of you. I hope you're proud of yourself too." She's getting tears in her eyes now, but I know they're happy tears.

"I was worried about getting in trouble for telling on Mr. K. and those guys. I'm still kind of afraid about that." I figure this is the time to tell her this, not to burst her bubble or anything.

"I know. It was a tough decision. The thing is, those boys *and* Mr. Kendall were hurting lots of kids. If nobody ever says anything, it never changes. I had a teacher in elementary school who gave us nicknames, but they were nice ones, and she asked us *privately* if we liked them before she ever used them. She even let us help her create them. And those boys calling you Pudge and Prude was bad enough, but those drawings definitely crossed a line. As it turns out, my court reporting job came in handy because I know lots of attorneys who would be happy to help us out —your uncle being at the top of the list. I might've mentioned that in passing when I talked to Ms. Winters. They need to know that if they let this type of thing continue to happen, there *will* be consequences."

"I've never seen you like this before, Mom. It's cool!"

She smiles at me. "When someone hurts my kids, Mama Bear comes out big time, and that brings me to my next topic. We have an appointment with Dr. Melton on Wednesday after school. It's for your regular check-up and to talk about your weight loss. Not to make you worry, but sometimes sudden, unexplained weight loss can be a sign of something serious, like diabetes."

It's hard not to smirk. "I don't have diabetes, Mom."

"How do you know?"

Shame washes over me. "Because I've been *trying* to not be pudgy." Tears fill my eyes. "Even if no one calls me that anymore, it's hard not to believe it. I must've been pudgy on the first day of school, otherwise Mr. K. wouldn't have called me that." I sniffle loudly, and Mom gives me a tissue.

"Well, Mr. K. is an ass," Mom says, harshly.

"Mom! Language!"

She laughs and shrugs. "Well, he *is*! Just don't say it at school, okay?"

"I love you, Mom."

"I love you, too, Leah-loo. And please remember that you can always come to me with anything, okay? I know you told Momo all of this before you told me, but I need to know these things. Don't worry about upsetting me. I'm a tough cookie, you know." She reaches across the table and squeezes my hands.

"I know. Mr. K. might be an ass, but you're a *bad*ass!" She gives me a big grin. "By the way, Mom, what nickname did your teacher give you?"

Her grin grows even bigger, and she gives me a wink. "Tough Cookie."

Hope

Sept. 2, 1966

Dear Daisy,

It's Moving Weekend! It's Labor Day on Monday, so school starts on Tuesday. We're helping Dad move into his new house tomorrow. I'm so excited! The weather's been sort of cool which is lucky because then Dad won't wonder why I'm wearing jeans and a sweatshirt. It's just easier if he doesn't think I look thinner. I *am* thinner, of course, but he won't understand why it's so important to me. Both he and Mom have been super distracted the past couple of weeks, so no one has paid much attention to what I do or don't eat; not even Pete. He's been super distracted too because he has a new girlfriend. That means we don't hang out as much as we did before, but it works out okay because he was starting to nag me about getting too skinny. His girlfriend is named Mary. She's really pretty and super tiny —thinner than I am, so my new goal is to get as thin as she is. I'm taller than she is (I said she's tiny!), so maybe I *should* weigh more, but I don't want to. I feel jealous of her when she's around, but she's nice to me, so it's not too bad. I actually feel bad about myself for feeling jealous *because* she's so nice. She's also a cheerleader and that's *so* cool! If I end up going to the all-girls high school we won't even have cheerleaders. The trouble is, I've never been one of the popular kids and that's usually who gets picked for that stuff. It wouldn't matter how thin I am—unless the popular kids want me to be in their group this year. Maybe they'll decide I'm cool enough if I'm thin enough. I can only hope! Time to go! I'll be back later!

Love,
Hope

Later....

Dear Daisy,

What a day! Moving is really hard work even if there isn't a lot of stuff. The beds Dad bought for the three of us are brand new because he said used beds are gross. He bought some other stuff at rummage sales and thrift shops. He also got some stuff from some guy he works with who was getting rid of a sofa and other things. I feel bad for my dad having to get used stuff, but he doesn't seem to mind. He said he'd rather have money for the house itself than what's inside it. Those things can be replaced later on. That makes sense.

I got really tired hauling things up to my new room, even though there wasn't that much besides sheets and pillows and some boxes. Dad kept asking me if I was hot since it's hot upstairs, but I was fine. I'm actually kinda chilly most of the time even though it's summer, so it works.

I didn't eat breakfast today, so I was really hungry by lunchtime. It made me wonder if running up and down the stairs will make me hungrier when I'm staying here. That would be good because I'd burn more calories, but bad if it makes me want to eat more. Usually, if I wait long enough the *hungries* go away and then I don't need to eat anymore. I knew that today we'd be stopping to eat lunch since Pete is a bottomless pit when it comes to eating. Dad also likes to eat, so that's why I planned ahead and didn't eat a thing.

Something really unusual happened before lunchtime, and I'm only telling you about it, Daisy. I had just finished putting the sheets on my bed, and when I stood up after being bent over, I got really, really dizzy. I've never felt that way before, so it was kinda scary. I sat down on the bed until I felt a little better, but when I stood up to go downstairs, it happened again. Dad kept calling me to come down for lunch, and it was *really* annoying. I was afraid to answer him because I knew my voice would sound wobbly and worried and then *he'd* get all worried. It took another minute or so to feel okay enough to go downstairs. When I got down there, I got the third degree.

"What took you so long, sis?" Pete said, as he paced back and forth. "I'm starving!"

"You're always starving," I said, which is true.

"Can you hear us okay when you're up there, Hope?" Dad asked. "Because if you can't, that's a problem."

I rolled my eyes and sighed. "I heard you. I was just busy making my bed."

"And you can't talk and make your bed at the same time?" Pete snickered.

"I guess not," I said, as I elbowed him in the side.

"Okay, you two—that's enough. Where should we go for lunch?"

"How about Beek's Pizza?" Pete looked at Dad, pretending to pray.

"Sounds good to me. You okay with that, peanut?"

Pizza is on my list of forbidden foods, but Dad and Pete don't know that. I felt a little panicked because you can't fake eating pizza; there's no moving it around on the plate.

"Sure," I said, totally lying.

Lunch was a disaster. Dad kept bugging me about what I wanted on the pizza, and I really didn't care. We finally ordered an extra large pepperoni and black olive with extra cheese, and we each got a large pop. All I wanted to drink was water, but Dad made me get pop anyway, so I got a Tab. I was relieved he let me get diet pop so I could do my "drink diet pop to feel full" trick.

The pizza came and it looked and smelled so yummy. I can't remember the last time I had pizza, so I decided it would be okay to have some. (I mean, I kinda *had* to.) I started slowly, eating the toppings with a fork first. I wanted it to last as long as possible so I wouldn't have to eat another slice. Pete and Dad wolfed down several slices in the time it took me to eat one. As soon as I finished mine, though, feelings of panic and shame bubbled up, and I felt really yucky. I ran to the restroom and once I got in there, I threw up all of my lunch. At least I made it to the toilet! Realizing I'd just thrown up in a public toilet made me throw up again. It was so gross! I hate throwing up, but once I did, I felt sort of relieved. I'd been able to eat like a normal person but now I didn't have to worry about the pizza making me fat. It was gone! I could see where this might come in handy when we're staying at Dad's, but since there's only the one bathroom, that might be tricky to do without anyone knowing. As soon as I realized that, my stomach started to hurt.

When I walked out of the restroom, Pete was already in the car, and Dad was waiting by the door to the outside.

"You okay, peanut?" There was definitely a worried look on his face.

"Yep, I'm good." I smiled my biggest, best smile.

He put his hand on my shoulder and said, "Okay, but you know you can tell me anything, right?"

I just nodded. If I said even one word, I'm pretty sure I would've cried.

I can't tell anyone anything about this—nobody but you, that is. People will think I'm a freak if I tell them—even my family—so it's got to stay our secret, okay, Daisy?

Love,
Hope

Leah

Wow. Every time I read an entry in Daisy lately I have that reaction—that *Wow* reaction. Her dad just said to her exactly what my mom said to me the other day—that I can tell her anything. It's so weird that lots of what happened in Hope's life is similar to what's happening in mine. In a way, I like it, but it also scares me. Hope worried about being a freak. If I want to lose weight does that make me a freak? I have enough problems without adding that to the list, especially the throwing up part. That's just nasty! The thing is, dieting seems like something everyone does sooner or later. It seems completely normal and that's all I'm trying to be.

I have my doctor appointment today, and I'm dreading it. I should be excited because I get to leave school early and miss gym class, but I'm not. They're going to weigh me, and I *really* don't want them to. I know what I weigh. I made a point of not eating or drinking *anything* today because I don't want to weigh too much at the doctor's office. I know I'll weigh more than I do at home because I'll have clothes on, but still. It's strange because even though I *know* that, it makes my heart pound really hard.

I meet Mom by the main office at two o'clock. She smiles but doesn't hug me. That's a relief because it would be *so* embarrassing.

"Hi, sweetie!"

"Hi, Mom."

"How was your day?" she says as we walk out to the car.

"Okay, I guess." I really don't feel like talking.

"Do you still have the nice sub in math?"

"Yeah." I buckle my seat belt and stare out the window.

"Well, that's good."

It snowed last night so Mom is very focused on the roads and doesn't talk too much. Otherwise, she'd be chatting the whole way there. It's not that I don't love my mom or anything, but sometimes I like it quiet. I've noticed that more and more, now that I'm home by myself after school. I like having my own quiet time. Obviously, I'm not having it today.

The first thing they do at the clinic after they call us back, is make me get on the scale. I've been coming to this doctor's office since I was a baby, so I've sort of gotten to know some of the nurses. Margo is my all-time favorite, but she's not here today. Instead, it's someone new who is young and blonde and super thin. She's wearing lots of makeup which makes me feel really plain and ugly. I slip off my shoes and step on the scale. I was going to keep my eyes shut, but I need to know what the number is. It's a half-pound more than I was at home this morning. I'm a little bummed, but whatever. I notice that Mom's eyes get sort of wide when she sees the number, and I assume that's because the number's too high. The nurse jots it down on my chart and then leads us into an exam room after she measures my height.

"What brings you in today?" she says as she logs in to the computer without looking at us.

"Well," Mom says, "we're here for Leah's annual checkup. We're sort of late because we moved—"

"Is she on any medications?" The nurse, who hasn't told us her name, stares at the computer screen and waits.

"No, just a multivitamin."

"Any allergies?"

"No."

"Any concerns or problems?"

"Well, yes. Leah has lost some weight recently."

The nurse shifts her eyes to me and looks me up and down. I feel like I'm on display and wish I was thinner than her. Instead of saying anything, she just types something into the computer.

"The doctor will be in soon," she says, taking a blue and white gown out from a drawer in the exam table. "Put this on. It opens in the back. You can leave your underwear on." She leaves the room.

I look at my mom, mortified. She's my mom and all, but I really don't want to undress in front of her. After all, I *am* nearly twelve.

"I'll close my eyes," says Mom, sensing my dismay.

I quickly change into the gown and then sit on the end of the exam table, my feet dangling over the edge. Just then there's a soft knock on the door, and Dr. Melton walks in.

"Well, hello, Peterson ladies!" She gives us a warm smile. "I've missed you, Leah. How have you been?"

I feel my cheeks turn warm and know I'm blushing. I hate it when that happens. It makes me feel like a big, round tomato.

"Good," I mutter, managing a weak smile.

"You're in middle school now, right? How's that going?"

I shrug. "Okay." I can sense that my mom is getting frustrated by my one word answers, but I can't seem to find any more words.

"Well, that's good because middle school can be tricky. Lots of kids struggle at least a little bit, so it's lucky that you're not." She smiles at me again and turns her attention to the computer screen as she logs in. "Hmm—it says here

that your weight is down from the last time I saw you."
Now she looks at me again. "And you've grown two
inches."

Mom and I look at each other; neither of us says a
thing. Since Mom is the parent, I think she should talk first.
After all, this appointment was *her* idea, not mine.

"Yes, well, that's actually one of our concerns, Dr.
Melton. Well, it's *my* concern. I want to make sure Leah's
not diabetic or something." She's fidgeting with the strap
on her purse and tapping her feet under her chair.

Dr. Melton nods and looks at me again. "Is it a concern
of yours too, Leah?"

I shrug again. "Not really."

"Have you gotten your period yet?"

Now I *really* want to die. I just nod, hoping Mom will
talk for me.

"Yes, she got it on the first day of school."

"Whoa! That had to be interesting, huh? Two big firsts
on the same day!" Dr. Melton smiles and shudders a little it.
"How has it been going? Is it getting easier?"

"Well, she—"

Dr. Melton turns to my mom. "Actually, Mom, why
don't you go check out some of the magazines in the
waiting room. I'm pretty sure the new People is out there.
Go and relax."

Mom looks at me and then at Dr. Melton, unsure of
what to do. I just nod to let her know it's okay. I mean,
what else can I do? I can't act like a baby and say I want her
to stay, can I?

Dr. Melton turns back to me after Mom gently closes
the exam room door. She's leaning forward with her elbows
on her knees. "Do you have any questions about your

period? Sometimes girls have questions they're uncomfortable asking their moms."

"I don't know," I say, quietly. "I only got it the one time. My mom said that's normal. Is she right?"

"Yes, Leah, she is. At first, it can be really sporadic because your body is getting used to the hormones and everything, so yes, that's perfectly normal. Any other questions?" She stands up, taking the stethoscope from around her neck. It has a tiny stuffed koala bear hanging onto it which makes me smile. That same koala bear has been there for as long as I can remember.

Putting the stethoscope on my back she tells me to take a few deep breaths, then she does the same on my chest. After that, she just listens to my heartbeat. Next, she takes the little hammer out of her pocket and gets ready to tap my knees to check my reflexes, something that's always made me giggle.

"I had the best blueberry muffin in the world for breakfast this morning. What did you have?" She taps my left knee.

I feel myself turning red and can feel my stomach growling. "I didn't have time for breakfast this morning."

"Some mornings are hectic, aren't they?" She taps my right knee and together we watch my foot jerk toward her. "I bet you were really hungry by lunchtime. What was for lunch today?" She grabs the flashlight for looking in my throat and waits for me to answer.

My heart is thumping now, and I'm relieved that she's already listened to it. I squirm a little, wishing I had eaten something so I don't have to lie. I'm a terrible liar.

"I didn't really eat much lunch."

"Really?" she says as she peers into my left ear. "Weren't you famished?"

I shrug because I don't want to tell her that I was so hungry I felt nauseous and dizzy.

"I always find it really hard to concentrate if I'm super hungry. Sometimes I even get *hangry*. Does that ever happen to you?"

I have the distinct feeling that she's onto me. "Sort of, but the feeling goes away after a while."

She places the instrument she was using on the counter and sits down on a stool that has wheels on the bottom.

"Leah, honey, do you think about food or how much you eat very often?"

I nod and pick at a hangnail.

"How often do you think about it during the day? All the time, sometimes or not very much?"

"All the time." My voice sounds really squeaky.

"When did you start thinking about it so much?" Her voice is very calm and cozy, sort of like a warm, fluffy blanket that just came out of the dryer.

"After a teacher called me pudgy and then some kids started calling me Pudge." Tears fill my eyes, making the room get all blurry. "It happened on the first day of school."

"Oh my," says Dr. Melton, "that's awful, Leah. I'm so sorry that happened to you. That was certainly a rough day, huh?"

Suddenly, I'm telling her everything about everything: the bullying, Nora and April and how I've been trying to lose weight. As she listens, the expression on her face remains kind and calm. It seems like she's heard stories like this before, and it helps me feel like less of a freak.

"Leah, it's normal and healthy for girls to gain anywhere from 40 to 50 pounds during puberty and to grow as much as ten inches. Because you've gotten your period, you're officially in puberty. Gaining weight is *supposed* to happen." She reaches out and takes my hands in hers. "I'm so sorry you were made to feel otherwise. It's hard to be one of the first ones, isn't it?"

I nod, making the tears slip out of my eyes and run down my cheeks. She hands me the whole box of Kleenex.

"I'm so glad you came to see me today, Leah. You're lucky to have a mom who doesn't put things off or ignore them. Because this is so important, I'm going to suggest that you schedule a visit with someone who helps kids who worry about their weight and their changing bodies. I'm telling you about this without your mom here to see what you think. Parents sometimes overreact to this stuff and that's normal because they love you. Would you like to be able to talk to someone like that?"

I shrug a little and then nod.

"I'm not going to lie, Leah. They'll help you restore the weight you've lost because your body needs that to be strong and healthy. Does that still sound okay to you?" She looks at me, cautiously.

"I don't know. I like being thinner, but I don't like thinking about it all the time," I admit. "Does this mean I have an eating disorder?"

For a split second she seems surprised. "You've heard about eating disorders?"

"Yeah, my grandma had a friend when she was my age who had one. Or she *thinks* she had one. She said they didn't talk about it very much."

"Well, Leah, that's why I want you to see my friends. They know way more about this stuff than I do. I suspect that you might be at the very beginning of one and now is the best time to deal with it. Are you okay with that?"

"It would be nice to be like I was before, when I ate whatever I wanted to. Mom's made sure the bullies were dealt with, so that's over, I hope."

"I hate to break it to you, Leah, but there will always be bullies. The key is to not let them have any power over you; then they're just insecure people saying stupid things. It's so hard to feel good in your body when other kids are on diets they don't need or when you see super skinny people on You Tube, television and in magazines. But none of that is real or healthy, okay?"

Wow. This is a lot to take in all at once, but I feel the knot in my stomach untwist a smidgeon. It's also a little easier to breathe than it was a few minutes ago.

"Okay, but does it cost a lot?"

"Oh, you don't need to worry about that."

"Well, I do because we don't have a lot of money. My mom has a good job, but we just moved into a new house and—"

Dr. Melton takes my hands again and gives them a firm but gentle squeeze. "That is not something you need to worry about, Leah. That's not your job; that's your mom's job, and I'm confident she can handle it, okay? Should we bring her back in?"

More tears sneak out of my eyes when I nod my head. It feels so good to hear an adult say these things to me. I just hope she's right.

Hope

September 6, 1966

Dear Daisy,

Today was the first day of school, the first day of 7th grade! It's really cool to finally be in the upper grades. My school has first through eighth grade, but 7th and 8th grades are thought of as "junior high." We're not little kids anymore!

The day started out really great because my uniform skirt was even bigger than it was the last time I tried it on. Yay for me! Mom was surprised in what seemed like a good way because she didn't get mad. We found some big safety pins to fasten it shut and actually pinned the skirt to my blouse. She said she'll teach me how to move the button over myself. That's fine with me because I'd like to learn how to sew—then I can make lots of new clothes, like tent dresses and miniskirts, that fit me as I get thinner.

We don't have hot lunch at my school, so we have to bring our lunches from home. I used to feel bad about that but not anymore since it will be easier to control what I eat. I told Mom I'm old enough to make my own lunch now and that makes her really happy since she spends so much time getting ready every morning. She only does that on the days she works at the insurance office; otherwise she sleeps in. She worked today so she was up, but she said that since I'm so responsible she'll let me make my own lunch every day. I must be growing up because last year that would've really upset me. This year I'm good with it—excited even!

When I was ready to leave for school, Dad surprised me by showing up to take the "first day of school picture." (Pete insisted he's too old for that now, so Dad didn't push it with him.) Mom was surprised too. They ended up having an argument about it on the front steps, all because Mom had forgotten about the "tradition" as Dad called it. Good grief! How humiliating! By the time they got done arguing there was only time for a quick picture, and Dad ended up driving me to school because he planned on doing that anyway. He got all emotional when I was getting out of the car, saying things about his little girl growing up and all that. It was weird because Mom used to be the one who got all emotional about stuff, and Dad was more distant. Now it's the other way around, and it feels really strange. I never know what to expect anymore.

There's two 7th-grade classrooms, and I'm excited because Reenie *and* Jill are in mine! We don't sit very close to each other, but we get to switch classrooms for science, and we can choose our own seats in there. Mrs.Olsen, our science teacher, is so cool that way. (She also teaches us music, but I've already told you about her, haven't I?)

At lunchtime, the three of us found a spot near the end of one of the long tables in the lunchroom. All the grades have lunch at the same time and are organized by classroom. We're not exactly in the popular group, but we're not outcasts either; we're somewhere in the middle. Reenie was all excited about her peanut butter and banana sandwich, which I have to admit, sounded pretty tasty, so I tried to ignore it. Instead, I focused on my Ry-Crisp crackers and celery sticks. Jill looked up from her thermos of spaghetti, frowning at my lunch.

"Is that all you're eating, Hope?"

Her spaghetti smelled *so* good.

"Yeah, I ran out of time to make more because my dad stopped by to take my first day of school picture." I was hoping to get them on another topic.

"Parents are so weird, aren't they? Mine did that, too," said Reenie, as she held her sandwich in mid-air. "I can't decide if it's lame or not."

"I think it's kind of fun to see the pictures from year to year," said Jill, who has four brothers and two sisters.

"Yeah, it must be fun to see how you all grow every year," said Reenie. She took another bite of her sandwich.

My mouth began to water as I watched her chew, and I quickly took a bite of my Ry-Crisp. I told myself it tasted okay, but it sure was dry. At least it was crunchy and took a long time to eat.

After lunch, was recess. The 7th and 8th graders always dominate the playground. There are two playgrounds that are really just parking lots for the church. The boys have the big playground, and the girls have the smaller one. There are hopscotch and four square games painted on ours, but the boys have nothing on theirs. They usually just run around and play football or whatever, and the girls are expected to play hopscotch, four square and my favorite— jump rope. Last year there was an 8th-grader named Georgia who was the Jump Rope Queen of the school. Seriously—she could jump better than anyone I've ever seen, and I've been watching girls jump rope for years!

During the summer, Reenie, Jill and I practiced so that *we* could become the new jump rope royalty. I hoped that by losing weight I'd have an easier time sailing over the jump rope and also doing other jump rope games like double-dutch. The three of us got pretty good at it but that was just with the three of us. At school, there's *all* the other girls who might have practiced all summer, and it made me really nervous! I was afraid to even get in line to jump. Reenie pulled me along, though, reminding me the whole time how good I am at every jump rope game. She's such a good friend, Reenie is.

When it was my turn to jump in on *Not Last Night But The Night Before,* I was so nervous I thought I was going to throw up, but I jumped in perfectly and made it the whole way until I had to jump out. It was great! The only thing was that afterward I felt super dizzy, and my heart was beating really fast. I sat down on the curb to rest, afraid that if I didn't, I'd fall over.

"Are you okay, Hope?" Reenie said as she and Jill sat down on either side of me. "You don't look so good."

"Yeah," said Jill, "maybe you should've had a bigger lunch." Jill is always talking about food. I think it's because there never seems to be enough to eat at her house with all those brothers and sisters.

"I'm okay," I said. "I was just super nervous." That was when I noticed that my knee-highs were in puddles around my ankles. I pulled them up quickly, hoping nobody noticed.

"You were jumping so hard your socks fell down!" Reenie said, giggling. "You were amazing! You're going to be the new Jump Rope Queen for sure!"

I was thrilled! It sort of made how awful I felt worth it, but when I tried to stand up, everything was spinning.

"Maybe you should go to the nurse's office," said Reenie. "Like I said, you don't look so good."

I was worried that if I went to the nurse's office, they'd call my mom and she hates to be called when she's at work. If they called my dad, then he'd be all worried about me. I didn't like either of those options.

"I'll be okay," I said, hoping it was true. We took it easy the rest of recess and just sat on the curb.

Pete was already there when I got home since the high school gets out earlier than mine. As usual, he was having an after-school snack large enough to feed a family of four. It's amazing that he can eat like that and not get fat. I wish it was like that for me.

"How was school?" he asked, right before he bit into a nasty-looking bologna, cheese and pickle sandwich.

"Fine. How about you?" I stood just outside the kitchen door because being too close to food felt kinda scary. I was so hungry, even the bologna smelled good, and I *hate* bologna.

He nodded and gave me a thumbs up because he had food in his mouth. That must've been all he had to say because he immediately took another big bite and turned his attention back to the MAD magazine he'd been reading.

My stomach was growling so much I could hardly stand it. Just seeing Pete eating that sandwich made me realize how little I'd eaten all day. Glancing at the clock on the wall in the living room, I saw that it was only 3:30. How was I going to last until 6:00 when we eat dinner? I always look forward to the one small but "normal" meal I let myself eat each day.

Just then, the phone rang. From the living room, I could hear Pete answer it. He didn't say much, but from what I could tell, it had been Mom. She probably called to see how our first day of school went.

"Hey, sis!" Pete called from the kitchen. "Mom's not gonna be home for dinner, so we're on our own, okay?"

My heart sank. How could Mom not want to come home to see us on the first day of school? How could she not even want to talk to me on the phone? She always used to be so excited to see how our days went. Now she didn't seem to care at all. I went to my room and slammed the door, even though door-slamming is not allowed. With no parent there to hear it, who cares? Then I heard the phone ring again.

"Hey, sis!" Pete shouted. "It's Dad! He wants to talk to you!"

I wiped away the tears and went back to the kitchen. (That's where the only phone in the house is.) Pete looked kinda surprised to see I'd been crying, but just handed me the phone.

"Hello?"

"Hi, peanut! How was the first day of 7th grade?"

"It was good! I might become the new Jump Rope Queen at recess. At least that's what Reenie and Jill said." I tried really, really hard to sound excited and bubbly. "And the three of us are in the same class, so that's good."

"That's great! I'm glad to hear it! Say, I'm sorry about the argument your mom and I had this morning. That's not a good way to send you to school, especially on the first day, so I want to apologize for that."

"That's okay, Dad." For some reason this made me want to cry more, but I held it in.

"Well, I've got to get back to work, but we'll celebrate being Jump Rope Queen next week when you're at my house, okay?"

"Okay, Dad."

"I love you, Hope."

"I love you too, Dad. Bye."

I rammed the phone receiver back in its holder and hurried back to my room, slamming the door again just because I felt like it. Within seconds, Pete was there, knocking.

"Hey Hope, can I come in?"

"I don't care." I quickly wiped away the new tears that had filled me up while I'd talked to Dad.

Pete came in and stopped in his tracks. Seeing me sprawled on my bed crying probably wasn't what he was expecting. I have to hand it to him though—he didn't bolt. Instead, he came over and sat on the edge of the mattress.

"What's wrong, sis? Did Dad say something to upset you?"

"No, he was really, really nice." I sniffled loudly and grabbed a Kleenex.

"What's wrong then?"

I sat up and faced him. "I don't know. I guess I feel sad that Mom's not coming home after work. And *both* Mom and Dad seem to have forgotten about our "First Day of School" dinners." I blew my nose.

"Oh yeah," said Pete. "I sorta forgot about that too. I didn't know it was such a big deal to you. I always thought they were sort of lame." He laughed at himself. "Well, I guess I liked them until high school, now that I think about it."

"Yeah, well, it just reminds me of how different everything is now, and I *hate* it!" I punched my pillow for dramatic effect. "If Mom and Dad can't be married anymore, at least I wish Mom was still Mom." I could feel a new crop of tears growing.

"I know, sis. I do too, even though I might not act like it." He tossed one of my throw pillows in the air over and over again. "Tell you what. I have some money left from my birthday. Let's order a pizza and have our own First Day of School dinner!"

"Really? We can do that? But how will we get it?"

"They deliver it to the house, silly."

"Really?" We'd never, ever done that before.

"Yes, really!" he said, laughing. "Just because Mom and Dad never do it doesn't mean we can't. Let's do it and have our own party. We'll start a new tradition!"

I was so touched by Pete's kindness, I made sure to eat lots of pizza. One reason was because we didn't want there to be any leftovers in case Mom got mad, but the other reason was because I didn't want to hurt Pete's feelings— and I was starving. I also had a new trick in my bag. If I felt too full afterwards, I could make myself throw up. And that's exactly what I did.

Love,
Hope

Leah

I've had a few appointments at the eating disorder clinic and so far, so good. They said I'm in the early stages of anorexia nervosa. They also said it's good to catch these things sooner rather than later, so it's good that I'm there. I meet with a team that includes a psychologist/therapist, a dietitian and a medical doctor. Sometimes, when kids are really sick, they go and live somewhere else to get help, but they said if I do okay with what they call *family-based treatment*, I won't need to do that. Even though I'm really worried about gaining weight, I promised Mom that I'll try my best to get better. I'd feel terrible if she paid for this and then I didn't do a good job. I'm also learning that we don't just talk about food and eating. We talk about all kinds of stuff—basically anything that's on my mind.

I'm also going to group therapy once a week. I was nervous about going to that for all sorts of reasons: What if they don't like me? What if they think I'm too fat to be there or not thin enough? I've looked up some stuff about anorexia online and some people get really, really thin; so thin that they look like skeletons. I don't look like that, but my therapist told me that it's valid for me to be there and not to worry. Hannah, my therapist, even said that some people with anorexia don't look thin at all. She said if I absolutely hate it, I don't have to do it or we can try a different group. It's scary that there are so many kids feeling like I do. Another cool thing I can do if I want is go to a yoga class they have at the clinic. I've never done yoga before, but Hannah says it's helpful way to deal with stress or anxiety and that it just feels good in your body.

When I walked into the group meeting this week, I was shocked to see Nora sitting there looking sort of lost. Nora! At first, I wanted to turn around and leave, but then decided to be brave.

"Hi," I whispered as I sat down next to her.

She almost jumped out of her skin before she gave me a tiny smile. "Hi, Leah."

We sat there in excruciating silence for a few seconds and then she turned toward me a little bit. "Your mom called my mom."

Mom and I hadn't discussed it, but I wasn't surprised she'd done that, just humiliated. "Sorry about that."

Nora shrugged and said, "It's okay. My mom was always on my case about how thin I was getting and stuff, so this probably would've happened eventually."

"Did my mom call April's mom too?" I was terrified to hear the answer to that question.

Nora scoffed and nodded. "I guess so, but April's mom didn't want to hear about it. She seems to think that being thin will help April get into one of the fancy ballet schools in New York." She paused for a second and glanced around as though April was hiding in the shadows. "Between you and me, April's not that good of a dancer; no amount of weight loss will help that."

I tried really hard not to laugh. I also couldn't decide if I could trust Nora not to tell April anything negative that I said about her, so I kept my mouth shut and picked at a hangnail instead. If you can't say something nice…

"Leah, I'm really sorry about all that bullying stuff. You know how April can be, and I was too afraid to stand up to her. You didn't deserve any of that. I'm really sorry." She sniffled a little, like she was starting to cry.

"Thanks, Nora." I handed her a box of Kleenex from the chair next to me. "I get it. I never thought it was your idea."

"Well, I should've been a better friend to *you*, not April. And what's the deal with her liking Johnny Morgan anyway?"

I chuckled and gave her an exaggerated eye roll. I would've made the "gag me" gesture but figured that would be wrong since we were in an eating disorder therapy group. The rest of that meeting was even better than the other ones I'd been to because it felt like I had my friend back, at least once a week. Before we left, Nora said she'll call me, but I'm not exactly sure I want her to just yet. My trust level is still pretty low, so I'll give it some time.

It scares me to read what Hope's been going through lately. It sounds like she's having a really tough time with everything that's going on in her family. It's hard for me to remember that all of that happened back in 1966, it feels so real. Hope would be in her sixties now, just like Momo. That's another thing that freaks me out. Momo said she knew someone who they thought had an eating disorder of some kind she was my age. How many people could there have been way back then who worried about that kind of stuff?

I'm sort of afraid to tell Momo about the diary even though I really want to ask her about Hope and everything. The trouble is, if I tell Momo that it's making me anxious, she'll make me tell Mom and then they might take Daisy away from me. I couldn't stand that! I guess I could tell Hannah about it, but she'll say that if it triggers anything for me, I should stop reading it, and I don't want to do that. Not yet, anyway.

Christmas didn't seem that important this year. It *was* important because it was the first Christmas in our new house, but I wasn't into it very much. Sometimes, I get really, really scared about gaining weight and when I'm like that, nothing makes me feel better, even Christmas. Mom and Clara are almost *too* nice to me now that I'm seeing a therapist. (Maybe they don't want to give me new things to talk about!)

One snowy afternoon during break, Prudy, Tabinda and I were hanging out in my room. A large plastic container of beads sat on the floor between us, as we worked on creating new masterpieces.

"Hey, Leah, can I ask you something?" Prudy said, looking up from the orange and yellow beads in her hands.

"Sure!" What can you say besides that when a friend asks that question?

"I've noticed that you've been less fussy about eating lately, and I'm wondering why. Don't get me wrong—I think it's great—I'm just curious about what's changed."

Before I could say a word, Tabinda chimed in with, "Me too."

I took a very deep breath and told them all about everything, even about Hope and her diary. They listened silently, hanging on every word.

"Yikes!" said Prudy. "I feel so bad for you, Leah, and for Hope."

"So do I," said Tabinda. "How awful to feel like that about yourself. I'm so glad your mom took you to the doctor."

"I wasn't very happy about it at first. It still makes me mad sometimes. It's really scary to eat more, but Hannah has a lot of ideas to help with that." I paused for a second and took another deep breath. "Now can I ask you guys something?"

They looked at each other, shrugged and then nodded.

"Have you guys ever felt bad about your bodies or food or anything?"

They both sat there, playing with anything within reach —beads, the fuzzy purple rug we were sitting on, any loose threads on their clothes. I felt sort of nosy asking them, but I had to know how I compared to them. Hannah has a phrase, *Compare and despair,* to remind me of how dangerous it can be, but I still asked.

"Well," said Tabinda, "I've felt uncomfortable at times, especially this year, but more because of my skin color and my religion than my body size. I can't and don't want to change either of those things, so maybe it's different that way."

"Yeah," Prudy added, "I guess it's different to feel bad about something you might be able to change because then you feel like you should." After pausing a beat, she said, "Can I tell you something, Leah?"

I nodded and waited for her to continue. Prudy repositioned herself on the floor, sat up taller and cleared her throat like she was going to give a speech.

"I'm not saying this to make you feel bad or anything, but since you've been getting thinner and have been eating next to nothing, it's made me feel like there's something wrong with *me*—that I eat too much or that I'm a big slob for not being like you." She looked down at the rug and sniffled as a tear ran down her cheek.

Tears stung my eyes and my heart at the exact same time. It had never occurred to me that my losing weight would have affected my friend like that. I'd been so focused on myself that I hadn't even thought about it. Shame bloomed from somewhere deep inside. I realized that I had been doing to my new friends what my old friends had done to me. I felt terrible.

"I'm so sorry, Prudy! I never thought of that, really, I didn't." I reached over to give her a hug. I was so relieved when she hugged me back. "Tabinda, did I make you feel that way?"

Tabinda wriggled. "A little bit, I guess. I mostly wondered why you thought you needed to change at all. I thought you were perfect the way you were the first day we met. I guess I was more worried than anything—you know, that you were going to turn into April and Nora or something."

"I'm sorry! I'm so sorry! I never meant to make you feel bad or worry. And being like April and Nora would be the worst thing ever. I *never* want to be like them!" I scooted over to give her a hug.

"The thing that's so weird is how something like Mr. K.'s calling you Pudgy had such a big effect on you," said Prudy. "I mean, his calling me Prudent wasn't the greatest and it bugged me, but it didn't make me want to change anything about myself. It's like I said that day, I've heard that stupid joke like a million times."

"You've never wanted to change your name because of that?" Tabinda asked with a tiny smirk. When Tabinda has that smirk on her face, we know she's kidding.

"Nope! It actually makes me like it even more. Maybe since I've heard it so many times, I'm used to it. And my mom says having brothers who've teased me since I was little has helped me grow a thicker skin." She rolled her eyes. "But having Johnny and Collin bully me about it still didn't feel good. If Mr. K. hadn't said it in the first place, those guys never would've thought of it on their own."

"That's for sure!" Tabinda said, laughing. "Those guys probably have the vocabulary of a gnat!"

We all had a good laugh for a minute but then stopped ourselves, all at the same time.

"I feel kind of bad for making fun of them," I said, wiping the tears of laughter from my eyes. "Does this make us as bad as them?"

Prudy shook her head. "No, because we're not going to bully them and call them names. Let's make a pact to never say it again." She put her hand out and Tabinda and I did the same. We all shook on it and then pinky swore, just to be on the safe side.

"It's very scary how it all came together and made you get sick so fast, Leah. I mean, between the nickname, the bullying and April and Nora, it's like it was too much at once," said Tabinda.

"I've talked with Hannah about that a lot because I think it's scary, too. She said that if you have the right ingredients for developing an eating disorder, it doesn't take a whole lot to make it happen."

"That's what scares me," Tabinda continued. "How do you know if you have the ingredients? I mean, Hope had no idea and neither did her parents."

"It makes me wonder how many kids at school have the right ingredients," said Prudy. "You didn't know you did, right?"

I shook my head and hugged the fake fur pillow in my lap. "Not to sound creepy, but it was like someone else took over my brain. I'd never thought about it at all before that. And you know what's really strange? When I was reading about Hope's eating disorder, it never dawned on me that I was doing the same thing. How strange is that? I felt bad for her and all that, but I never saw myself in it.

Hannah says it's because I wasn't ready to see it, but if my grandma hadn't told my mom about it, I might still be doing it."

"But what if you started fainting like Hope did and stuff like that? That would've made you stop, wouldn't it?" Prudy shivered. "It's terrifying to think that you could *die* from it."

Then it was my turn to take a deep breath and sit up taller. "You know what I want to do? I want to see if Ms. Winters could start a group at school where kids could meet and talk about this stuff. Lots of kids our age, especially girls, think about this stuff a lot. And it can start even younger than we are. Hannah said that like 80% of girls dislike their bodies because of what they see online and in ads and stuff. Another thing is that people of all sizes can develop an eating disorder, so how many people get missed or think they're fine because they're not super skinny? It's really sad."

"I'll say!" said Tabinda. "That's a great idea, but even if Ms. Winters doesn't start a group, you know you can talk to us, right? Because I want you to stay well and keep eating."

"Definitely!" added Prudy. "We've got you, Leah!"

It felt good to tell them everything, and I feel like we're better friends because of it. I never would've felt safe sharing any of it with April or Nora. There might be hope for Nora since she's getting help, but her loyalty to April still scares me.

Winter break is over and we go back to school today. Johnny and Collin will be back after being suspended, but who knows about Mr. Kendall? I have so many questions about what it might be like and so do Prudy and Tabinda. They both say they aren't worried, but I think they are. We couldn't tell if other kids thought we were heroes for telling or if they'll be angry and start bullying us again. We don't even know if they suspect it was us who spoke up. There's no way to know for sure until we get there—that's why my stomach is hurting today.

"Good morning, sunshine!" Mom says in a sing-song voice as I walk into the kitchen for breakfast.

I give her a hug and slide into the breakfast nook.

These days Mom's been making sure I eat a good breakfast each morning, *and* she's been making my lunches. Her boss let adjust her hours a little so she doesn't need to leave home so early in the morning. Clara likes it because she can sleep in a little bit. This morning, we're having French toast, fresh fruit and Greek yogurt. One really nice thing about this new routine is that Mom sits down and eats breakfast *with* us. I've never really seen her eat breakfast before, except when we go to a restaurant. She told Hannah that she ate it before we got up, but I'm not sure I believe her. Hannah told her that she needs to set a good example for both Clara and me by eating *with* us. She also packs herself a lunch, usually the same thing she makes for Clara and me, unless we get school lunch. That's a new thing for her as well. At first, I resisted eating the amounts she served me. More than once, I stormed out of the kitchen and stomped up to my room, sobbing and shouting about how mean she was being to me. Mom was patient, though. She waited out the tantrum and then sat with me while I ate whatever meal it was. I still wasn't happy about it, but it helps me feel safe knowing that Mom won't back down. I'm figuring out where my stubborn streak comes from, that's for sure!

On Christmas, I overheard Kathy saying that Mom's going to gain weight along with me now that she's eating more. I heard Momo tell Kathy in no uncertain terms that she needs to stop saying things like that because that won't help me get better and that it wouldn't hurt Mom *or* Kathy to gain a few pounds. Of course, for all I know, Mom might throw her lunch away every day at work, but I don't think she's doing that. She's a stickler for not wasting food, so I'm pretty sure she's eating it. The other reason I think she's eating it is because she doesn't come home from work so *hangry* anymore. She just seems to be in a better mood in general. Who knows? Maybe eating regularly is making all of us feel better. All of us except Clara, that is, because she never stopped eating like a normal person. I'm going to make sure she never goes through anything like I have. Just like Mom was told to set a good example for me, I'm determined to set a good example for Clara. I *never* want my little sister to have an eating disorder.

I climb up the steps of the bus, not knowing if I should look at anyone or not. Johnny's stop is before mine, so he's always on the bus first. Will he be here today? In my dreams he's banned from the bus forever, but dreams don't always come true.

No sooner have I cleared the top step, when I see Johnny in the first seat, kiddie-corner from Fred. He now has an assigned seat which is what happens to kids who misbehave on the bus. I bet he's really mad about that; I know I would be.

"Good morning, young lady!" Fred's in his usual jolly mood.

"Hi, Fred!" I say, smiling.

I make my way down the aisle to my usual seat. Johnny didn't really look at me, but he didn't sneer at me or anything either, so that's encouraging. I sit down in my seat, eager for Tabinda to get on. When she sees Johnny sitting right up front, I catch her eye and she gives me a curious look after she greets Fred. Johnny also doesn't look at her as she walks past him.

"I see someone's sitting in the time-out seat," she whispers as she plops down beside me. "That's a relief, huh?"

"I haven't decided yet, although it should be a nicer bus ride."

She glances toward the back of the bus and then says, "Things seem pretty calm back there too."

I have to agree. The back half of the bus is unusually subdued, especially after having ten days off. Normally, everyone is really excited to see each other, and it gets fairly noisy. Not so much today. It makes me wonder just how big of an influence Johnny has had on everyone.

The bus slows to a stop, and Prudy climbs up the steps.

"Hey Fred!" she says.

"Hi, Prudy! How was your break?"

"It was great! How was yours?"

"Excellent! Thanks for asking!"

Fred continues to welcome kids as Prudy walks toward us. I can tell she's bursting to comment on Johnny's new seat assignment. At the next stop, we all look up to see Collin saunter onto the bus and sit down in the seat across the aisle from Johnny—the seat right behind Fred.

"Yikes!" Prudy whispers to us, her eyes huge. "That's epic!"

Tabinda shrugs. "I just hope it doesn't make them worse once they get *off* the bus."

She said the exact same thing I was thinking. I've been terrified to go back to school because of the weight I've gained (*restored* is the word Hannah encourages me to use).

If Johnny and Collin bullied me for my fat ass before, what will they do now? Will they even notice? I've restored some weight—I don't know how much because they don't tell me, and Mom has gotten rid of the scale—we actually smashed it with a sledge hammer! The new outfits Momo bought me still fit okay, so Mom says not to worry about it. Not worry about it? Seriously? Hannah assures me that I won't always worry about it so much which I find hard to believe, but I'm trying. I also got some new really cute clothes for Christmas in a size up from the ones Momo got me when I was super thin. I got those big enough to hide my weight loss, which is why they fit now, so that all worked out really well. Kind of like karma, is what Momo says.

When we get to school, before anyone can get off the bus, Fred gives Johnny and Collin a signal to leave, something I've never seen done before. I crane my neck to see and catch a glimpse of the principal *and* the assistant principal waiting to escort them into the building. As soon as they're gone, the bus is buzzing with the hum of kids' voices—happy voices, I might add. What a way to start the day!

As we make our way to our lockers, we pass Ms. Winters in the hall. She smiles warmly and sort of winks at us as she goes on her way.

"Did you guys see that?" Prudy whispers, her head down.

"See what?" Tabinda whispers, that tiny smirk on her lips.

"You know—that! Her!"

"Who her?" Tabinda loves to mess with Prudy, and it makes me giggle.

"You mean Ms. Winters?" I say because we're already at our lockers and Tabinda has to keep going.

"*Yes!*" Prudy hisses, clearly exasperated with the two of us.

Tabinda and I look at each other and grin. "Yes, Prudy," Tabinda says. "We did."

"Well, then why did you act so clueless?"

"Just to have a little fun," says Tabinda.

"That's just great, Tabinda! We solve the Johnny and Collin problem only to have the Tabinda and Leah problem take over."

A dark cloud passes over Tabinda's face; she appears truly devastated. "I'm so sorry, Prudy. I didn't mean to—"

Now it's Prudy who giggles. "Gotcha! I'm just having a little fun!"

For a second, I can't tell if Tabinda is upset or not. When she high-fives Prudy and laughs, I know the answer.

"Geez, you two! Way to scare a person!" I say, stuffing my bulky down coat into my locker.

"See you guys at lunch!" Tabinda says, laughing and continues down the hall to her locker.

It's nice to have friends who can kid around with each other; it's something I'm not used to at all. They haven't kidded around with me very much yet—maybe because I'm seeing a therapist—but I hope they do. With April and Nora, there was always so much drama. Momo called it *cat fights*. Mom told her not to say that because it's insulting to women, but whatever. April and Nora are insulting to women all the time, so I guess it fits.

In homeroom, Johnny is very well-behaved which is a big surprise and a relief for Prudy and me. Ms. Wilcox has changed our seats around, and I'm guessing it's no coincidence that Johnny is right up front, directly in line with her desk. The other awesome change is that Collin is no longer in our homeroom. How fantastic is that? Maybe that's what Ms. Winters was winking about. Just like before winter break when Johnny and Collin were suspended, the rest of the kids seem calmer and even nicer. Some of the ones who laughed along with the nasty comments are still being nice even though Johnny's back. A few of them are even talking to Prudy and me which is really something new and different. I'm not sure if I want to be friends with people who are so easily influenced, but I'm going to try not to hold it against them. After all, nobody's perfect; they aren't supposed to be. That's something else I'm learning from Hannah.

Hope

June 7, 1967

Dear Daisy,

I'm sorry I haven't written to you in such a long time. I can't believe that I hardly wrote to you at all during 7th grade. Well, I guess I wrote *once*, but that barely counts. That last time was a couple of days before everything went wrong. I wanted to tell you about it, but I couldn't. You see, Daisy, I wanted to write to you more than ever, but they wouldn't let me. The thing is, I don't know how much I'll be able to write because I'm sneaking to do even this.

I'm at my dad's right now—that's how I can write to you. I had hidden you in the window seat bench. They wanted me to give you to them, but I acted dumb and said I didn't know where you were. Sorry Daisy, but once or twice I even said that maybe I'd thrown you away. If they find out I still have you, and if they see what I've written in you, that will be really, really bad. I'm *not* going to let that happen.

I guess I should explain to you what's been going on, but I don't know if I want to think about it that much. I know I've caused my parents and Pete a lot of trouble and cost them lots of money. Mom was the most upset about that part, even though Dad kept telling her not to worry. It's hard to know who's telling the truth about all that. I can usually count on Pete to be honest, though. He's been really, really nice to me during this time, and that's helped a lot.

Uh-oh! I can hear someone coming. I've got to go, Daisy. Back in your spot you go!

Love,
Hope

Leah

What's Hope talking about? She hadn't written in Daisy for nine months or so. I wonder what happened? I feel kind of sick when I remember that it takes nine months to have a baby. Could Hope have had a baby? That seems really crazy! Did Neil get her pregnant? That thought makes me feel even sicker, and my heart begins to race. I'd *die* if that happened to me!

A strange feeling comes over me as I sit on the window seat, holding Daisy in my hands. All of a sudden, I feel very protective of not just Daisy, but of Hope. She'd found a really good hiding place for Daisy, and I don't want to let her down by letting anyone find it. It would be terrible if Daisy was taken away from me. It also sounds like Hope was in trouble—bad trouble.

Momo is coming over for dinner tonight and will be here pretty soon. Mom has a dinner meeting for work, so Momo is going to hang out with Clara and me, *and* we're ordering pizza for dinner. Part of me wants to show Daisy to her—or at least the last thing she wrote. Keeping Daisy a secret was very important to Hope, so I don't know if I should spoil that now. Hannah has told me that eating disorders thrive in secrecy, and I sure don't want *that* to happen. As much as I hate to admit it, because Momo told my mom about my weight loss, I owe my getting better to her. Some days I love her for it, but sometimes I hate her for it as well. Hannah says that's normal. I don't feel too guilty about it, but sometimes the guilt still creeps in. I guess that's normal too.

Since Mom isn't home, Momo uses our safety routine, calling from her cell phone when she's *at* the front door. Our rule is not to answer the door for *anyone* when we're home alone, even if they say they're the President of the United States or God. Momo also has a key for our house to use in case of an emergency, but this isn't an emergency.

"Hi, Grandma Mo!" Clara says into the phone by the breakfast nook. She loves answering the phone, mostly because it's never for her. "Leah will let you in!"

Upon hearing my cue, I scurry to the front door.

"Hi, Momo!" I open the door and give her a big, long hug.

"Hi, Loo-loo," she says, hugging me back. "How's my girl tonight?"

"I'm good! Come on in!" It's so nice to say that and really mean it.

She walks through the front porch and into the living room, hanging her huge purse on the coat tree. One thing our house doesn't have, is a front closet for coats and stuff. Mom almost didn't buy it because of that, but the breakfast nook won her over, thank goodness. Clara is already next to us, percolating with excitement. Momo picks her up off the floor in a huge hug.

"Are you ladies hungry? Should we order the pizza now or wait a while?"

We decide we're very hungry and order not one, but two pizzas. Clara is still at the plain cheese pizza stage, and Momo and I like more toppings. We order two large pizzas because leftover pizza of any kind is always good. It makes me a little worried to be so excited about eating, but I know Momo will help me handle it if I run into trouble.

Momo makes sure we've finished our homework while we wait for the pizzas to arrive. She says that *back in the day,* which is code for when she was younger, some pizza places would give you your pizza for free if it took longer than thirty minutes for it to arrive.

"Did you ever get a free one?" Clara asks, looking up from her coloring sheet.

"Nope! I didn't know anyone who did either. They'd speed and drive like crazy so they wouldn't have to give away a free pizza. I think the cost came out of the driver's pay which was really unfair. They didn't make much money to begin with."

Just then the doorbell chimes, and Momo peeks through the living room window.

"Here they are!" She hurries to the door to get the pizzas while Clara and I set the table in the nook.

There's no other smell quite as delicious as piping hot pizza! My mouth begins to water the moment the pizzas are in the house. We're using regular plates instead of paper plates because as Momo says, 'What are we, animals?' (She has so many sayings!) The pizza is so yummy I don't even think twice about having a second slice.

It's a school night, so Clara goes to bed at eight o'clock. Mom said she wasn't sure when she'd get home, so I don't know how much time Momo and I will have by ourselves. I decide that now's my chance.

"Momo," I say as we sip chamomile tea in the breakfast nook, "can I show you something? Something you promise you won't tell Mom about?"

She smiles at me as she blows on her tea to cool it down. "As usual, kiddo, I need to know what it is first. I don't make blind promises, you know."

I let out an exasperated sigh. "I know. Okay—it's in my room. Let's go up there."

She shrugs and stands up. "Okay. Can we bring our tea with us?"

"Yep!"

We climb the stairs to my room after Momo peeks in at Clara. Clara's snuggled up with her teddy bear, snoring softly. She's so adorable when she's asleep.

Making herself at home in my comfy chair, Momo sets her tea mug on a coaster on my desk. I set mine next to hers and then go to the window seat for Daisy.

"I found this in the window seat bench the day we moved in," I say, handing the diary to her. "I haven't told Mom about it."

Momo takes the diary from me, turning it over in her hands. "Can I open it?"

"Of course! That's why I'm showing it to you. I want you to look in it. I'm wondering if the girl it belonged to, was your friend. You know—the one with the eating disorder. It has a lock, but no key. It wasn't locked when I found it."

My grandma is terrible at hiding her emotions even though she thinks she's really good at it. I can tell in an instant that something is wrong. She's become really, really quiet as she stares at the diary's cover. When she looks up at me there are tears in her eyes. This isn't good because I've hardly ever seen Momo cry. She cries mostly at happy things, like military surprise homecoming videos and long lost pets finding their way home. I wait for her to say something, afraid to push her.

She opens the diary and sees the first page where Hope's name is neatly written in blue ink and tenderly runs her fingers over the letters. There's something about this whole thing that makes my heart hurt. Finally, Momo's gaze settles on me.

"I did know Hope, Loo-loo. We were very good friends."

Not knowing if Hope shared any of her struggles with Momo or her other friends, I have no idea how much of the story my grandma has heard. Even if she knows all of it, it's been over fifty years, so she might have forgotten. The thing is, by the way she's reacting, I'm afraid she remembers all of it.

"This was her dad's house." She surveys the room with a faraway look in her eyes, like she's picturing her younger self there. "We had a couple of wonderful sleepovers up here." She smiles at the memory.

"Why didn't you say something to us?"

Her eyes become even sadder. "I didn't know if I should, Loo-loo. Hope went through some hard times, especially from sixth grade on. I wanted you to have only happy feelings about this house." She pats my leg. "But you've had some hard times of your own, haven't you?"

I think about that for a second and wonder if my problems would be worse if I didn't have Daisy to read or a friend in Hope, as weird as that sounds. I also wonder if there's bad juju in this house or something, but I don't want to think about that, not now or ever.

"Yeah, but I think hers were worse. Is she the friend you thought had the eating disorder? She wrote a lot about losing weight and stuff." Right then, a light bulb goes on in my head. "Are you Reenie?!"

Momo nods. "Yes, I'm Reenie. I *hated* being called Maureen back then. And yes, Hope was that friend. That's why I was so alarmed when *you* started losing weight. It was a huge red flag to me. I didn't know if I should say anything more about Hope because I didn't want to worry you or your mom." We sit in silence for a moment and then she says, "Is there anything you want to ask me?"

"First, let me ask if you're going to tell Mom about this. I don't want her to take Daisy away from me."

"Why on earth would she do that?"

"Because she'll worry it could make me want to lose weight again. Hannah calls it a trigger."

"Do you think that will happen?"

"I don't think so. If anything, it makes me want to get better even more."

"I'll make a deal with you. If it triggers you, will you tell Hannah about it? You can tell me too, but Hannah's the expert on this subject. If you promise to do that, I'll keep your secret." She winks and smiles at me, but her eyes are still so sad.

"Thanks, Momo." I lean over and kiss her cheek. "I do have a couple of other questions, though. There are nine months between the last entry I read and the one before it. Did Hope have a baby or something? I mean, she didn't write in Daisy for *nine months*." I wrap my arms around my stomach.

"As far as I know, Hope never had a baby, but that's a logical question given the timing. She was gone for most of seventh grade, except for a few days here and there. I hadn't seen her as much the summer before seventh grade, and I never knew the reason why. It was strange. On the first day of school, I remember being shocked when I saw her. She was *so thin!* She had to pin her skirt to her blouse to make it stay up. After she jumped rope at recess her knee-highs fell down around her ankles because her legs were so skinny. There were lots of things that had changed over that summer. Anyhow, after she collapsed at school one day, her dad came to get her and we didn't see her for a very long time. My mom told me that she was in the hospital and was very sick. Jill and I worried that she had cancer or something and that's why she was so thin. That's pretty much what everyone thought."

"What made you think she had an eating disorder?"

Momo shrugs. "I didn't understand it at the time, but something clicked when you started losing weight and when you told me about April and Nora being on diets. It made me remember how Hope started not eating certain things. She also stopped wanting to hang out with Jill and me as much. She would always scold us for eating potato chips and cookies. The other thing is that if she had had cancer or some other disease, they would've said so. We would've had a bake sale or paper drive to raise money for her family. As it was, nothing was said."

"Why wouldn't they have said anything if it was an eating disorder?"

"I don't know if doctors knew very much about such things back then, but anything to do with mental health was very hush-hush. People were made to feel ashamed for needing help."

"That's so sad! I guess I still kind of feel like that, though—like if the kids at school found out I was seeing a therapist, I'd get bullied big time. I mean, I'm not exactly shouting it from the rooftops." I can feel my cheeks get hot at the thought.

"Well, Loo-loo, I bet there are lots of kids at your school who see therapists for one thing or another and if they're not, they should. It's never a bad thing to get help with mental health. We go to the doctor for physicals regularly, right? And I bet that lots of kids, mostly girls, at your school are struggling with their changing bodies. What did they say at the clinic? That half of teenage girls and a third of teenage boys do something unhealthy to control their weight?"

"Yeah, and that anorexia is the mental health disorder that people die from the most. It's really scary."

"It is, which is why I'm so happy you're getting help! Your entire life will be so much happier if you don't have to struggle with this."

"One more question, Momo, and this one is kind of freaky. Did Hope ever get…um…well…raped?" The word barely squeaked out of my mouth.

Momo is definitely shocked at this question. "Why do you ask?"

"There's something she wrote in her diary about someone maybe trying to do that to her mom, and I just wondered because the guy was her mom's boyfriend. He seemed really creepy, so I wondered if he ever tried to do anything like that to Hope. She wrote that he hugged her a lot." I can't help but cringe.

"I don't know, honey. That would have been horrible. I remember her talking about that guy. He was her mom's boss, wasn't he? No, I think her brother kept a close eye on things and so did her dad. I'd forgotten about that. Yeah, that was really upsetting for Hope. It seems like that was at the beginning of her troubles, now that I think about it. It was heartbreaking."

Just then we hear noise from downstairs and glance at each other: Mom's home. Either that or Clara's on her way up here. I pop up to put Daisy back in her hiding place, relieved to know that I'll feel less stressed out the next time I read her. I rush back to give my grandma a hug.

"Thank you, Momo. I love you."

"I love you too, Loo-loo!" She gives me a quick squeeze and a sloppy kiss on my cheek. "Tell you what—maybe we can read Daisy together sometime."

"I'd like that."

I'll sleep better tonight just knowing that I'm not alone, that my Momo will be there with me—and Hope, of course.

Maureen

Hanging out with Leah and Clara tonight (I'm not allowed to call it *babysitting* anymore) was full of surprises—some nice and some not so nice. My older grandkids are young adults now, so I must be out of practice anticipating all the curve balls teenagers can throw at you. Leah isn't officially a teenager yet, but she's well on her way. At the beginning of adolescence when the hormones start surging, everything is exaggerated, both the good and the bad. Seeing Leah so excited about ordering pizza was a really good thing. After her reluctance to eat much of anything for what felt like forever, watching her dive into that pizza was truly a joy. Later on, after Clara went to bed, the not so good part happened. It made me stop in my tracks, took my breath away and any other cliché one can think of.

Leah had tried to make me promise to keep something from her mother again, which I refused to do until I had more details. I'm sensing a pattern of this with Loo-loo, so I've decided to be very cautious. I definitely don't want to conspire against my daughter!

Being in Leah's room when Diane had first looked at the house, had brought back a tsunami of memories from when I was a girl. Memory upon memory swooped over me, which I made every effort to hide from Diane and the girls. When Hope had lived there, I'd had some very memorable times in that room. The sleepovers were the best. We only had two of them, but they were wonderful. It would've been nice if there had been a bathroom up there back then, but there wasn't, so we had to sneak downstairs for that. It always made me nervous because Pete's room was right by the bathroom. It would've been so embarrassing to run into him while I was down there! (I had a *huge* crush on Pete.)

I made my way over to what Leah calls her comfy chair and sat down, carefully setting my mug of tea on Leah's desk. My Loo-loo, being the perfectionist she is, has coasters available, so I made sure to use one. She's definitely her mother's daughter in that way. I'm not always as careful about that sort of thing at my house, but when I'm a guest, I follow the rules.

Leah immediately went to the window seat, opened it, and reached inside. She walked over to me, holding a small red book in her hands. Kneeling down next to the chair, she handed it to me. It looked exactly like Hope's diary! That was the first time my breath was taken away that evening. I hadn't seen that diary for decades. I just sat there, speechless. Seeing Hope's precise handwriting after so many years brought tears to my eyes. I reached out and gently ran my fingers over the letters, feeling as though my friend had just appeared before my eyes.

Leah was staring at me like she'd seen a ghost. I realized that she'd probably never seen me cry so easily before. At her father's funeral I had to make myself squeeze out a few tears, which was really hard to do because I don't cry in public. (Don't ask me why, I just don't.) Seeing Hope's diary, however, brought back so many feelings, it was impossible to hide them. Right then and there I decided to tell her that Hope had been my friend, that I had been in this house before, and that I'd kept quiet about it. That was tough to explain, but she seemed okay with it. We'll see if she still feels that way after she's had time to think about it.

Hope's dad bought the house right before the beginning of seventh grade. It was close to Hope's mom's house, but not too close. It would've been strange if it had been across the street or something, especially the way her mom was behaving. I always felt so sad about that because before the divorce, her mom was amazing—or so it seemed to me. Looking back now, I realize how little I knew as a kid. In those days, divorce was really frowned upon, especially by the Catholic church. It must've been hell for her parents. I can empathize, although I'm widowed, not divorced, but I digress.

By the time they moved to her dad's house, Hope had already lost a lot of weight. I never knew how much, but for a self-absorbed almost-teenage girl to notice, it must've been significant. I can't recall feeling jealous of her, but I do remember feeling more aware of my own budding breasts and changing body. I had an older sister, so I thought it was kind of exciting and couldn't wait to get my first bra, but it was different for Hope. She didn't talk about it, but it seemed as though she hated growing up.

It's so sad to realize how many women start hating their bodies when they're just girls. Just about every woman I know, at the very least, dislikes some part of her body. I often find myself thinking that way as well and have to consciously make myself practice more self-compassion. Seeing what Hope went through back then, although I didn't know what it was at the time, made body positivity a priority for me when I was raising my girls. It's hard to know how well it worked because they were still inundated by diet culture from every angle. Sadly, it's even worse today because of social media. It's such a waste of time and energy. It's become my new mission in life to do whatever I can to combat the soul-crushing effects of diet culture and weight bias, and I'm starting with my Loo-loo. I just pray it works.

Hope

June 14, 1967

Dear Daisy,

Here I am again—finally! It's been hard to find a good time to write to you because everyone is watching me like a hawk. Pete and I have been staying at Dad's because Dad doesn't trust Mom to keep a good enough eye on me. They don't think I know that, but I do. Their fights are *not* what you'd call quiet now that they're divorced. It's really frustrating. It almost feels like Mom doesn't love me anymore because she keeps saying I'm fine. She's pretty much said that the whole time, even at the worst of it. I know that Dad thinks it's because she'd rather spend time with Neil, and I have to agree. Even though I think Neil is super creepy, in some ways I'd rather live at Mom's *because* she ignores me. All this attention is getting on my nerves! I also get the feeling that Mom is kinda scared of Neil, which makes me feel even more out of control. That is *not* good for me, according to the doctors I saw when I was in the hospital. (You didn't know about that, did you?)

Yeah, I was in the hospital because I got too thin. I thought it was so ridiculous and mean of them to do that because I was just fine, just like Mom says. So I'd lost some weight? So what? I guess I shouldn't have jumped rope at recess every day. That, and the tiny lunch I had (according to the doctors) made me weak and made me faint. Long story short, they put me in the hospital and gave me medicine that made me really tired. They made me stay in bed all day long and forced me drink these really nasty milkshakes. They also gave me some other medicine that made me all light-headed and shaky a little while before the milkshakes. One of the nurses said it was supposed to make me hungrier or something. All it did was make me sweaty and feel icky. The milkshakes tasted awful, so giving me that medicine didn't work very well. Maybe if they'd given me something worth eating it would've worked better, but who am I kidding? I'm not dumb, Daisy. I know the reason I had to go to the hospital was because I wasn't eating enough in the first place, so if I'm being honest, there's not many things I'd want to eat anyway. I just can't eat much of anything without feeling sick even if I *want* to eat it, which I don't. It's weird.

After a month in the hospital I gained enough weight to be able to go home, but *just* enough. If I lost *any* of it, I'd have to go back into the hospital again which I ended up doing because I lost two and a half pounds. How did I know that? Well, one of my parents has to weigh me every day. It's a major pain. After my dad caught me putting stuff in my pockets so I'd weigh more, I now have to be weighed wearing a nightgown that has no pockets. It's so annoying! I'm not even supposed to drink water or anything ahead of time—and it's at the same time every day—another reason they watch me so closely. Mom thinks all this monitoring is as dumb as I do, which is why I'm living with Dad. He's really serious about it. He keeps telling me it's because he loves me, but I don't know. I think he's being mean.

After a couple of stays in one hospital, I was brought to another type of hospital—a *mental* hospital. (It was actually just one floor of a different hospital, not the whole hospital.) Apparently, they have more doctors trained to take care of people like me at that place. They still tried to get me to eat and when I didn't or couldn't, they put a tube in my nose that went down my throat and into my stomach and fed me that way. Ewww! I *hated* that thing! It felt really weird and because I knew it was making me gain weight, I hated it even more. Once I pulled it out, which felt horrible, and they threatened to tie my arms down if I ever did it again. They told me that if I didn't gain weight, I could die. Yeah, right. They're just trying to scare me. But honestly, Daisy? Some days I'd rather die than gain weight. I mean, what if I gain weight and never stop? I might get fat and I'm *terrified* of that happening. *Terrified.*

At the new hospital, I didn't get to lie around in bed all the time. Even if I was tired they made me get up and go to meetings with other patients like me. We also did some other stuff like write down our feelings, kinda like I do with you. I felt kinda guilty writing about that stuff in another diary, Daisy. The problem was that they actually read what I wrote! The doctor I saw by myself is the one who read it. He was nice enough, but really—how much can a middle-aged man understand about a girl not wanting to be fat? I'm pretty sure *he's* never felt that way. No one knows this but you, Daisy—I never wrote my real feelings in that thing. I wrote what I knew they wanted to hear so I could get out faster. It sort of worked, I think. I got out faster and have even convinced everyone that I'm better! Maybe when I grow up I should be an actress because I'm really, really good at pretending.

Love,
Hope

Leah

"Yikes!" I lean back in my comfy chair. "That was a lot!"

Momo's arm is around me, and I'm grateful for that. Since we decided we'd read the next part of Daisy together, I've been both looking forward to it and dreading it. It's been tricky to get the time to read it without letting Mom in on the secret. I still feel sort of guilty about hiding it from her.

"It worked out well that Clara and your mom have Daisy Scouts tonight," Momo says, her voice sounding kind of funny. "Kind of ironic, isn't it? We're *reading* Daisy while they're *at* Daisies."

I look over at her and see that she has tears in her eyes.

"I had no idea that Hope had been suffering so," she says, wiping away an escaped tear with her pinky. "I wasn't a very good friend to not notice."

I sit with that thought for a minute. I hate to see Momo so sad.

"But you didn't know. Nobody knew that much back then, Momo. She never told you anything, did she?"

"No, she didn't. Jill and I saw she was getting thinner and thinner, but when we asked her about it she got angry, so we stopped asking. We also stopped trying very hard because she withdrew so much. I've always felt bad about that, but had sort of forgotten about it until *you* started losing weight."

"Well, you said something about me to Mom and me, so that's good, right?" I'm desperate to make her feel better.

Momo nods and smiles. "Yes, I did, Loo-loo. Knowing Hope helped me think of it. I just had no idea that the treatment was so extreme back then. Maybe that's a good thing because I might've been afraid to say anything about you. Your treatment hasn't been like that, has it?"

"No, it's been really good! Hannah is amazing. She really gets it. And remember, Momo, they said I'm in the *early* stages of anorexia. We're trying to keep it from getting worse by catching it early. I don't think they did that back when you were my age." I surprise myself with how smart I sound, and I like it.

Momo glances at her watch. "It looks like we have about an hour before your mom and Clara get home. Should we read another entry or is one enough for tonight?"

"I think I can handle another one, if you can."

She gives me a long hug and kisses my cheek. "Okay then. Let's read."

Hope

July 1, 1967

Dear Daisy,

I'm so excited! Last night my dad told me that if I gain at least two pounds by August 3rd, I can go to the Monkees concert! I love, love, LOVE the Monkees—especially Davy Jones! I can't believe Dad got tickets for it! It's on August 4th at the St. Paul Auditorium. He got three tickets so that I can invite Reenie and Jill, but he said I shouldn't tell them until I've actually earned the reward. That's so unfair! I threw a fit when he said that part, but he assured me that he's already checked with their parents. That made me even madder! I don't want the world knowing about my problems!

"Don't worry, peanut, I didn't say *why* you're earning a reward, and their parents won't tell them ahead of time in case it doesn't work out," Dad said as he tried to calm me down. "Not that I think it won't. I have the utmost confidence in you."

My stomach started to hurt when he said that because with the way things have been going, I don't have much confidence about gaining any weight. It's like this urge to not eat has taken control and no matter what I do, it's stronger than I am. After being in the hospital three times, I don't know what else to do. With all the talking and groups and tube feeding and everything, I still have a really hard time eating anything. It's even gotten hard to swallow, and that's a *really* scary feeling.

I know my dad's just trying to think of ways to get me to eat and gain weight, and I love him for it, but I'm so afraid I'm going to fail. I feel so ashamed of myself, Daisy. I know I'm costing my parents a *lot* of money—wasting their money. The way they look at me when they don't think I'm watching makes me really sad. They don't understand why I'm doing this to myself but they don't get it; *I'm* not doing it—it's the monster inside of me that's doing it, and I don't know how to make it stop.

So I'm going to try my best to eat everything they want me to and more. I won't make myself throw up either. I'll keep thinking about seeing the Monkees and how wonderful that will be. I've never been to a concert before and neither have Reenie or Jill. It's going to be so cool!

Love,
Hope

August 4, 1967

Dear Daisy,

Today is the official weigh-in day before the concert. I'm *so* nervous! I just wanted to tell you that before I get weighed instead of after. Of course I'll tell you how it turns out either way. How could I not do that?

I'm at Dad's house, which is where Pete and I have been for the past week. We were at Mom's for most of July because Dad had to go out of town for work a bunch of times, so the whole eating and weighing thing was less strict than it is when Dad's in charge. I really have tried my best, Daisy. It was harder at Mom's because she doesn't cook as much as she used to, meaning that Pete and I did most of the cooking. That should be a good thing for someone trying to gain weight because we mostly made spaghetti and Rice-a-Roni and hot dogs, but that stupid voice in my head kept screaming at me when I tried to eat—and it wasn't telling me *to* eat. It was telling me just the opposite, so yeah —it was really hard.

Dad said I didn't have to do the weigh-ins for the whole time because we both know that even though the goal is to gain weight, there was a good chance that if I saw that I *had* gained, I'd freak out, so I've been working without a net in that way. Dad said I should go by how my clothes fit. If that's any way to measure, I'm worried.

I also did a really dumb thing, thinking it would make me try harder: A week ago, I told Reenie and Jill about the concert.

"Oh my gosh!" screamed Reenie when I told her. "We'll get to see them in person?! Oh my gosh!" She was jumping up and down so much I thought her love beads were going to fly right off her neck.

"Are you serious?" Jill said, keeping her excitement under control until she knew it was safe. She's super cautious.

"Yes, I'm serious! Why would I joke about a thing like that?"

We were upstairs in my room at Dad's house. Reenie and Jill had ridden their bikes over and we spent the afternoon hanging out. I haven't seen them very much this year, with being in the hospital and all. It's been a weird year for sure.

"The thing is, there's a catch," I added. My heart was beating so hard I thought I might throw up.

Reenie stopped jumping and sat down on my bed, looking worried. "I knew it was too good to be true." She sounded really disappointed.

"Just wait til she tells us before you get all bummed out," said Jill, sounding more like an adult than a kid.

"Well, this is the deal—I wasn't supposed to tell you guys until the actual day of the concert, but I'm too excited to wait. I also thought that it might help to tell you sooner." They looked totally confused which made me wish I'd kept my mouth shut. "You know how I've been sick a lot this year?"

They both nodded and looked down at the floor instead of at me. It made me feel ashamed and defective. For a second, I wished I had cancer; then I wouldn't have to keep it such a secret.

"Well, my dad got the tickets as a reward for me if I do everything the doctors told me to do to get better. I've been trying really, really hard. I thought if I told you, then I'd be really motivated—not that I'm not motivated already, that is." I felt like such an idiot.

"What do you have to do? Maybe we can help," Jill said as she sat down on floor next to me.

"Yeah," said Reenie. "One question: If you don't do what you're supposed to do, does that mean none of us go to the concert?"

"Reenie!" Jill snapped.

"Well, it's a fair question, isn't it? At my house, if one of us doesn't earn the reward, nobody gets it. I just wanted to know. Sorry, Hope." Reenie's face had turned bright red.

"It's okay, Reenie," I said before Jill could scold her anymore. "I don't know. If I ask my dad, then he'd know I blabbed. Can we wait until Friday? That's when I find out for sure."

Reenie and Jill looked at each other and shrugged.

"Okay," said Reenie. "Micky Dolenz has waited for me this long—what's a few more days?"

Jill and I burst out laughing and threw pillows at Reenie. She's always got something funny to say. I just wish I felt as happy on the inside as both of my friends are on the outside.

I never did have to tell them how or why I need to earn the reward because just then Jill's mom called and said it was time for her to go home. Whew! That was a close call! Part of me wanted to tell them, Daisy, but I was so afraid they wouldn't understand. It's such a hard thing for normal people to understand. I don't even get it, so how could they? I just hope and pray that I don't end up being a disappointment to them.

"Hope!" my dad just called upstairs. "It's time!"

Well, here goes, Daisy! Time to go downstairs and get weighed. I'll know in a few minutes if I get to see the Monkees. Say a prayer for me!

Love,
Hope

Leah

The diary slips from Momo's hands onto her lap. Her hands are over her mouth and her eyes are wide with shock.

"Oh my God!" she says in a really quiet voice. "It all makes sense now."

Needless to say, I'm confused about a lot of what Hope wrote. I also want to cheer Momo up because she's so distraught.

"Who are the Monkees?"

A grins slides across Momo's face and her eyes look all dreamy.

"Oh, they were a singing group sort of like The Beatles, but that probably doesn't help much, huh?" I shake my head. "They also had a television show about these guys who were in a singing group."

"Was it a reality show like American Idol or The Voice?"

Momo chuckles. "No, honey, it was a sitcom. Sort of like art imitating life. Anyhow, Hope, Jill and I *loved* them. We each had a favorite—mine was Micky. Hope loved Davy and Jill loved Peter."

"There were just three of them?"

"No, there were four, but Mike was married, so he was off-limits. In our twelve-year-old minds we were each going to marry our favorite. How ridiculous is that?" She laughs. "We were so clueless and innocent."

"How old were they?"

"In their early twenties. We were convinced they'd wait for us. It was delusional daydreaming, but it was harmless fun. Naturally, when Hope told us that we might get to go to their concert, we were over the moon."

"Did she ever tell you what she had to do to earn the concert? I'd want to tell Prudy and Tabinda, but I also wouldn't want to disappoint them."

"No, she didn't. I think she was going to that day, but then we had to leave."

Momo stares off into the distance, lost in her memories —or at least that's what I think is happening. Right then and there, I'm so grateful to have Prudy and Tabinda as friends. They were both so kind and understanding when I told them about the eating disorder. We all talked about how we think it's really, really awful that diet culture makes us feel like there's something wrong with us just because our bodies are changing. Prudy's tall because height runs in her family. Tabinda has a rounder shape, but so do her grandma, her mom and her older sister, so she figures that's why she looks that way. She said she loves those people so why wouldn't she want to be like them? She's so lucky to feel that way and it makes me wonder why I don't. I make a mental note to ask Hannah about that.

"Yoo-hoo! We're home!" We hear Mom's announcement drift up the stairs and know that it's time to put Daisy back in her hiding place.

"Well, it's been quite a trip down Memory Lane for me tonight," Momo says as I tuck Daisy safely away. "Are you going to be okay?"

I give her a quick hug. "Yes, Momo, it makes me realize how lucky I am for so many things."

She puts both of her arms around me and squeezes me tight. "That's a good thing to realize, Loo-loo. A very good thing! Now, should we see what those two did at Daisies tonight?"

After saying goodbye to Momo, I go back up to my room fully intending to get ready for bed, but instead, am drawn back to the window seat. Reaching in, I pull Daisy out, hoping Momo won't mind if I keep reading. I know I won't be able to sleep until I know what happened next.

Hope

August 4, 1967

Dear Daisy,

These pages are probably going to be all blurred and runny because I'm bawling my head off right now. I thought I'd run out of tears, but they just keep coming. In case you don't know—why would you, you're a diary—I'm *not* going to the Monkees concert. I didn't earn my reward. I hate my life! I hate myself!

This morning, when I went downstairs to have Dad weigh me, I felt like I was going to the electric chair or something.

"Well, kiddo, this is the big day!" he said, all happy and excited. "Let's see how you did."

I stepped on the scale with my eyes shut tight. I was afraid to look. I do this every time I'm weighed now that the number is supposed to be going *up*. There's just no joy in it like there was when it was going *down*. If I've been a "good girl" and have gained something, Dad does a little happy dance as though I'm a potty-training toddler. I don't blame him; he means well. He thinks it will help me want to gain more and more. Guess what? It doesn't.

There was no happy dance, though. No big deal made. Just silence. I pried open one eye and peeked down at the scale. I was *down* three and a half pounds.

I looked at Dad, afraid to say anything, hoping he was feeling generous.

"Well, peanut, I'm sorry. No concert tonight." He looked almost as bad as I felt, if that was even possible. "It's good that Reenie and Jill won't know what they're missing."

I felt instantly queasy. "Um, Dad? They do know. I told them last week. I thought it would keep me motivated."

His expression went from disappointed to *really* disappointed mixed with angry. It was an expression I hope I never see again.

"Hope, I told you not to tell them! I shouldn't have even told you, but I thought it would help you eat more. Obviously, I was wrong!" He picked up the scale, ready to put it back in its hiding place.

Tears clogged my throat and made it ache right along with my stomach. I'm not at good anything—not a good girl, a good friend or a good daughter. The only thing I'm good at is the thing I'm *not* supposed to do. The fact that I did it even when I was trying so hard not to, is terrifying.

"But Dad, I tried! I really did! Ask Pete! I ate everything he made while we were at Mom's, even if I didn't like it! I didn't throw up at all! Not once! Please let me go to the concert! Please, Dad, please!" Tears were streaming down my face.

"Sorry, but no. We made a deal, and I want you to know that I keep my word."

"But what are you going to do with the tickets? Pete won't want to go! Please, Dad, please!" Snot was running out of my nose along with the tears.

"Stop begging, Hope. *You're* not going to that concert, but you know who should go?" He looked at me and waited for an answer.

"Reenie and Jill?" The words got stuck in my throat like thick peanut butter.

"Yes, but only because you already got them excited about it. They can invite another friend to use the extra ticket. I'm not doing this to be mean, peanut. You know that, right?" His voice sounded a little softer.

Did he really expect me to believe that? My heart was breaking into hundreds of teeny tiny pieces as it was, but then he said he'd give the tickets to my friends anyway and that they'd bring someone else? That was worse than not getting to go! It brought on a whole new crop of tears.

"Can I go to my room now?" I asked in-between sobs.

"Yes, honey, you can, but come here a second."

It was nearly impossible to make my feet move in his direction, but I did. I hated him right then. When I reached him, he put the scale down and gave me a long hug. I didn't hug him back.

"I love you so much, Hope. You'll understand when you're a parent." He kissed the top of my head, which only made me cry harder.

I ran up the stairs as fast as I could and threw myself on my bed like they do in the movies. I cried like I've never cried before—even more than when Mom and Dad told us they were getting divorced. I didn't have any control over that, but I did over this, and I failed. I proved to myself and to my dad and my friends, that I'm not good enough, even when I try my hardest.

I talked Pete into talking Dad into letting him and me go to Mom's house. She was out of town with Neil, but Pete promised he'd look after me. I didn't want to be anywhere near my dad. He took away the one thing I had looked forward to for a really, really long time. Nobody will believe how hard I tried, not even my dad. The part that makes me so mad and that's so scary is that I really DID try, Daisy. It's like my body is doing what it wants no matter what I do.

Love,
Hope

Leah

Clara's Daisy meetings have come in very handy now that Momo and I are reading Hope's dairy together. Even though I'm able to be home alone, it's nice to have Momo hang out with me. I think Clara might be getting a little jealous, but I figure we're even, since we could never afford for me to join Daisies, Brownies, or Girl Scouts. Another perk for her is that Mom is one of the troop leaders, so Clara gets more time with her than I ever did.

Clara's meeting is at six-thirty, so she and Mom leave right after dinner. It's worked out because Momo comes and eats with us and then she and I clean up the kitchen together. Momo usually brings dinner with her, and tonight it's Subway, so clean up is fast and easy.

"I brought a little surprise tonight, Loo-loo," Momo says as she hangs the dish towel on its rack. "Let me go and get it."

She comes back into the kitchen with her purse, reaching inside as she walks.

"Ta-da!" She holds up a small, red book. "My diary from 1967!"

"Are you kidding me? That's so cool! I didn't know you had a diary!" I'm relieved for the distraction. I've been stressed out for days not only about how to tell Momo I read ahead in Daisy, but about what was written. It broke my heart.

We settle into the breakfast nook side by side. "I didn't want to tell you about it before I was sure I could find it. You know how my closets are!" We both chuckle at her legendary disorganization. One time, one of the shelves in her craft closet broke because there was so much stuff on it.

"It looks just like Hope's." I trace the gold lettering on the front with my fingers.

"It was a really popular style back then. Once I saw Hope's, I pestered my mother into getting me one just like it. I did the dishes every night for a month to earn it." She nudges me with her elbow. "And we didn't have a dishwasher."

"Wow. That was a lot of work. You must've really wanted it."

"You bet I did! It was worth the dishpan hands I got. I loved this thing."

"Can I look? Or is it too private?" I suddenly feel ashamed for even asking. Of course it's private!

"Well, Loo-loo, it was private when I was twelve, but I think it's okay to share it now. I wrote a *lot* about the Monkees. I also wrote more about Hope than I remembered. I can't believe I'd forgotten so much."

"That's okay, Momo. It was a long time ago."

"Yes, with an emphasis on *long,* for sure." She flips through the pages until she finds what she's looking for. "Should we read it down here or in your room? I don't think it's a big deal if your mom and Clara see it. I can just tell them we took a stroll down Memory Lane."

"Sounds good to me!" I snuggle into her side like I always do when we read together. "But there's something I have to tell you first, Momo. I read ahead after you left last time. I just couldn't wait to see what happened. I'm sorry."

She looks at me and smiles. "That's okay, Loo-loo. I had a feeling you might do that. How did it make you feel?"

"Terrible! I cried myself to sleep that night and vowed I'd never read ahead again. It would've been so much better to read it with you."

"No worries, kiddo. I'm sorry it upset you so much." She kisses my cheek. "Oh, and just so you know, I also named my diary after a flower."

August 4, 1967

Dear Buttercup,

Hope's dad just called with the bad news. Hope didn't earn her reward so she can't go to the concert. OH NO! At first, I was really upset because I was SO excited about it. I didn't even wait for my mom to explain anything—I just ran to my room and slammed the door. Luckily, my mom was feeling sorry for me so I didn't get punished for the door slam. (As you know, Buttercup, I do that a lot...) Once I stopped crying, she told me that Mr. McMillan said that he's giving us the tickets anyway so that Jill and I can still go! We can even bring another friend along, although I don't know who that would be, especially on such short notice. I mean, the concert's TONIGHT!

"But Mom," I said, "what was it Hope had to do to earn the reward? She never got a chance to tell us."

"Well, Reenie," she said, rubbing my back, "she had to gain at least two pounds over the past month and she didn't. She *lost* weight instead. Such problems to have, huh? Lord knows I'd have absolutely no trouble gaining a couple of pounds. I just *look* at food and gain weight!" Then she patted my bottom lightly. "It looks like you won't have that problem either."

I get so tired of hearing my mom complain about her body. She's never, *ever* happy with herself, and is always trying new diets. It's so annoying! Now she's going to start in on me? I don't think so!

"I just don't know what's wrong with that girl," my mom said. "She just needs to eat more! Why is that so hard? She's just doing it to get attention."

I felt like screaming at her to stop talking about my friend like that, but I knew that might keep me from going to the concert, so I bit my tongue.

"All I know, is that she's gotten really sad and really thin, and I feel really bad for her. She can't help it if her family fell apart. She was fine before all that happened."

"Well, she's putting her parents through *h-e-double-hockey-sticks*, that's for sure."

I don't know exactly what's wrong with Hope, but trying to tell my mom to be kind to her is pointless. My dad always says that I get my stubborn streak from my mom. That might be true, but right now I'm vowing to never be so judgmental and mean to people, especially behind their backs. You can hold me to that, Buttercup!

Luv ya,
Reenie

"Who else did you bring with you since Hope couldn't go?"

"Nobody. Jill and I decided to keep that seat empty for Hope, as if she was there. Mr. McMillan didn't care, and our parents were okay with it. Since the tickets were Hope's to begin with, it felt wrong to bring another friend."

"That was nice of you. I bet Hope appreciated it." I feel all warm and gooey inside hearing about my grandma's kindness when she was my age.

A strange look falls over Momo's face. "Tell you what. Before we read any further, let me show you exactly who these Monkees were." She pulls her phone out of her purse.

"Oh, I already did that, Momo."

"What did you think?" Momo raises one of her eyebrows as she waits for my answer.

I thought they all looked kind of dorky in an old-fashioned way, but assure Momo that they were definitely cool, and that I could see why she liked Micky so much. What else can I say?

"Okay, then let's keep reading."

August 4, 1967

Dear Buttercup,

The concert was SO GROOVY! I still can't believe we actually saw the Monkees IN PERSON! It was the best day of my life!

First of all, our parents actually let Jill and me ride the city bus to the concert! Jill's dad drove us to the bus stop on Bloomington Ave. and Lake St. so we just had to take one bus. Otherwise, we would've had to transfer buses and that seemed like a lot. Anyhow, lots of other girls had the same idea because there were TONS of girls all going to the concert like we were. TONS! After the concert we took the same bus route back, and my dad picked us up.

When we got to the St. Paul Auditorium, it was just crazy! Teenage girls were EVERYWHERE! Neither of us had ever been in such a big crowd before. An usher helped us find our seats which were right up near the front. Mr. McMillan must've bought the best seats in the house! The seats were on one side of a stage that jutted out from the main stage where the curtain was. We were sitting there getting more and more excited, when we heard some girl scream, 'There they are!' She was pointing to the stage where the curtain had moved a tiny little bit. We didn't see anything besides the curtain move, but the whole place erupted in screams. If everyone got that excited when a *curtain* moved, what would happen when the actual Monkees came out onto the stage?!

We found out about fifteen minutes later when they burst onto the stage RIGHT IN FRONT OF US!!!!!!!!! They were singing and playing the theme song from their TV show and everyone went WILD! I never thought I'd scream like the girls in the audience did when The Beatles were on The Ed Sullivan Show, but Jill and I screamed our heads off along with the rest of the crowd. Whenever one of the guys looked in our direction, we went especially crazy! Buttercup, I felt like Micky was looking RIGHT AT ME—it was so groovy! I thought Jill was going to faint when Peter smiled at us. (That's not exaggerating because lots of girls actually DID faint!)

They did THREE encores! I never even knew what that was until tonight. I guess at the end of a show or a concert the audience gives the performers a standing ovation in order to get them to do another song (that's what my dad told us on the way home) but the whole audience was standing and screaming the whole time, so they must just plan on doing the extra songs. Either way, it was SO GROOVY! When Davy looked at us, I felt sad that Hope wasn't there to see it. She would've LOVED that!

Jill and I were pretty quiet on the bus on the way home; *everybody* was. I think it was because we were all so hoarse from having spent the last two hours screaming at the tops of our lungs. It was strange to have a bus packed full of teenage girls—we ended up having to stand in the aisle— and have it be so quiet. My dad said that alone would've made it worth it for him to go to the concert with us. Hardy-har-har, Dad!

Jill and I bought a souvenir program for Hope at the concert. We each have one too, so it will be fun to sit and look at them together. Jill thinks it might make her too sad, so we'll have to see. I sure don't want to make her feel any worse than she already does.

Well, Buttercup, I'm going to sleep now and dream wonderful dreams about Micky and me. Hopefully my ears stop ringing soon!

Luv ya!
Reenie

I lean back in the nook with a whole new image of my grandma. It's hard to picture her screaming her head off like that. She gets excited at our school events, but she *never* screams.

"*Groovy?* And all that screaming? You were wild back then, Momo!"

She blushes and shrugs. "It's amazing how powerful peer pressure is, isn't it? Jill and I just got caught up in the frenzy. It was one of the best and one of the worst events of my life. We had a great time, but it was overshadowed by the fact that Hope wasn't there with us."

"Yeah, that must've been hard," I say, trying to be sensitive and mature about it. "Did you give Hope the program?"

Momo's eyes fill with tears. She wipes them away before she says, "No, Loo-loo, we didn't."

She doesn't say anything more, but just sits there, staring down at Buttercup.

"You didn't want her to feel bad?"

Momo sniffles and then turns to face me. "No, Loo-loo —we never saw her again."

My heart begins to pound like crazy. "Why not? Did she go back into the hospital?"

Before Momo can answer, I slide out of the nook and run upstairs. I can hear her footsteps behind me as I race to the window seat. Flipping open the lid so hard that the cushion flies onto the floor, I yank Daisy from her hiding place. Frantic, I find the last page of the last entry I read, throw the diary on the floor and burst into tears. The rest of the pages are blank.

"Oh, honey, I'm so sorry." She walks over to me and wraps her arms around me. "Let's go sit in your comfy chair, okay?" She leads me over to it, and we sink down into it together. "We didn't see her again because—well, because Hope passed away."

I pull away from her, shocked. "No! When? Not the night of the concert!"

The expression on my grandma's face tells me she's regretting this whole diary thing, but it's too late now. I'm going to ask her every question I can think of, and I'm going to make her answer them.

"Did you *forget* about that? If Prudy or Tabinda died I'd never forget it, *ever!* How could you forget that?"

Momo slumps back in the chair. It seems like all the bones in her body have turned to jelly. She grabs a tissue from the square box on my desk and blows her nose. When she looks at me it's weird because it's like I can see her twelve-year-old self right there in her grandma-body.

"I've never forgotten Hope, Loo-loo. I admit I buried that memory way down in my heart, but I've never forgotten any of it. It's resurfaced over the years sometimes, but not very often because it's too painful. When you started talking about dieting and began to shrink before my eyes, my memories of Hope grew in a big way." She puts her hands on either side of my face, wiping away my tears with her thumbs. "Like I told you, when the three of you moved in here, of course I remembered being here with Hope. If I'd known you'd been reading her diary, I would've told you about her sooner. I didn't want to borrow trouble unless it was absolutely necessary." She leans in and kisses my forehead. "Do you forgive me, Loo-loo?"

"Yes," I say, even though there's nothing to forgive. "Can I ask you another question?"

Momo nods, her mouth sagging in a sad line.

"How did she die?" I'm kind of scared to hear the answer, but I have to know. There's a girl in my therapy group that hasn't been there the last couple of times and this makes me really afraid for her.

A long sigh escapes from Momo, and she takes both of my hands in hers. "I don't have all the information because the adults wanted to shield us kids from it. All I know is what I overheard at her funeral. Hope had anorexia *and* bulimia nervosa. As she wrote in her diary, she went to the hospital several times. The last time was the night of the concert. They rushed her to the emergency room because she wouldn't wake up. I guess her heart just stopped." She wipes away more tears. "It was the first funeral I'd ever been to and by far the saddest. It was such a terrible loss of such a remarkable life."

The first and only funeral I've ever been to, was my dad's. It's weird because I don't remember a lot about it, except for a bunch of adults, some I knew and most I didn't, coming up to Clara and me and giving us hugs and sadly shaking their heads. We'd never been hugged so much in our lives, and I hated every second of it. Another thing I remember is the slideshow that was playing at the wake. There were pictures of my dad from when he was little, all the way to when Clara was a baby. I liked it because it only showed the good times. There was one picture of him and me when I was about five or so at Minnehaha Falls. Just the two of us had gone there for a breakfast picnic right before Clara was born. It's one of my best and favorite memories of my dad. He had asked a stranger to take our picture so that we'd always remember what a great day it had been. I didn't understand it at the time, but now I do. It's important to have pictures of the good times, especially when the bad times come.

"It must've been really sad. I can't imagine going to a funeral for one of my friends or a kid in my class—even someone like Johnny Morgan."

She nods. "Yes, it was. It didn't help that Hope's mom was already so troubled. You've read about some of that in the diary, but it was much worse than Hope realized. Again, the adults tried to protect the kids. Given the circumstances it was probably a good idea, but Hope really struggled during the times she and Pete lived with their mom. You might think it's a pain to have a mom as vigilant as yours, Loo-loo, but believe me, it's a blessing. As you know, she and Pete were alone at their mom's the night of the concert. Pete found Hope unresponsive and called for the ambulance. Their mom couldn't get home until the next day, after Hope had died."

"That's awful! Poor Pete!" I feel like I sort of know Pete, even though I obviously don't. "Was he okay after that?"

"I can't really say. I do know that he lived with his dad full-time from that point on. Hope's mom moved away; nobody heard from her again."

"Wow. It's all so sad. And to think that it might've been prevented makes it even sadder." Now it's my turn to reach for a tissue.

Momo dabs at her tears. "We need to remember that they didn't know as much about eating disorders and how to treat them back then. It was easy to blame her parents, especially her mom, but that's what they did back then. You have a perfectly wonderful mother who is always here for you, and you developed an eating disorder, so who knows how or why they start?"

"Yeah, I guess."

We sit there for a few minutes, lost in our thoughts. I'm guessing that Momo is thinking about her friendship with Hope, wishing she could've helped her more. I wish she could have too.

Maureen

How did I not seeing this coming? How did I spend time reading Hope's diary with Leah and not realize that I'd have to tell her how it all ended? Leah had demanded to know how I could forget such a tragedy, and she was right to ask. I'm sure it seemed that way to her. I mean, who in their right mind leads their granddaughter down such a tragic path? The thing is, Leah had already been reading Hope's diary, and I knew she'd have questions when it ended so abruptly. I just didn't expect it to be so emotional for both of us.

Sharing my diary with Leah was only supposed to be about the Monkees concert; that was my plan. Of course, my naturally inquisitive granddaughter asked perfectly logical questions; that's the part I can't believe surprised me. It's as though we skipped ahead to the end of a book, although we didn't—not really. The last entry in Daisy was the one Hope wrote about her not being able to go to the concert. That was the end of her story; she died on what was supposed to be the best night of her short life.

I brought my diary home with me because I didn't want Leah to read the rest of it by herself. In fact, she told me to take it home. She knew she'd wallow in it if it was there. Before I left, however, I told Diane all about Hope. Leah didn't want me to, but I wasn't going to let her be alone with all the big feelings she was having.

"Leah's been reading this diary since we moved in?" To say that my daughter was alarmed is an understatement. I knew she'd react like that. "Oh my God! Did that cause her eating disorder?"

I led Diane to the breakfast nook and made us each a mug of chamomile tea. I didn't want her rushing up to talk to Leah in her panicked state of mind. The last thing Leah needed was to absorb all of her mother's anxiety.

"Listen to me, Di. Leah's upset now, but she's going to be okay. She thought of the diary as a new friend. She didn't tell you about it because she thought you'd make her stop reading it."

"Why did she think that?" Diane's fingers were laced around her mug.

"Because diaries are private and all that. It wasn't locked, so it's not like she broke into it. Look—I don't think it's a big deal. I know you feel slighted because she didn't tell you, but that's not the issue. I actually think it helped her with her own problems. She didn't feel so alone."

"But she's been reading it with you behind my back." She eyed me with disdain and then shifted her gaze to the table.

"Honey, I know you don't want to hear this, but sometimes kids don't want to tell their parents every little thing—even if they have a mom as wonderful as you are. I seem to remember being kept out of the loop about certain aspects of your life when you were Leah's age." I gave her a quick little wink.

"I know, Mama. It's just upsetting to know that she's keeping things from me."

"She's trying to protect you, Diane. She knows how much you care and how much you worry. At least she told *someone* about it, right? She said she's told Hannah about it."

"Well, *that's* good to know." Diane sniffled and took a small sip of tea. She was trying so hard to keep her tears inside.

"You're a good mom, Di. You're getting Leah the help she needs and that's what's important. Not all parents do that. It's hard to admit your kid is struggling with anything. You've stepped up for her at school with the bullying and have been her safe place to land, *always*. Give yourself a break here, okay? She loves you so much. You know that, right?" I reached across the table and grasped her hands.

"Yeah, I guess so."

"And I have *both* your backs, a*lways*. You know that too, right?"

She nodded, unable to speak because she had started to cry. Oh, my dear, sweet Diane—she feels things so deeply.

"Let Leah sit with this for a little while. Maybe check on her after I leave. I'm bringing my diary home so she won't have that to keep her up tonight."

"Okay, Mama. Thanks for being there for her—and for all of us. If it weren't for you, I don't know if I would've picked up on her eating disorder until much later."

"And I wouldn't have picked up on it if I weren't for Hope. I knew it made an impression on me, but I sort of put it on the back burner for a long time. I think it's good that Leah knows what happened to Hope. If Hope's death can save her from getting deeper into this thing, then Hope didn't die in vain. She saved our Loo-loo."

After I got home that evening, I decided to postpone the laundry that was almost begging to be done and curled up in my reading chair with Buttercup. Call me a glutton for punishment, but ever since my conversation with Leah about Hope's funeral, I felt compelled to revisit that day. It had been the first funeral I'd been to and it made an indelible mark on my heart. My mother hadn't wanted me to go, but our class was going to sing, so I sort of had to.

Those were the days before they had grief counselors come to school to help kids cope with the loss of a classmate; we just had to muddle through on our own. Yes, Hope died during summer vacation, but still. I always wondered why they could manage to organize our class to sing but they couldn't offer us any help with our grief. I took a deep breath and began to read.

August 8, 1967

Dear Buttercup,

Well, it was Hope's funeral today and it was the saddest thing ever. Our class, or the kids they could get to come since it's still summer vacation, sang a few songs during Mass. They were songs that Mrs. Olsen had taught us during the school year. I'd like to think that they were some of Hope's favorites, but the truth is, she missed so much school, I don't think she knew any of them.

Hope didn't have a ton of friends—I think Jill and I were the only ones—but boy, did some of those girls act like they were her best friends. The popular girls were the worst, crying on the popular boys' shoulders. Jill and I *were* her best friends and we hardly cried at all, maybe because we were all cried out. It just made me mad how kids that never gave a hoot about Hope were acting so sad. I *did* cry when I watched her family walk in. They had to make their way down the center aisle of the church after everyone else was seated. Hope would've *hated* that. She never liked being the center of attention. I felt the saddest for Pete. He looked like he wanted to die too. And you should've seen the girls that were "comforting" him! Good grief! Oops—

I shouldn't have said that. There's nothing good about grief
—nothing at all.

The absolute worst part of the whole thing was Father
Fremont's sermon. He's the grouchy old pastor that always
reads our report cards out loud in front of the whole class
while we stand there, humiliated. He's really, really mean
and we're all afraid of him. If he ever catches you stepping
on the grass around the playground, you're in BIG trouble.
He got up there and talked about how much money
everyone should give to the church and how Hope's family
was behind in their giving and that maybe this was God's
way of teaching them a lesson. He actually said that! I
couldn't believe it! When he said it, I could hear everyone
in the church sort of gasp. I guess nobody could believe it.

He didn't say one kind word about Hope and how nice
she was, how she'd always help anyone even if they weren't
nice back to her. He didn't say anything about how funny
she was or how she was the new Jump Rope Queen. He
didn't say that blue was her favorite color or that cotton
candy and pizza were her favorite foods. He also didn't say
that she hated tomato, cabbage and hamburger hotdish or
that she loved Davy Jones. He didn't know her at all. Jill
and I would've been happy to tell him about her but it's like
it didn't even matter. That *she* didn't even matter. When he
did talk about Hope, aside from the fact that her parents
didn't give enough money to the church, he hinted that she
had been selfish and vain and that she died because she
only cared about her looks. I thought I was going to go up
there and punch him when he said that! He topped it all
off by reminding her parents that since they're divorced,
they couldn't receive communion at their own daughter's
funeral and that went for any other 'people who don't
follow God's teachings.' What a jerk! I might go to hell

because I said that, but I don't care. Hope and her family deserved better than that.

I have to hand it to my parents—neither of them went to communion and neither did Jill's parents. Since they didn't, neither did Jill or I. My parents are usually pretty strict about everything to do with church, but I think that put them over the edge. My mom didn't understand Hope's illness like a lot of people didn't, but she loved Hope because she was my friend. She liked her because Hope was a good person. She told me after the funeral how angry the sermon made her and that she was going to give Father Fremont's a *big* piece of her mind. I've never seen her so mad!

It was such a sad day in the first place and that mean old priest had to go and make it worse. I'm pretty sure nobody was even thinking about Hope anymore—at least not how they should've been. Everyone was upset by the sermon, Buttercup. I figured that they were upset like my parents were, but on the way out, I heard some people whispering about how awful it was that Hope's family was getting a "free ride" and how they still hadn't paid all of Hope's tuition for the past school year. Can you believe it? I could definitely go to hell for this, but I wanted to kill them, or at least have one of their kids get sick and die. I better go to confession ASAP for thinking such terrible things. Maybe Hope will put in a good word for me since she's in heaven now. (Yes, heaven, not purgatory like they teach us in religion class. Hope was perfect, so I know she bypassed purgatory and went straight to heaven!)

Well, Buttercup, I better sign off. I don't want to ruin you with all the wet splotches from crying. I guess I'm not cried out after all.

Luv ya,
Reenie

I laid my head back on the chair, wishing I had a box of tissue on the end table. Evidently, I'm *still* not all cried out. I must've locked the details of Hope's funeral far, far down in the recesses of my mind and heart where traumatic memories reside, buried underneath all the other thoughts competing for attention.

After taking this one out and dusting it off, other memories snuck out, like the one where my parents decided to pull me out of the Catholic school. So did Jill's parents. We were going into eighth grade and would've been the oldest kids in the school, but instead, we were going to go to the public school and be the middle grade, since the public junior high went from 7th-9th grade. At the time they decided, we were all still wound up about how Hope's funeral had been ruined, and Jill and I were on totally on board. When the first day of school rolled around, however, we were both terrified. A bunch of new clothes for school sort of helped, (no more uniforms!), but it was still scary. Come to think of it, I'll never know if the decision was made *by* my parents or *for* my parents by the Parish Council, but it turned out to be a good thing. There's no way I could've handled being in that school where I'd spent so many years with Hope, knowing she was never coming back.

A fresh start in a new school helped more than I ever could have known. We were the new kids, but back then it seems like kids were nicer than they are now. Either that or we were just lucky. Maybe it was a little easier because we had each other; not like it was for Leah, starting at a new school all by herself. Thank goodness for Prudy and

Tabinda. My constant prayer is that they'll keep Leah from following in Hope's footsteps. I wish I'd been there for Hope when she needed a friend the most. Instead, I was at the concert she wasn't allowed to attend, having the time of my life without her.

Leah

I don't know what to do after Momo leaves. I know she told my mom about Daisy and Hope and all that, and that makes me a little nervous. Since there's no more entries in Daisy, I guess it's not a big deal if she takes Daisy away from me, but I'd still miss her. Now that I know what happened to Hope, however, it makes me want to go back and read Daisy all over again.

I pick up the faded red diary and flip open the latch like I've done so many times before. Hope's small, perfect handwriting makes my heart hurt as I tenderly touch the words. She must've felt so alone while she wrote every single one of them. From her parents getting divorced, to her mom's awful boyfriend, how did she get through it all? Momo and Jill were her best friends, but they couldn't help her very much because she didn't tell them anything. Everything might have turned out so differently if she'd felt less alone, if she'd just told her friends what was going on.

I feel goosebumps ripple along my arms when it occurs to me that if Hope *had* told Momo and Jill or *anyone* about what was going on in her head, she might have never written about any of it in her diary. She also might not have needed her diary at all. My next thought feels really selfish, but what would've happened to me if she hadn't had Daisy? Finding Daisy on that first day in the new house was like finding a friend—the first one I had in the new house and the new neighborhood. While reading about Hope's troubles, I felt less alone with my own, even Johnny Morgan and the bullying. Her mom had problems after the divorce, but her dad turned out to be really nice. I can feel my face grow warm when I realize that while reading Daisy, I pretended that her dad had been mine—or at least that my dad had been more like him. Guilt slithers through me until I remember that my dad was actually pretty wonderful —if only it could've stayed that way.

Suddenly, I feel a hand on my shoulder. For a second, it feels like it could be Hope.

"Hey, Leah-loo," Mom says, her voice barely more than a whisper.

"Hi." I reach up and pat her hand.

"How are you doing, sweetie?"

"I'm really sad." I sniffle some tears back in.

Mom sits down on the floor next to me and puts her arm around me. It helps to have her here with me; it also helps that she's not saying a word. After all, what is there to say? I cuddle closer and lay my head on her shoulder. She smells like lavender and vanilla, just like she has for as long as I can remember. It makes me feel safe and loved.

"Are you mad at me for not telling you about Hope and the diary sooner?"

She gently pushes my hair back from my forehead. "Nope, not even a little bit. I'm just glad you found a new friend when you needed one."

We sit quietly for a little while longer, listening to the sound of the wind moaning in the trees outside. I imagine Hope sitting here as she told Daisy her deepest thoughts and feelings, especially that last time. Tears sting my eyes when I remember how she said she hated herself and hated her life that day. No one should feel that way ever, but now I know that lots of people do. A tear slides down my face and hangs on my chin before it falls to my shirt.

"I hate that Hope died feeling so bad about herself and her life. She never really let her anger out and the first time she did, she ended up dying. She died hating her dad. They never got the chance to make up. How sad is that?"

Mom rubs my arm and gives it a gentle pat. "It's very sad, but we don't know for sure that they didn't make up, do we?"

"That's true. Maybe Pete helped her understand why their dad wouldn't let her go to the concert. He was really good at calming her down. Maybe she even talked to her dad before she went to sleep that night."

"Sometimes it can help to make up your own story about things," Mom says, her voice cracking a little. "There's no harm in doing that if it helps you move forward." She brushes a tear away from the corner of her eye and kisses the top of my head.

"Yeah, I guess. It's just such a waste, you know? Hope was so amazing. She was spunky and funny and really kind. It makes me wonder what she would've been like when she grew up. I mean, Momo's pretty much the same as she was back then, right?" I pause and take a shaky breath. "And then there's the scariest part of all."

"What's that, sweetie?"

"It's how Hope disappeared bit by bit throughout the diary. By the end of it there was nothing much left, not just of her body but of *her*, you know? That's what the eating disorder did. It's like her wish came true—she got smaller and smaller until she was just *gone*."

Mom hugs me closer. "It's the scariest and the most heartbreaking. I'll be forever grateful to her for keeping that from happening to you."

"Yeah, I think she saved me—her and Momo. And how cool is it that Hope and Momo were friends?"

"It's very cool—sort of like it was meant to be, huh?"

"I know, right?" Then a thought occurs to me out of nowhere. "Maybe Dad was looking out for me too. You know, keeping me safe."

Mom looks at me with tears in her eyes and smiles as she takes my face in her hands. "Maybe he was, sweetie. Maybe he was." She kisses my forehead. "That's a beautiful thought."

"I love you, Mom."

"Love you back, Leah-loo." She straightens up and says, "It's getting late. Are you going to be able to sleep okay?"

"Yeah, I think so." Even though I'm really tired, I feel too wound up to sleep just yet, but I don't tell my mom. I know she'll worry about me dwelling on all this by myself.

She walks to the top of the steps and then stops and says, "When you're ready to share her, I'd love to read Daisy. I'd like to meet Hope."

"Okay, Mom. I'd like that too."

"Sweet dreams."

Once I hear the door at the bottom of the stairs close, I grab Daisy and pad over to my desk. Turning on the lamp, I sit down at the desk, take a sheet of paper out of a notebook and begin to write:

Dear Daisy,

I was going to write IN you, but after I thought about it, it felt sort of disrespectful to you and Hope, so I'm writing on this separate sheet of paper instead.

You must have been wondering where Hope has been all this time. I want you to know that she didn't forget about you or get tired of writing in you. You were very, very important to her. I'd even say that she loved you. The reason Hope hasn't written is because she was very sick and died shortly after the last time she wrote in you.

I found you in the window seat bench the first day I moved into the house where her dad lived. From the amount of dust on you, I'm guessing nobody had touched you since Hope last hid you. You and Hope have helped me a LOT since that day, Daisy. You see, Hope had an eating disorder and so do I. It's a really weird coincidence. I'm so grateful to both of you for so many reasons, mainly because meeting Hope through you was like making a friend when I really, really needed one. Also, finding out the end to her story has made me even more determined to recover from this eating disorder so that there's a happier ending to mine. Even though Hope isn't here anymore, I'll always carry her with me, in my heart.

Thanks again,
Leah Ann Peterson

Once I'm finished writing, I fold the letter and slip it between a couple of blank pages near the back. I close the diary and set it on my desk where I'll see it every day; there's no reason to hide her anymore. Daisy will be my reminder not only *of* Hope, but to *have* hope. Her battle didn't end well but that doesn't mean I won't be able to conquer mine. As it turns out, hope is everywhere—I just have to remember to look for it.

I stand up and stretch, feeling a little lost now that I no longer have Daisy to read at night. That's when a glint of gold from the window seat catches my eye. Curious, I tiptoe over to see what it could be. I come to an abrupt halt when I see a small red book laying on the cushion. It has a shiny gold latch with two gold keys dangling from a red ribbon. The cover is gently embossed with flowers that look like roses. Kneeling next to the window seat, I just stare, not knowing if I should pick it up or let it be. Where did it come from? It wasn't there when I ran up here to get Daisy. Now that I think about it, I don't remember putting the cushion back in its place either. How did that happen? My heart pounds as I reach for the book. I'll never find out what's going on if I'm not brave enough to look at it, just like when I first found Daisy. Taking a deep breath, I pick up the book and turn it over in my hands. I push up the round button on the lock, just as I've done with Daisy so many times. What I see when I open the book makes me smile and cry at the same time. There, on the first page, is written:

This diary belongs to Leah Ann Peterson…
…with Love and Hope,
Momo

The End

Acknowledgments

I'd like to extend my sincere thanks to those who took the time to read this novel in its early stages: Chuck M., Lindsey M., Amy K-V., Joan E. (my sister), Jackie K., Joan E. (my friend), and Karen N. It's not always easy to critique the writing of a relative or friend, and I appreciate them taking the risk and for the valuable feedback they shared with me.

Heartfelt hugs to my lifelong friend Roxy M., for the inspiration her childhood home and bedroom provided for this story. Many wonderful memories were made in that house, memories I will carry with me always.

Last of all, I want to thank everyone who has supported me in my own eating disorder recovery during the past two years. While this novel is a work of fiction, I can attest that all the feelings are painfully real. I know, because I've lived with them for decades. The good news is that recovery is possible, no matter what age help is obtained. It's never too late to take that step.

If you or anyone you know might be experiencing any eating disorder behaviors or thoughts, there is help. A good place to start is:

The National Eating Disorders Association (NEDA)
nationaleatingdisorders.org

CPSIA information can be obtained
at www.ICGtesting.com
Printed in the USA
LVHW011923121022
730564LV00002B/177